GHOSTED BY TEXAS

LOVED FOR THE HOLIDAYS
BOOK TWO

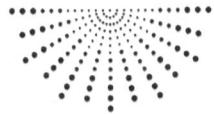

ANNE STORM

with
CHRISTINE MICHELLE

Cover Design © Christine M. Butler / Christine Michelle
Cover *Art/Photography* licensed via Deposit Photos

Paperback Edition
ISBN: 979-8-89706-003-0

ABOUT THE BOOK

AUSTIN
Loyalty to a life-long
friendship cost me everything!
I wasn't sure if Becs would ever allow me to atone for my
screwups, but I was going to use every trick in the book to earn
the only treat I ever wanted.
Her!

BECS
My heart ached for the loss of
the man I once loved.
It ached even more when I
found out I was carrying his baby.
Finding out the reason he
ghosted me...
That made my heart hurt worse.
He had been tricked.
Could I love a ghost?
There was only one

For everyone who complained about the original cover. The second edition is cheesy too, but there aren't any balloons. 🫠 Hopefully, you enjoy the story anyway.

PROLOGUE

As I scanned the party for Clea, who was supposed to meet me there twenty minutes earlier, my eyes landed on the man of my dreams.

It felt as though I could melt right into the rich, warm depths of dark brown that stared right back at me. When his lips kicked up into a lazy half smile, I swear to all that is right in the world, I freaking swooned. My legs threatened to give out, my heart stuttered in my chest, and stupid palms started sweating for no good reason.

He stood at least a good eight inches above my much smaller frame and those broad shoulders that tapered down to his trim waist only made the size difference seem that much more – wow. Yeah, that was the right word for him. He was all kinds of wow. A leggy sorority girl, who was much closer to his height, leaned into his arm and whispered in his ear. All the while, he never took those mesmerizing eyes off mine.

"Austin!" I heard the woman whine as she slipped away from his body and stomped her prissy foot into the ground. She couldn't be less subtle if she yelled, "Pay attention to me, dammit!"

ANNE STORM

He did not pay her any mind, and instead, made his way over to me. Our eyes never wavered from one another's as he moved closer. The jeans he wore clung to his frame in all the right ways, not too tight, but not so baggy that you couldn't tell his thighs were shaped with sturdy muscles underneath. He had a golden star shaped badge clipped to the black belt that ran through the loops of his jeans. A black t-shirt adorned his torso and boy did I wish it hadn't. Why couldn't the man have worn a costume that meant he needed to go shirtless like some of the meatheads running around the party?

Still, happy birthday to me! I'd consider him a present that I had to unwrap, if given the chance.

"You looked like the best kind of trouble from across the room, so I had to come find out for myself."

Oh shit! As far as pickup lines went, that struck a nerve. It was a different approach than the usual, "Hey beautiful" or "Did you fall from heaven?" bullshit that I'd heard at parties during my years at university.

"Is that so?" I asked.

He laughed at my question instead of answering it, and then reached out to push gently on my button.

Oh! I was a fucking idiot.

Clea and I decided to go against the grain and not wear super slutty costumes, like ninety-nine-point-nine percent of the other women on campus. We went with a boardgame theme. She was the Game of Life, and I was Trouble, the boardgame with the big button in the middle that you had to push to make the die inside bounce. The same button that my mystery hunk was playing with.

I laughed along with him. "Honestly, my best friend was supposed to be the Game of Life, but she hasn't shown up yet. Would you believe that I forgot what costume I was wearing?"

He grinned down at me. "As bulky as this thing is, it's hard to believe."

2

"Well, your sheriff's costume had me stunned stupid for a minute, so there's that," I admitted shyly.

"U.S. Marshall. Sheriffs have to wear uniforms." He winked at me as he pointed to all the yummy goodness hidden behind his street clothes, not a uniform.

"What would I ever do without you to school me on the differences?"

"Maybe you should stick close, just in case you need help with anyone else's costumes."

"I don't think I noticed anyone else's." Holy fucking word vomit. My cheeks flushed with heat. I wasn't normally a shy person, but I also wasn't the bold type of woman who outwardly came on to a man so strongly. There was just something about him that tugged at this cord inside me, almost like we were meant to be attached. If he tugged, I moved closer. If I tugged, he would too. I didn't doubt that for a second.

"I'm Austin."

"As in Texas?" I asked.

"The very same," he chuckled as he admitted that, and it felt like there was a story behind Mr. Texas's name that embarrassed him a little bit.

"I'm Becs," I told him.

"I think I'll stick to Trouble for now, and we'll see where the night takes us."

Yep, it was a very happy birthday for me, indeed.

CHAPTER ONE

BEFORE

Mr. Texas was far from perfect. That didn't change the fact that he seemed perfectly suited for me.

"Are you sure you don't want to watch the," I swear, the man almost gagged while trying to say the word, "romance."

"I promise, that is the last thing that I want to watch with you right now. It sets women up with unrealistic expectations and bores men to death." I pushed a fly-away piece of my very expensive, yet slightly grown out, dirty-blond dye job out of my eyes. "Besides, there's nothing like an adrenaline-fueled, action-packed movie to build up to the exciting part of a date, right?" I asked him, as his tongue all but rolled out of his mouth in cartoon fashion.

"Can we just skip the movie and go get married?" He teased.

"Are you sure you don't want to watch the romantic comedy?" I retorted as his grin widened while I teased him. "That sounded like a cheesy line from one."

Austin – otherwise known as Mr. Texas – moved in closer and tucked the stray hairs of my too-long bangs behind my ears as he catalogued everything about me. "Is your hair normally darker?"

I nodded. "It was naturally blonde when I was younger, and gradually darkened until the only way it goes blonde now is with some chemical help and a lot of sunshine. I don't get out in the sun as much these days, so this is thanks to chemical help. I guess I need to go get it touched up again."

My cheeks heated with embarrassment as I realized he must have taken notice of the roots that had grown out just a tad too much, since I had to pay for books a few weeks ago when the semester started and couldn't get the touch-up I needed.

"It looks good as is, but I bet you look just as stunning when it's naturally dark."

The heat in my cheeks was for an entirely different reason as his compliment settled in. Most men I'd dated had preferred the lighter hair and seemed displeased if I allowed my darker roots to show. It was encouraging that Mr. Texas didn't feel the same.

"You know, normally I'm not a movie for a date kind of guy," he stated as his hand engulfed mine and he tugged to get me moving in the direction of the ticket line. "Since this is our third date, I figured we should do something different, though."

"It's weird because the movie date is so cliché, but I've never actually been on one."

"You've never been on a date to see a movie?" He sounded shocked by that admission.

"Nope. Never."

"Huh, well, we're about to change that and hopefully, it will be a night you'll never forget."

Austin was already well on his way to becoming a man I'd never forget. This was date number three, in less than two weeks. That was something unheard of for me. I was the date-around and never get serious girl. Sure, I wanted that romantic forever just as much as the next girl, but I'd never met someone who would fit the bill of the leading man in my romantic story. That changed when Mr. Texas came breezing into my life at the Halloween party I'd gone to on my birthday.

There was no way I could say no to a man who had seen me through that horrendous costume while surrounded by scantily clad angels, demons, and pirate wenches. It was weird to think that had been two weeks ago, because it felt like I'd known him forever. I wanted to punch myself in the mouth for feeling that way, because it wasn't normal and felt more like one of those unrealistic romantic comedy movies I'd just avoided. I loved those movies when I was with my bestie, Clea, watching them. They wouldn't do for a date though because I would compare what was going on with Austin to them.

Kind of like what I was already doing in my head.

"Do you want popcorn and a drink or something else?" Austin asked as we approached the counter.

"Can people watch a movie without the obligatory popcorn and soda?"

That grin that I couldn't get enough of popped to full effect as he turned to order a large tub of buttered popcorn and two drinks. "Reese's Pieces too, please."

"Sure," he agreed easily. "Can you add a box of the Reese's Pieces?" He asked the girl working the counter who tripped over her own feet because she was too busy staring at Austin to function properly. Me too, girl. Me too.

"You're not allergic to peanut butter or anything, are you?" I asked as an afterthought.

"Nope."

"Good. Do you mind if we dump the candy into the bucket of popcorn?"

"Seriously?"

I nodded. "Trust me. It's the best thing ever."

"I'll try almost anything at least once," he answered, though the dubious look he threw at the box of candy said something entirely different.

"You won't hate it," I promised.

Once we took our seats, Austin hesitantly started to dump the candy into the popcorn. I took it from him, shook the bucket, then dumped some more and repeated the process a few times until the box of candy was empty.

"I see there's a system." He chuckled as he eyed the bucket in my hands. The answering grin and nod of my head confirmed.

"There needs to be equal displacement, otherwise it just all sits there on top and that's no fun. Half the experience is dipping your hand in for some popcorn, once the lights go low, and ending up with a mouthful of salty-sweet goodness instead."

Austin leaned in so quickly, it took me until his lips landed on mine to process the move. Once I did, I was already lost to his kiss as his tongue teased at the crease of my mouth until I opened and invited him to explore me further. He groaned and pulled away far too soon for my liking.

"That's more my kind of a salty-sweet surprise, since we're sharing the things that we love."

"I seem to be a fan, too." My voice sounded breathy and not at all like it usually did. I'd never had a kiss that took my breath away before.

As the lights dimmed, Austin reached over and took my hand in his. "I've never connected so easily with anyone else on this planet," he admitted. I turned to see him ducking his head, almost as if he was embarrassed by admitting something like that to me.

"I feel the same," I agreed. "I don't know why. Normally," I paused, hesitating to say the rest.

"Normally?" He prompted.

"When I date," I groaned in frustration with myself over what I was about to say. "I could take them or leave them and mostly, if I'm being honest, leave them. It's been about three years since I went out on a third date with anyone because they usually just feel lackluster in some way."

Austin leaned in and kissed me again as the pre-movie local commercials swapped to a preview of the latest super-hero blockbuster. As our lips parted, he smiled warmly at me. "You took the words right out of my mouth, Trouble."

It was probably a good thing that the lights were too low for him to make out the blush that stole across my cheeks in the wake of his agreement. I was stuck in my head, thinking about the tingly sensation left behind on my lips, when his groan of pleasure forced me to look his way again.

Austin's eyes were on mine as his jaw worked while he chewed. "You were right. Now, I wonder why I never thought to do this before."

"Do what?" I asked, still in a kiss-induced la-la-land.

"Add the Reese's Pieces to the popcorn. The hot popcorn kind of made it slightly melty, but the candy coating resisted the melt and held it all together until it got in my mouth. Mixed with the buttery popcorn, it's the best thing I've put in my mouth, next to your lips." He winked and grabbed another handful from the bucket.

Austin raised the arm of the theater seat that was between us and pulled me closer to him so that I ended up snuggled into his side for the duration of the movie as we munched, occasionally trash-talked a character, and just enjoyed being with one another. I never knew movie dates could be so damn perfect.

As we walked out of the movie theater, and into the parking lot while holding hands, Austin stiffened and looked nervously toward where we'd parked earlier. He spun me, so that my back was to the car, and I faced him. It was such a quick move, that I giggled, thinking he was trying to be romantic and steal another kiss.

I continued to think that, until I noticed that he was watching something, or someone, over my shoulder with what seemed like trepidation in his gaze and maybe a little guilt. The butterfly feeling in my gut moments ago, transferred into something heavier, souring the popcorn and candy I'd ingested during the movie.

"Is something wrong?" I asked Austin. His eyes came down to meet my own briefly before he sighed and shifted his gaze to stare at his feet. I took the opportunity to glance over my shoulder, where I found a woman standing there with a hurt look on her face. She wasn't so much standing as leaning on a car parked right behind Austin's. It was obvious, by the popcorn bag still in her hands, that she had just been in the theater to see a movie as well. The problem was, her sullen look shifted to a scornful one as her eyes left my date's and moved to take me in.

"Who is that?" I asked before turning my attention back to Austin.

"She's, fuck, it's hard to explain."

"It's really not, Austin. Who is she to you?"

"She's been my best friend ever since I could remember," was his answer. That wasn't so bad. Maybe he had blown her off to go on our date. If that was the case, I could understand her being angry with the situation. "We've grown into something more though," he admitted which completely burst the platonic bubble I'd been shaping around them.

"Something more?" I prompted, hoping he meant anything other than what it sounded like.

"We're not dating, serious or anything, Becs. It's not like that. It's just that when neither of us is seeing someone, we sometimes hook up, too."

"So, that's your fuck buddy over there giving me the evil eye?" I snipped at him.

"Don't say it like that. We've done nothing wrong," he insisted.

"It sure does feel like you're doing something wrong, considering the death glares that are heating up my backside," I argued.

"We're not like that. She has no right to be angry or jealous or whatever the hell is going on. We're friends," he tried to reiterate.

"You are friends who fuck. Didn't anyone ever tell you that

you can't be fuck buddies with your best friend? It doesn't work like that. There are feelings involved."

"I promise, it isn't like that."

"Oh? Then you don't mind calling her over here to straighten that out while I'm able to hear her confirm?"

"What? No, that would just be cruel and awkward."

"Cruel to whom?"

"What do you mean?"

"If she's just a friend, then clarifying the fact that you are only friends, who happen to fuck when you're not seeing someone else, shouldn't be cruel to anyone. If you're lying, then I guess it would be cruel to both that woman and myself, Austin. I'm telling you now, either you call her over here and get this out in the open, or whatever we started between us ends here."

Austin stared at me for a moment, as if I might change my mind, and then his shoulders slumped and he took a step to the left and crooked his finger, inviting the woman to join us.

My stomach had gone from being filled with beautiful butterflies to lead balloons, and now it felt like a bottomless pit about to suck me into a hellscape of my own making. Why had I thought confronting the other woman in Austin's life was a good idea? Shoot. Wait. Was I the other woman? He was dating me, but they were lifelong friends and fuck buddies for who knew how long. Dammit, logistically, that made me the other woman.

My cheeks flushed with embarrassment at the thought as I turned to greet the naturally blonde girl who stood only a few feet behind us.

"What's going on, Aus?"

"Jordan, this is Becs," he introduced *her* to *me*. That didn't sit well because I was his date for the night. It felt like that introduction should have gone the other way.

"And?" She turned that one word into an effective question with the attitude that dripped from it. If I thought she resented me spending time with Austin, it was proven by how she responded.

"And, since you're throwing around so much attitude, my date had questions about our relationship," he added.

Jordan glared my way before turning her attention back to Austin and smiling viciously. "Did you tell her we were best friends?" She asked, to which Austin nodded his head, and I could almost see the relief alleviate some of the sag that weighed his shoulders down. His bestie wasn't quite done, though. "Or that we fuck? A lot," she tacked on those last two words before turning her venomous smirk back my way.

"Why are you being like this?" My date asked the woman. "I told her that we had an arrangement whenever we weren't seeing anyone else."

"Yeah? Well considering we exercised our arrangement just a few days ago, and had plans tonight that got cancelled unexpectedly, I wasn't aware that our arrangement was paused again."

A few days ago? That lead balloon feeling morphed to something far worse as I felt the need to hurl my popcorn and candy mixture.

"It's been weeks, not days," Austin corrected as he huffed out a frustrated breath. The woman grimaced and shrugged her shoulders, as if that little fact changed anything. It did, in a way. At least he hadn't been having sex with her while he was trying to date me. That would have been a lot worse.

"I wasn't aware there was any arrangement with another person before five minutes ago," I explained to the woman. "I'm sorry for that because I never would have gone out with him had I known."

Jordan ducked her head, seeming almost embarrassed by my admission. Austin turned on a dime and reached out to take hold of my arm and stop me from moving any further away from him.

"Becs?" He questioned with a hint of desperation in his voice. "Please, stop. I don't want you to leave. It's not like I've been seeing you both at the same time. I haven't even seen Jordan since last week, and that was only in the gym on campus. I haven't been with her since before the day I ran into you."

Jordan sucked in a breath, no doubt realizing that he cut her off, apparently without a conversation about it, the day he met me.

"It looks like you have some things to work out with your *friend*. That was something you should have done before asking me out," I scolded him. "This is an awkward position for me because you made me the unknowing other woman. You should have clarified a bit better when I asked if you were dating anyone."

Austin cut me off, but that was all I had to say to him. "I told you that I wasn't seeing anyone, and that was the truth."

I scoffed. "That was your cue to come clean about having a regular fuck buddy. Don't try to bullshit me with semantics, Austin."

"It's the truth, though. I never would have touched Jordan again while dating you."

"But the minute we end things, you'll be right back in her bed, right?" I asked, hurt on Jordan's behalf that he could so callously dump her and then expect to pick right back up when she was convenient again. He shrugged sheepishly and I turned to look at the woman whose cheeks were flaming with embarrassment.

"We've only ever been friends who have sex when we're both single," she admitted while kicking at a pebble that seemed to be taking all her concentration.

"When was the last time you were the unavailable person in your little arrangement?" I asked out of curiosity. The woman glanced up at me, a pained expression in her eyes, and I knew the answer without her having to say a word. She hadn't been dating other people. Jordan was waiting for Austin to take their relationship seriously and become more than a fuck buddy or his friend.

"I can't do this," I told Austin, before turning and getting the hell out of there as quickly as possible. I ignored Mr. Texas as he pleaded for me to come back. There was no way in hell that would ever happen. It was a damn shame too because there was a spark with Austin that I'd never experienced with another man in all my years of dating. We clicked on this crazy, other-worldly level that I dared to call magical when I told my best friend about him. Unfortunately, the magic turned out to be a healthy dose of deception and disappointment.

CHAPTER TWO

Clea was my best friend. I should have told her what happened with my date, especially since I had waxed poetic about him being my soulmate and a bunch of magical crap that turned out to be a load of bullshit. I wasn't the type of girl to delude herself into thinking things were true that weren't. I certainly had never been the type to fall in love at the drop of a hat. I'd never been in love. We were in college, I'd dated. Okay, I'd dated a lot of men and a couple of women. There hadn't been any that I would ever say anything magical, poetic, or even a single lovey-dovey sentence about. Not one. Not until him.

My epic failure stared me in the face as Clea waited to hear all about my date the night before. What to tell her? Shit. I had nothing.

"Well?"

I sighed. "Maybe he wasn't as magical as I originally thought," I admitted.

"The date didn't go well?"

"No, it did, right up until we came out of the movies, and he spotted a friend of his."

My best friend rolled her eyes in solidarity with me. We'd all been there before, when a perfectly datable guy screwed it all up by answering his phone, texting, seeing a friend and forgetting you existed, or in my case, when he saw his BFF-slash-fuck buddy and things got awkward.

"Tell me the bastard didn't ditch you for his friend."

I shrugged my shoulders noncommittally and allowed her to assume that was exactly what happened. There was nothing good that could come from telling my bestie that my date for the night had run into his fuck buddy, who was all too quick to tell me how often and how recently they'd fucked. My heart hurt just thinking about it.

"I hate him for you." Clea announced before her eyes glanced up from where she was focused on painting her toenails. "Unless he comes back with some amazing, grand gesture to show how truly sorry he is," my best friend tacked on when she saw my downtrodden expression.

"I don't think he can make up for the epic fail at the end of our date. I expected another kiss that sent me into orbit, or possibly an all-night, orgasm-laden romp in the sack at his place. Our third date had gone so well up to that point, I'd have married him on the spot. Then, instead of my date taking me to his place, I ended up with a ride-share driver who smelled like straight up canned tuna and farted twice on the thankfully short ride back to campus."

Clea couldn't hold in her giggles, and honestly, there was no blaming her. If she had come home with the same story, I would have flat out laughed at her. Then again, now I had to wonder if she left off the important details about her dates, too. Not that she had many of them. Clea wasn't a casual dater, or even into serial monogamy. When she agreed to a date, it was because she saw it going somewhere long-term. That meant her agreeing to one didn't happen often.

The one time that I thought I was heading in the 'Clea direction', and taking things seriously, it blew up in my face. My best friend was precious, but her outlook on men and relationships just wasn't for me. My phone dinged with an incoming text as the thought sent a wave of depression straight to my chocolate craving center.

> Dickhead Scumbag: I'm sorry. Please, let me explain. I fucked up.

> Becs: Since I'm the other woman, I don't think you owe me the explanation or the apology.

> Dickhead Scumbag: You were never the other woman. I fucked up by not telling her I was seeing someone, but she knew the score.

> Becs: Well, that makes it all better.

I wished he could see the way I rolled my eyes at that comment, so that the sarcasm could really shine through. Texts sometimes sucked that way. Then again, I really didn't need the asshole to see the hurt in my eyes either. He didn't deserve to know.

> Dickhead Scumbag: Please, Becs! Meet me for coffee, so I can explain everything. I don't want to lose you. We might have only been out on a few dates, but you are so far under my skin, I can't think straight. Don't make us both lose out on that because I messed up when I thought I didn't need to let Jordan know I was seeing someone. I honestly thought my absence over the past couple weeks spoke for itself, since it has in the past.

Becs: You almost had me, until that last line. I don't want to be just another reason you're off again with a woman who clearly worships the ground you walk on. Maybe, you should fix things with her, not me, since you're such good friends and already intimately acquainted.

Dickhead Scumbag: There's a reason she and I aren't anything more than friends who scratch an itch when we're free. I don't feel that way about her.

Becs: Then you're an asshole for stringing her along the way you do. I can't do this. You said she's your best friend. That means she'll always be around. It means I have to smile and be nice to the woman who has already had sex with you, for years, while I've never even done more than kiss you. That's asking a bit much, Austin. Were you even going to tell me if she hadn't been there? Or were you just going to let me get to know the woman who is in love with you and has already had you in probably every possible sexual position?

Dickhead Scumbag: Please, can we do this in person? I really need for you to see that I'm sincere in what I have to say to you.

Once again, my eyeballs attempted to roll in their sockets. Not because of anything the dickhead said, but because I was curious and hurt enough to want to hear him out. There was a word for people like me. Masochist.

Becs: Where?

Dickhead Scumbag: Fresh Pot on Main? I can be there in thirty minutes.

Becs: I can be there in an hour.

My counteroffer was about me being difficult. Technically, I could be there in about ten minutes. I just didn't want him to think I was desperate.

"You're going to see him?" Clea asked, startling me.

"Jesus!" I yelped as she giggled.

"Forgot I was sitting right here while you had your heated text exchange?"

"Something like that."

"So? Are you going to see him?"

"Yeah. He wants a chance to explain, in person." I shrugged my shoulders, as if I were indifferent to what he had to say already. While that couldn't be further from the truth, I refused to get Clea's – or my – hopes up.

"You know I'm here, if you need me." Her worried tone let me know that I wasn't fooling anyone, least of all her.

"I know." My sullen reply followed me to the bathroom, where I made myself look beautiful. If I had to meet with the man who could have owned my heart, but broke it before we could go further, then I was going to look unforgettable. By the time I left to meet up with Austin, there was no trace of the sad girl who spent most of the night silently weeping into her pillow. I owed a lot of thanks to the icepacks I'd used this morning to get the swelling down.

Exactly forty-five minutes after I ended my text session with Austin, I made my way into the Fresh Pot coffee shop on Main Street. I thought that I'd be able to beat Austin there and grab a latte that I could enjoy while I waited. There was little hope of choking one down while having to hear him explain to me about his conveniently forgotten fuck buddy again.

Unfortunately for me, Mr. Texas had already snagged a seat, two coffees, and the attention of a sorority girl I didn't mesh very well with. It wasn't her involvement with a sorority that bothered me, I was friends with plenty of people who chose the Greek life. It was that she ate, breathed, and lived the life while thinking that she was better than everyone that made me want to bounce a steaming pot of coffee off her head. Then again, it could also be the jealousy.

Austin grinned up at her from his seat, where he was kicked back in a relaxed position. The minute Gracie-Lou's hand landed on the chair across from him, I turned to leave.

"Becs!" I heard Austin call out. That didn't stop the hasty retreat I planned on beating out of the place. "Becs, wait a sec!" He called again, only his voice sounded much closer. A hand landed on my bicep, halting me from leaving. I swore under my breath and turned to face the man of the hour, who had been with yet another blonde-haired woman when I found him. I was beginning to think he had a specific type, and it wasn't really me, despite his false platitudes about wanting to see my hair in its naturally dark brown state.

"What?"

"We were supposed to meet here. Why were you leaving?"

"You were busy, and I didn't feel like wasting my time. Again." I tacked the last word on to emphasize how I thought our last date had been a waste, considering the ending.

Austin glanced back to the table, where a stunned Gracie stood staring at us. The damn man couldn't even wipe the grin off his face, which only worked to infuriate me.

"That chick just came up to my table to ask about a class we're in together, but I think she had me confused with my brother."

I cocked my head to the side, not believing that for a second.

"Houston?" Gracie called out to him. "I thought you were single. My friends said that Houston Mercer was single now." My jaw dropped at her audacity, not to mention the inaccuracy. The woman didn't even know that she had been propositioning the wrong Mercer brother.

"And like I told you a minute ago, I'm not my brother," he insisted with a roll of his eyes.

"What kind of game are you playing?" She asked while eying him suspiciously.

"He's not playing any games. Houston is his brother. You have the wrong Mercer boy," I stated coolly, hoping to get her gone, so that Austin and I could have our conversation. Then, I could go throw up the piece of toast I managed to choke down for breakfast.

"Are you single too?" Gracie asked with a glimmer of hope in her eye.

"No," he told her without hesitation. "My girl is here to have coffee with me this morning and she's getting pissed that you're interrupting our time together."

I almost laughed at his assertions, but it was close enough to the truth that it worked. Gracie glanced between us for a minute and then huffed and stalked off.

"You might want to warn your brother that he's being hunted down, and Gracie is seriously attending college to obtain her MRS Degree."

Austin chuckled. "Nah, I think I'll let him discover that on his own the same way I did."

"So, you don't like your brother?"

"Love the asshole, but he's been through some shit recently and I have a feeling that Gracie is going to come out on the losing end when she attempts to approach him the way she just did me. He just got rid of Samantha, who reminds me a lot of Gracie."

"Maybe she's his type then."

"Not anymore. Samantha cheated and got knocked up by another man. I think he's had enough of the husband hunting type."

"That sucks."

"It really does because my brother is one of the best people I know."

"Sounds like my best friend, Clea."

"I got coffee for us, but they're probably cold now." I glanced over toward the table where he'd been seated when I first walked in and someone else was already sitting there.

"Looks like the table went cold, too. Maybe, we should go somewhere else?"

"Do you want to go back to my place?"

Without realizing what I did, my body took an inadvertent step backward. Austin cringed at my reaction. "Just so we have privacy to talk, that's all. Plus, I can make us both some fresh coffee."

My stomach dipped and twisted at the prospect of putting coffee in it while my anxiety was ramped so high. "How about if we just talk for now and not worry about coffee or anything else that might need to go in my stomach."

Austin nodded. "Do you want to follow me?"

"Is it far?"

"A few blocks," he explained.

"I walked here from campus."

"I'll drive then, if you're okay with that?"

"That's fine," I agreed and proceeded to follow him outside and down the street to where his car was parked.

Once we got to the apartment he shared with his brother, Austin and I sat down on a cozy leather couch that had seen better days. It took a minute of him fidgeting before he finally glanced up at me and our eyes locked.

"I'm so fucking sorry for how things went down last night, Becs. That should have never happened, and it's all on my shoulders that it did."

There was really nothing I could say to that. Sure, there were plenty of responses at the ready, especially as my sarcastic tongue wanted me to bite down hard and come out swinging. That was my hurt trying to speak for me, so I kept my mouth shut and waited for more.

"The thing with Jordan and me is stupid," he started to say.

"Pretty sure that she would disagree with that."

He nodded but refused to meet my eyes again. "The thing is, she's the one who suggested the friends with benefits thing a few years ago. At first, I told her that I wasn't interested because I thought it would ruin our friendship. Our moms are best friends."

I sighed at that news because it meant their mothers had probably already planned out their wedding, future children, and more. That meant being with Austin in any romantic capacity would be next to impossible.

"We never went there with one another until her mother passed away. She was grieving and needed something more." He cringed before adding, "I gave it to her. It was always with the understanding that we were never going to be anything more than friends. That was two years ago."

"So, you've been fuck buddies for two years?" I asked, unable to keep the shock out of my voice. How in the hell the man thought having a sexual relationship with his life-long best friend, for two whole years, didn't mean more to her, was beyond me.

"Not two solid years. I've dated a few people here and there."

"She didn't, though."

"No, I guess she didn't. I never even noticed until you asked her that question last night. Jordan has never been real forthcoming about her dating life with me."

I laughed at the ridiculousness of what he'd admitted. He couldn't be that blind, could he?

"What's so funny about that?"

"You're so clueless. She hasn't been forthcoming because she hasn't dated outside of you."

"She went out with a few guys when we were still in high school."

"Likely to make you jealous," I surmised.

Austin stared at me as if I were speaking another language. Then, he shook whatever thought he had off and took one of my hands in his.

"I honestly didn't bring you here to talk about Jordan's dating history."

"It's relevant, Austin."

"How so?"

"You said yourself that your moms were best friends. The two of you grew up together in that regard. I'm sure your parents had a whole life of you two becoming a future couple planned out." The grimace he wore was enough indicator that I was correct.

"There's this huge history there, and you complicated it so much by adding a sexual element to your friendship. She has certain expectations, that her late mom probably had a hand in fanning flames for before she passed. Any woman you date will have to deal with the insurmountable obstacle that is your family, your best friend, and all their expectations going unfulfilled."

"It's my life to live, not any of theirs."

"That's true, but you gave her hope that they were all right." He shook his head, as if remaining in denial about what I pointed out would make it less true.

"She's not wrong," another man's voice spoke up from over by the kitchen. I damn near jumped off the couch at hearing another person, since I thought we were alone.

"I'm Houston," he remarked as I put a hand over my heart, as if that would calm the damn thing back down so it would stop beating the hell out of my ribs.

"Houston, I didn't realize you were still here," Austin said as he got to his feet. "This is Becs," he introduced as I also stood and moved beside him to hold my hand out to Houston.

"Good to meet you," he told me. "I was just about to head out. Didn't mean to eavesdrop on your conversation," he apologized to his brother before turning his attention back to me.

"You have good reason to be worried and very valid points,

but for what it's worth, my brother has never talked about a woman so much as he has you. I feel like I already know you and that means a lot. He's a bit clueless where Jordan is concerned, but I don't think that will be an issue anymore, if you're willing to give the idiot another chance."

Houston didn't wait around for my response. He moved around us and left the apartment as quickly and silently as he had shown up.

"It's true. I talked to Jordan last night and told her that we're done with anything beyond friendship and we both agreed to take a little time away from one another. I think she needs that separation more than anything, to come to terms with whatever she thought was going to happen."

"I don't know, Austin. It's still a hell of a mess you created for me to have to walk into."

"What if we just take it slow, date, and don't worry so much about the future, family introductions, and whatnot for now?" The hopeful look in his eyes almost did me in, but the idiot kept talking.

"I'll talk you up to my family during that time and make sure they understand that nothing was ever going to happen between Jordan and me. Houston already knew that. I thought everyone else did, too. According to you and my brother, I thought wrong. I understand now, and I'm working on fixing any misconceptions. I don't want to lose what it felt like we were working toward. I've never felt that type of connection with anyone else, Becs. Please, don't take it away now because I messed up by being a clueless jackass."

CHAPTER THREE

HIS PLEADING STARE PULLED ME IN AND HELD ON TIGHT. HOW could I tell the man no, when I felt the sincerity coming off him in waves.

"Please," he pleaded with me.

"Can I be honest with you?" I asked quietly.

"I prefer it."

"Okay then. There's a part of me that really wants to give this a shot because I feel that insane connection to you, too."

"But?"

"But I'm not sure how to handle your best friend being someone you regularly have sex with."

"Had," he corrected as I rolled my eyes.

"It's all the same, Austin. It wasn't that long ago that you were rolling around in the sheets with her. She wants you, as more than just a friend or fuck buddy. That will be hard to deal with for both of us, even if you don't see it as a big deal."

"I already told you that we're taking a break away from one another. There will be plenty of space between us when she gets back."

I laughed at his ignorant assertion. "Seriously? You think that just a little time and distance will cure her of her broken heart or me of the fact that I'll never trust her around you?"

"You don't have to trust her. You need to trust me."

"And considering the fact that you kept your relationship with her a secret until it was shoved in my face, and likewise never told her about me or that you broke off your arrangement because you were seeing someone, I think we have a bit of a problem there as well." He leaned back almost as if I'd smacked him.

"It's the truth. We're brand new. There wasn't even time to establish any kind of trust with you before you lied by omission and put your friend and me in a very awkward position. Then, you want me to simply have faith in you, that when you say you're spending time with her, no matter how mundane, that nothing is going on. It's a huge ask and one I'm not entirely comfortable with. You have to see my point there."

"I told you that nothing sexual will take place between her and I while we're dating, and I meant it." He seemed incapable of processing the point I was trying to convey, so I decided to flip the script and allow his lizard-man brain to figure shit out the old-fashioned way.

"What if I told you Clea was a silly nickname for my best friend, Clarence, and that we sometimes have sex when we aren't dating anyone else?" The scowl on his face said it all, but I carried on because the only way to get him to understand my point of view was to make him feel a little of what I had at the end of our date.

"What if you met Clarence and realized that he was in love with me? Would you then be okay if I called him to come fix something in my apartment while we're there alone? What about if he asked me to go out to dinner with him? Would you want to meet my family if they were dead set on me marrying Clarence one day? What if we were innocently watching a movie and I fell asleep on his couch and spent the night there? I would of course, assure that nothing happened, but would you be inclined to believe it, if I told you that right now or even two weeks or a month from now?"

"Fuck no! Clea better be a chick."

"But you should trust me, though. Who cares if Clea is a man that I've had sex with often for the past couple years? If I say it won't happen again, that should make you comfortable with the situation, right? Plus, I just know that you and Clarence will become best friends, too. Who knows, maybe when I'm not around, my former fuck buddy bestie and you can trade tips and tricks on how to get me off. I bet that would happen because you know, jealousy games and shit."

It might have been petty to mock him, but he needed to understand how callously he was treating my feelings about the situation. Slowly, I watched as his reaction to the same exact scenario he'd placed me in, finally dawned on him.

"Okay, I get it. Fuck, I never even thought about it like that. Not that I don't trust you to be honest with me. As far as I'm concerned, you have my faith until you do something to take it away."

"You did do something to take away the little faith I would have given you at the start of a relationship. I had faith that I was the only person you were seeing, dating, and potentially screwing when we started hanging out. As it turned out, that wasn't true. Even if you say that you weren't physical with Jordan since before our first date, you never informed her of that change and certainly didn't tell me about your former arrangement. All those things should have happened before you ever attempted to move forward with me."

"I feel like such an asshole, and I never meant for it to seem like I was hiding anything. I swear, I would have told you about my past with Jordan before introducing you." He saw me noticeably cringe and inadvertently mimicked my response.

"Although now that you gave me that very detailed example using 'Clarence,'" he finger-quoted the name. "I'm guessing even the thought of being introduced to her in a different light is not the greatest idea." He blew out a frustrated breath. "I don't know what to do about her. It was stupid to start down any physical path. I never thought it would be a big deal with people I dated down the road, though."

"That's because you're the one who doesn't have feelings beyond friendship. She's dealing with unrequited love or whatever. Anyone you date is going to have to deal with her inevitable jealousy and the hate she throws their way. Kind of like she tried to do with me in the movie theater parking lot by talking so cavalierly about your sex life and insinuating it had been more recent than it was."

"I'm sorry that I didn't think everything through sooner."

"Austin, you said you dated other people during the two years when your relationship turned physical with Jordan." He nodded his agreement. "Why didn't it work out with any of those women?"

"I don't know. They all just kind of lost interest in me." He shrugged his shoulders, clearly embarrassed to admit that he'd basically been dumped by every woman he tried to date over the past couple years.

"So, your relationship not progressing with them was always on the part of the women?"

"There were only a handful of women I tried to date, and I broke it off with one because she was crazy," he explained. As he did, something dawned on him, though. His eyes met mine briefly before he quickly looked away.

"Let me guess, she made a bunch of claims about Jordan that didn't seem believable to you?"

"She's been my best friend practically my whole life," he argued, which was enough of an admission.

"Still, that's the uphill battle any woman who dates you will have to deal with. Even if nothing is going on between you and your friend while you're with someone else, I promise you that Jordan is probably filling them in with all the details of your past together. You missed the daggers she threw at me with her eyes the other night because your focus was on my reaction. I can just bet that all those women were run off by your bestie."

"Becs, I don't think..."

"I'm going to stop you right there. What you're trying to do now is why things will never work out between us, or with any other woman you try to date. Jordan will always come first. You will always defend her actions or pretend they never happened. You have a Jordan problem, Austin, and it's a lot bigger than you seem to think it is."

"I told you that she went away for a while. I think the distance will help put our relationship back into perspective for both of us. Please don't give up on you and me because I made a mess of things with her."

The niggling feeling in my gut should have been warning enough not to jump in with the man. The overwhelming urge to be with him negated most of the worry, though. There was no doubt in my mind that Austin was being genuine with me. I didn't think he had real feelings for his best friend, aside from normal bestie vibes, despite the fact that Jordan was dealing with a whopping dose of unrequited love, lust, or maybe just a weird obsession created by overzealous, matchmaking parents. Still, I went against my better judgment, and decided to take a chance on my Mr. Texas.

"How about we put all of our cards on the table and then we try going back to square one with a first date all over again?" I suggested.

"What exactly does 'put all our cards on the table' mean?"

"Austin, are you married?" He grinned and shook his head in response. "Dating anyone?"

"No and no."

"Are you currently in, or were you recently involved with and forgot to end it with your partner, a fuck buddy situation of any type?"

He sighed and shook his head with what looked like remorse written in his eyes as they met with mine again. "My best friend, since we were kids, is a girl. For the past two years, we've had a friends with benefits arrangement whenever one of us isn't seeing other people. I have broken that arrangement with her, and she isn't even in town right now."

"Well, my next question was going to be: Do you have a female bestie or close friend who might cause problems in our relationship, but the last question kind of answered that. How is your friend going to take me being in your life when she gets back?"

"She's going to have to deal with it." Austin didn't even hesitate as he gave his answer.

"Okay, so what will you do if she can't deal with it and tries to cause trouble to get me out of the picture?" I widened my eyes as if to reiterate my earlier point about why all the women he attempted to date broke things off or seemed to come at him with 'crazy' accusations about his bestie.

"I'll handle situations as they arise, but I won't tolerate that kind of interference with my potential happiness, Becs. If you have any problems with her, I expect that you'll be honest and communicate those things with me."

"Easy enough, but fair warning, Austin, if it comes down to it, and you refuse to believe me over her without communicating with me through the process, we're done."

He swallowed noticeably and I watched as his Adam's apple bobbed up and then back down. Maybe I was weird, but there was something about watching that action and did strange things to me. My eyes drifted to the pulse that thrummed not far from there. His heart rate ticked up with the prospect of losing me or dealing with his bestie. I didn't know which, but damn if it didn't sink that doubt about risking a relationship with him even deeper in my gut. The man would be dangerous to my heart and still, I jumped in with my eyes wide open.

CHAPTER FOUR

"WHERE ARE YOU HEADED TONIGHT?" I TURNED TO SEE CLEA eyeing me skeptically.

"Austin is taking me to dinner."

My best friend's sigh did nothing to alleviate the broody butterflies swarming around in my belly. The dirty blonde locks she had swept up into a high ponytail swished as she shook her head in disappointment.

"What? Just spit it out, Clea."

"I'm worried about you, Becs. You're my best friend, so that's my job. The first few dates you went on seemed to go well and you talked about this guy like he was the only one you'd ever seen." She chuckled. "And maybe that's true to a point. I don't think you've allowed yourself to see anyone else in a real way. Then you came home from that last date all depressed because he ditched you for a friend and you've been acting weird ever since."

"I'm just nervous. I've never liked a guy before. Well, you know, I've liked plenty of boys in my past, but never in a way where I saw them as a potential part of my future, too. It's freaking me out a bit, that's all. I swear."

In truth, I wasn't exactly lying to my friend. The prospect of having a long-term boyfriend, or possibly more one day, had well and truly freaked me out. It wasn't in a bad way though. It was more like I could feel hope returning for once. The icky part, and what I wasn't proud of, was keeping the whole Jordan situation from Clea. I knew she wouldn't understand. My friend was a bulldog when it came to protecting others. She would bite down on the offending person and not let go until they got well and truly gone from the situation.

"I'm here for you, whenever you need me." The dubious stare she leveled on me was enough to drill her point home. She knew I was holding back but was willing to give me time. "I won't even be mad that there's something you're not telling me because we all need to keep our own confidences sometimes. If and when that changes, I will always be here."

"That is why you're my very best friend in the whole wide-world."

My pronouncement made her smile, which was all I could ask for before the doorbell rang and I took off running. I don't know why, but I wasn't ready for Clea and Austin to meet just yet.

"Did you ever hear that anticipation makes things better?" She called out from behind me.

"If you knew Mr. Texas, you wouldn't keep him waiting either." I waggled my brows at her and then turned to open the door. Because my best friend was such an amazing person, she didn't even attempt to peek. That's where she was a better person than I was. I would have totally looked. Actually, I probably would have raced her to the door to force a meeting because my curiosity always got the best of me. I think that's why Clea, and I worked as well as we did. We were one another's counterbalance.

"Hey gorgeous, are you ready to go, or need a minute?" Austin asked.

I snagged my purse off the desk near the door and slipped out quickly. There was no missing the curious glance Austin threw over my shoulder. "I'm ready."

"Hmm," he hummed out his response as I locked the door behind me. "Not ready to introduce me to Clarence yet, I see," he teased to my complete amusement.

"Well, he's still a little touchy about the subject of me dating some other man and all."

"If you hadn't already told me about Clea on our first date, that door would be off its hinges." I turned to see he was completely serious.

"Remember that feeling and don't ever give me reason to experience the same," I warned. "I won't be ripping doors off hinges. It will just be the end of us."

"Promise, I won't."

"Good, now I do believe you owe me a fabulous second-chance first date." I winked at him as I turned to walk toward the parking lot

CHAPTER FIVE

"A blind date? You want me to go on a blind date for Valentine's Day! What is wrong with you?"

"Nothing! It's not like you'll look desperate or anything. He doesn't have a date either." I tossed a pair of high heels at my best friend, that she would never wear in a million years, but it worked as a distraction so she would stop sighing. She'd done it so much over the past twenty minutes that I was concerned it would turn into her hyperventilating.

"There is no way I'm wearing heels."

"You have to," I teased. "They go with the dress!" Poor Clea, she had no clue that I'd already thought about every tactic she would use to get out of the blind date, and I had a plan for every single one of her excuses. Mostly, it involved keeping her distracted until it was time for us to head out.

"Do you remember the last time I wore heels?"

"I can't remember you ever wearing heels, now that I think about it." Lies. All lies. How could I forget? That had been a disaster of epic proportions and Clea's date would probably never forget it either. I was certain the poor boy ended up with scars from that incident.

"Prom," I pretended to finally remember as I snatched the high heels back from my bestie. It was all a part of my grand time-wasting plan. There was no way I'd allow her to kill herself, me, or anyone else on the night I was finally going to introduce her to my perfect Mr. Texas. Yes, his name continued to grow in my mind. It would be hell to get that on our marriage certificate one day. Perfect Mr. Texas Austin -whatever-his-middle-name-was – Mercer. I'm sure it would have more of a ring to it once I found out his middle name. Weird that I didn't already know it after two and a half months of dating.

"Maybe, we'll just get you a cute pair of kitten heels."

It took some convincing, but once Clea realized she would get to meet my Mr. Texas, she was all in. Well, maybe not quite 'all in' but close enough.

WHEN WE GOT to the party, my nerves kicked in. What if Clea and Houston hated one another? Would that spell instant doom for Austin and me? My cold feet and worry about losing my boyfriend nearly made me text him our excuses and drag Clea back home.

"Where is your date?" Clea asked. It made me pause for a moment to look around before dragging her through the front door of the frat house where the party was being held. The guys were supposed to be waiting just inside the door, so we wouldn't have any trouble finding them.

"Inside already."

"Is it the Texas guy?"

I wiggled my brows at her suggestively. "Austin, and yes, it's him."

"Do you see that going somewhere serious?"

If only she knew that I'd been daydreaming about what name would go on the marriage certificate while we got ready for our night. I shrugged my shoulders at my bestie. It was my attempt at indifference, but she saw right through me, so I gave a small admission. "I really like him, so we'll see where it goes."

"That's a lot."

It was, considering I'd never even introduced her to anyone I'd gone out with, let alone admitted to liking them. If only she knew just how much I liked the man, she might drag me out of the party and save me from my near nervous breakdown that threatened to bring me to my knees.

Austin and his brother were supposed to meet us by the front door, so that we wouldn't have to keep up the mystery charade too long. Plus, if we left it up to Clea and Houston to find one another, it would probably turn into one giant mess anyway. We both knew that and planned accordingly, despite going through the whole ordeal of making them take headless photos so we could show the other what they were wearing.

Unfortunately, neither man was there as we entered, so I attempted to see over and around the ocean of people swimming around the room. Okay, they weren't really swimming, but that guy in front of me was doing a damn good job of imitating a garden sprinkler for some reason.

"Becs," Clea startled me as she spoke directly in my ear. "Did you forget something when you dressed me?"

I laughed at her because my bestie had just figured out the dress code and that she was in violation of it to the point where she would stand out to anyone and everyone in attendance.

"Nope. I figured you would stand out more this way."

"I'm going to kill you. Dead. As in no longer breathing, Becs!"

"That's usually what dead means, dipshit!" I tugged her toward the homemade bar the frat set up in the corner. I needed a drink to quell the nerves. If that was how I felt, then Clea had to be a worked-up mess, too. "First thing, we're getting you a drink to loosen you up." She didn't need to know that I was feeling a case of the nerves as well. Sweaty palms be damned.

"Becs! I think I see him!" Clea yelled. I turned just in time to see a bow and arrow wielding, blond-haired, diaper wearing, slightly familiar looking man push past. He must have bumped Clea because she was on her way to hitting the floor before I could even react. Before the startled noise she made even registered, a decent looking guy with great reflexes had Clea wrapped up in his strong arms, and maybe a bit more. Dammit. There was no way to contend with hero-worship. I glanced around, but still didn't see Austin or his brother. Why in the hell hadn't they been at the door, as promised?

"Are you okay?" I barely caught the man's question before Clea managed to spin to get a look at the man whose grip landed squarely on one of her breasts. "Oh shit!" He puffed out as he pretended to realize where his hand landed.

Yeah, right, buddy.

I had his number already. The jerk was smarmier than... well... a jerk.

"Sorry, I was just trying to catch you before your cute ass hit the floor."

"Thank you," my best friend eloquently greeted him back after staring him down with her wide doe-eyes that narrowed just a bit as she took him in. Thank fuck she had come to her senses about the guy because my douche-o-meter was pinging full steam ahead.

"Are you okay?" I finally managed to ask her. I'd hoped that it would be the perfect opportunity to pull her out of the clutches of douche-o-rama, so we could find Austin and his brother, but no.

"Yeah, I am now. Thanks to..." She left her words hanging in the hopes that the asshole would fill in the blanks and of course he did.

"Jeff," he offered her his name and his hand. I wanted to stomp on his foot with my heels, but that would draw too much attention.

"This is my best friend, Becs," she introduced us, but my attention was focused on finding the Mercer brothers before the night went completely sideways. It was already sliding in that direction, dammit.

"And that would make you?" The man asked her.

"Here on a date," I answered for Clea.

"Oh! The two of you are together?" I was certain that did not detract from Jeff's interest one little bit. The new sparkle in the bastard's eyes seemed to indicate I was right.

"No. I was supposed to meet a blind date here," Clea insisted. Dammit. A blind date could be ditched and judging from the smug smirk on the asshole's face, he would test the theory.

"Oh, well his loss is my gain."

"Wait!" I yelled. "He didn't lose, he's here somewhere."

"No," Jeff responded, looking the tiniest bit annoyed with me. "He lost because there's no way I'm letting this beautiful woman out of my sight now."

I huffed out a breath of frustration. "Do not go anywhere!" I growled the words through gritted teeth, hating the idea of separating from Clea, but knowing I needed to find Austin and his brother immediately or Houston would lose out on his blind date. Then, my boyfriend was bound to be angry with me for causing the situation, since I insisted that his brother and my best friend were perfect for one another.

It took me ten freaking minutes to track down Austin, and when I did, he was a sweaty mess who looked like he had single-handedly been running the show. Clea's supposed date for the night stood with him, looking just as harried.

"Hey, where have you been?" I asked when I got close enough to be heard over the music.

"Cleaning up messes our other brother made."

"Dallas is here, too?" I hadn't met the younger brother yet, but I heard he was a handful and then some.

"That would be the one." Austin glanced around me, as if looking for someone before he asked, "Where is Clea?"

"Shit!" I grabbed his hand. "Hurry, some frat douche was hitting on her when I left to go find you."

"Well, that doesn't sound good," he admitted, and I had to agree with him, though I refused to do so out loud. We moved over toward the corner bar where I'd left Clea and the jerk only to find that neither of them were there.

"Oh no!" I spun on my heels and glanced at every corner of the room. There were no black dresses in sight. "Oh no!" I groaned again.

"What?"

"I don't see her," I whined.

"Hey man, I'm wiped out from dealing with Dallas's shit. Did that chick show up or not?" I turned to see Houston, who looked just enough like Austin that they could be mistaken for one another, if you weren't paying attention to the differences, like the fact that Austin had darker hair and was the tiniest bit taller than his brother.

"Where's Clea?" Austin asked.

"I think she might have left. I don't see her anywhere," I admitted reluctantly.

"Figures," Houston groused dejectedly.

"Houston, man, I'm sorry. Don't take it personally."

"How can you not take being stood up on Valentine's Day personally?" He asked, though he laughed as he did.

"Fuck!" Austin growled.

"I need to go find her and make sure she's safe. We came here together. It isn't like Clea to leave a party without me."

"You go find her, make sure she's safe, and meet me back at my place in an hour, okay?"

I nodded my head. "I'll see you then." I turned to Houston after that. "I'm so sorry about this. Some asshole knocked her down before I went to find you guys and..."

He cut me off. "Don't worry about it." Houston turned and took off in the opposite direction and my boyfriend shot a glare back at me after watching his brother walk away. "You promised this shit wouldn't happen," he said.

"You promised to be at the front door," I countered.

"We'll talk about everything later. Right now, I need to go make sure you and your *friend* didn't do too much damage to my brother." The way he said friend made me worry. Austin had been growing impatient lately with the fact that I hadn't introduced him to Clea yet, even though I was open with him about why I hadn't.

It hurt that my boyfriend didn't even bother with a goodbye to me, let alone a kiss or anything, as he left me there alone at a frat party to follow his brother. Some Valentine's Day! Our first one together was a disaster and I had less than an hour to find and check on Clea before getting my ass to Austin's apartment to try to salvage what was left of the night. I knew he'd be mad that things turned out the way they did, but he would have to understand it was beyond my control.

I was a little miffed that Austin let me leave the party alone. That was safety rule 101 for college. Never leave a lone woman unattended to walk across campus to her apartment alone, right? I was just as angry with Clea though. She left me alone at a party, too. At least, where she was concerned, she thought she left me there with the man I'd been dating for months. She, however, broke safety rule 102. Don't leave a frat party alone with a strange dude while your best friend is left behind to worry about you.

She wasn't outside in the front yard. I grabbed my phone and dialed her number. No answer. I sent a text, instead.

> Becs: Are you okay? I can't find you anywhere.

No answer.

Dammit. I walked back to our shared apartment where I finally found Clea standing out front with the asshole, Jeff. Their lips were locked in a kiss that proved Clea was having a far better Valentine's Day than I was. I loved my best friend, but that shit made me angry.

"CLEA!" I yelled, which worked to startle them apart. I think Clea might have bitten him, or he bit her, because she swiped at her lips and frowned as her hand came away tinged with pink.

Then her startled eyes came up to meet mine and I saw the remorse there. "Oh, God! Becs! I'm so sorry."

"I should hope so. Do you know how worried I was when I couldn't find you and you didn't answer your phone?"

"I didn't even think, since you said Mr. Texas was there," she started to excuse her actions.

"We never leave parties alone! We never leave the other one. We almost finished out four years with a perfect safety record and you left with some asshole frat-douche you don't even know. Worse, you left me there to walk home alone."

"Where was Mr. Texas?"

"You didn't know where he was before you left either," I yelled at her. "Maybe he wasn't there at all."

"Becs!" My name was a whimpered plea. Part of me felt badly for coming down on her, but truthfully, she put us both in a potentially bad spot by running off with the asshole who gave me creeper vibes.

"I assure you that your friend was fine with me," the asshole stated.

"I don't know you from Jack. Plus, who was there to assure me that I'd be safe? If you were any kind of gentleman, you would have made sure her best friend had an escort home, too. At the very least, you should have made sure I knew you were leaving to begin with."

He chuckled, as if I were an amusement and nothing more. "If we waited around to find you, that blind date of hers might have materialized and ruined things." Clea blushed when he admitted that. "No offense, Bell, but I play to win and Clea is a prize."

"Becs," I corrected. "And this isn't a goddamn game."

"They don't call it the game of love for nothin'." He countered quickly. I swear to all that is holy, I watched Clea swoon over his answer. There was something truly wrong with my bestie's dickwad sensors if she was falling for his shit, but I had other things to worry about, like my relationship and the fact that my boyfriend ditched me because Clea left his brother feeling like a rejected asshat.

"It's not her fault," I muttered to myself.

"What was that?" Jeff the ass asked.

"Clea, are you good?"

"Yeah, I am. Becs, I'm really sorry about tonight."

"At least one of us got to enjoy Valentine's Day, right?"

She cringed, but I couldn't pull the sarcasm back. My night had been well and truly ruined. There didn't seem to be a way to salvage any of the night either because I was angry with Austin for being so callous and uncaring where I was concerned. Anything could have happened to me when he left me to go deal with his brother's hurt feelings. I felt bad for Houston, but dammit, he was a big guy. The chances of him being attacked on his way home were significantly less than mine.

"I have to go," I told Clea. "I'd appreciate it if you don't let a total fucking stranger into our apartment while I'm gone."

Clea's eyes widened, shocked by my attitude with her, no doubt. "I won't," she promised.

"You can come back to my place," Jeff suggested while leering at her breasts.

Clea missed the leering. "No, I think maybe we should just exchange numbers and go from there. Becs is right, we don't know each other, but I'd like to change that."

I didn't catch his response because I hopped in my car and took off for Austin's house. It had been nearly an hour, what with the walk home and arguing with dipshit. I was certain my anger with my roommate took up a few good minutes as well.

It took another fifteen minutes to get to Austin's apartment, since he lived across town. Thankfully, traffic was lite, and the cops usually placed themselves closer to the bars at that time of night.

I pulled up outside Austin's place and noticed right away that the living room light was on. At first, I thanked God for small favors, that he hadn't just gone to bed angry, but then movement in the window caught my eye. Jordan was standing there. She opened her coat, as if to take it off, and the only thing the woman wore was a pair of barely-there panties and a bra that failed at containing her tits.

"You have got to be kidding me," I mumbled to absolutely no one inside my car. I glanced to the side and found Austin, sitting in his comfy chair in the corner of the room. His relaxed posture with legs spread wide, body slouched down, and a beer sitting beside him, made it look for all the world as if he was waiting for a lap dance from his nearly naked best friend, fuck buddy, or whatever the hell she was to him these days.

He had lied to me again. She wasn't even supposed to be back in town yet. So, what was she doing at his house, in lingerie, on Valentine's Day when we were supposed to be out at a party together? Had he been planning on ditching me all along to come home to her? I swiped angrily at the tear that dove down my cheek. They were talking, her arms were flailing and then she smiled widely at him and moved forward, as if she were going to give him that lap dance scenario that I'd imagined moments ago.

The fact that I sat there watching the woman parade herself in front of him for more than ten minutes, and he never once showed her naked ass to the door, proved that he couldn't be trusted anyway. He would have flipped his shit if one of my exes showed up mostly naked and I didn't immediately send them packing or call the police to do it for me.

Part of me wanted to sit there and wait, to see how long it would take for him to get rid of her and call or text me to let me know what happened. The other part of me, the logical one, knew that I would see things that would break me even harder. I couldn't handle that. He was there, with his best friend and supposedly former fuck buddy, who was naked – or close to. The odds of nothing happening, when he hadn't already tossed her on her ass for daring to come to his place like that, especially knowing I was supposed to show up...

That thought stopped me cold. He knew. It had been almost an hour and a half since we left the party separately. I was supposed to be at his apartment thirty minutes earlier, and he had a naked woman parading in front of his living room window for all and sundry to see. Maybe, he wanted me to see her there. He was done with me, and this was his way of letting me know.

The disrespect came in only second to my heartbreak as I drove back to my apartment. When I got there, the impulse to call or text to ask for an explanation was there on the tip of my tongue. I wanted to yell and scream at him for breaking my heart and disappointing me again. I did none of those things because he already gave me a visual explanation. We were through and he went right back to his twisted fuck buddy situation with his best friend who was in love with him.

I was sure she would be happy in her delusions, but I honestly hoped he choked on them. It would take time for me to get over everything. Austin was a lesson learned where those pesky love type feelings were concerned. Never again. Eventually, I'd settle down with someone who complimented me enough that we could handle coparenting better than my parents had. All my future husband would need to do was be dependable and friendly enough. My expectations for everything else would remain low, so if he wanted to run off with his secretary on the weekends, it would be fine unless he missed Junior's soccer games or something. Then we'd fight.

Two Weeks Later

I PLOPPED down on the lawn to soak up some of the unseasonably warm sunshine for a bit. It was still too early in the year for nearly eighty-degree temps, but somehow, I thought maybe nature knew my soul needed a boost of warmth because I had started to flounder.

My heart ached in ways that I didn't think were possible. I closed my eyes and tipped my head back to catch as much of the sunny goodness as I could when I felt the presence of someone sitting down beside me. The feminine perfume kept me from going on alert the way I might have if an uninvited male sat there.

"Pleasant enough day for you?" The female asked. There was something familiar about her voice, though I couldn't place it.

"Soaking it up while it's here," I informed the stranger.

"Kind of like you tried to do with Austin, huh?"

The mention of his name forced my eyes to snap open and my head to whip in the direction of the no longer welcome person who was crouched down beside me.

"What in the hell are you doing here?" I asked Jordan.

She grinned at me. "You looked like someone kicked your puppy, so I wanted to let you know that your puppy is doing just fine – with me. I've been treating him well since Valentine's Day. He's enjoyed my body immensely and hasn't thought of you once since. Thanks for fucking up with your diabolical plan to embarrass him by having your friend reject his brother. That was priceless if I do say so myself."

"I never did anything like that, and there certainly was never a plan, you crazy half-wit."

"No? Too bad that's what he thought then, huh?" She chuckled to herself. "You can go tell him I made it all up if you want, but he won't believe you. You basically stopped calling and texting him, so it only reaffirmed that my theory about what you'd done was correct."

What could I really say? She was probably right. Whatever bullshit story she'd spun that night, along with her lack of clothing, had convinced him that I wasn't the woman for Austin. If nothing else had already killed our relationship, that would have. I warned him what would happen if he ever took her word over mine without coming to speak to me first. He made the choice to do just that.

"Nothing to say?"

"To you? No." When she stared at me, as if she couldn't believe I'd said that; I made my point. "You're not worth my time or energy."

"Funny, because I think you're just jealous of me. See, Austin and I have a pact that if neither of us has settled down by the time we're thirty, we'll marry one another. All I have to do is make sure he never settles before then."

"Why in the hell would I be jealous of you when the only way you can get the man to marry you is to trick him and then trap him?" I stood and grabbed my things. "I'm not jealous of you. I'm disgusted by you," I told her as I started to walk away, leaving her still crouched there with her mouth hanging open in shock. "Oh, and one more thing, if you ever come near me again, I will commit violence on you the likes of which you have never even thought of. Austin can visit what's left of your depraved ass in the hospital."

"He won't visit you in jail." Her snide remark missed its mark entirely.

"The difference is that I wouldn't expect him to. Stay away from me."

I stormed home and ignored Clea's worried look when I passed her as she was leaving with the giant turd she had for a boyfriend. When it looked like she might say something, I shook my head and went straight for my room, leaving her to lock up or not.

My best friend and I had a rift that built between us. She couldn't help that she fell for the doubchebag's charms, since seeing the best in people was what she did. It wasn't that I was angry with her for how things turned out. None of what happened between Austin and me was her fault. The rift was one of timing, on her part, and avoidance on mine.

Clea was busy with her new man.

I was occupied with hiding the fact that my miserable heart had been shattered beyond recognition.

*LINK TO BONUS Chapter 5 (Austin's POV of this chapter).

CHAPTER SIX

SIX YEARS LATER

My first instincts about my one and only love might not have been right, but they were accurate as fuck about Clea's boyfriend turned fiancé, Jeff. The bastard had been cheating on her. As far as she knew, it had only been for the past few months. My gut told me it had been throughout their whole relationship. Not that she would ever entertain my suspicions.

A few weeks ago, Clea and I went back to her office, unannounced, to grab her phone before heading to the cake testing for her wedding. The same testing that her piece of shit fiancé couldn't be bothered to go to with her. The reason he couldn't attend had been because he was too busy fucking Clea's assistant on Clea's desk, which was where and how we found them when we went to retrieve her phone.

I was honestly shocked that Jeff had been able to pull it off and hang in there with my bestie for so long, but I think a lot of that had to do with Clea being so busy launching her career. Plus, there was that whole fight she and I got into a few years back when she put her foot down and told me that unless I had proof that the asshole was doing her wrong, I needed to keep my mouth shut about him because she was tired of hearing my suspicions when there was absolutely nothing to back it up beyond the fact that I hated the guy.

There may have been mention about me being bitter that she met him the night everything fell apart for me and Mr. Texas – the only guy I ever confessed to her that I liked. If I had confessed the fact that I was falling in love with him to her, or been honest about how the aftermath crushed me, she might have been less heartless in her approach. Still, I'd kept quiet about my opinion of Jeff ever since to keep the peace. It nearly cost me the tongue I had to bite down on far too often, but at least my friendship with Clea was still intact all these years later. I was even a big enough person not to rub it in her face with a giant "I told you so!" balloon after we caught him fucking her secretary. Well, sometimes I might have rubbed it in, but not to hurt Clea. For instance, the news I heard recently was something she needed to know, in case she needed to be rechecked by her doctor.

"Have you seen the latest?"

"What now?" Clea asked as she glanced behind me, as if looking for her new assistant who failed to stop me from barging into her office for an unscheduled visit.

"There are three women claiming to be pregnant with his baby. Two have shown proof of their pregnancies, and I guess they're all still pending a DNA test to show that the babies are his."

Clea's jaw dropped. Her wide-eyed stare hit me and held for a few minutes before she was able to pull it together to ask, "Are you kidding me?"

I felt bad for hitting her with the news so callously. Yes, it was true that Jeff had never been my favorite person, but Clea always had. There was a better way to deliver the news and I'd fucked up. Unfortunately, there was no going back either, so I bucked up and asked the question that made telling her the news necessary.

"Was your doctor absolutely certain you're in the clear?"

"I made him test me for everything and then some," she confirmed.

"And then some?" I asked because what the hell did that even mean?

"Well, while we were there, I told him to go ahead and run shit for strep throat, the flu, rabies, freaking Lyme disease, and anything else that asshole might have possibly passed on to me."

I almost tipped my damn chair over when I leaned too far back from laughing so hard. "Oh…" I managed to get out, "My…" I was laughing too hard to make one tiny phrase come out properly. "God!" I held onto my sides to keep my ribs from hurting, though my abs seemed to get a good workout from my amusement. "Fucking rabies?" My all-out laughter died down to a light chuckle before I finally got myself under control again. "Did he actually do that one?"

Clea, who was clearly amused with my response, shook her head. "He threatened to throw water on me. When I told him to do whatever it takes, he said I couldn't have rabies because just the threat of water touching me would have made me angry."

I tucked myself into a tight ball in the chair because laughing could hurt if you did it too much, too hard, or for too long. "Oh shit, Clea! I think I just pissed in my panties a little bit," I admitted through my hysterical laughter.

Clea cleared her throat while I wiped away the tears from my eyes. No, wait, that wasn't right. It sounded like a man clearing their throat, not my best friend.

"Sorry, he said he had an appointment," Clea's kiss-ass assistant whined.

"Which is why Becs shouldn't have been allowed into the office, no matter how much she begged," Clea scolded her assistant in the nicest tone I've ever heard someone being chastised with.

"Oh, she didn't beg. That woman just walked right past me like I wasn't even there."

I sighed and offered a sheepish grin to Clea, whose attention was on whoever was still hovering behind me. When I heard the man chuckle, the humor-heated blood in my veins immediately turned to ice. I knew that sound. Even after all these years, it didn't fail to send tingles through all the lovely special places in my body.

I turned to see him standing there. "Austin?" I questioned as he moved closer.

"Becs," he shot back at me with a bit of attitude, as if I was the one who had wronged him all those years ago. That fucker! Like he didn't go straight back to enjoying his little best friend-fuck buddy before he even bothered to tell me we were through. In fact, he never did tell me. Maybe that's what he was standing in Clea's office for. No. Wait. That was ridiculous. The asshole probably hadn't even thought of me once since he went straight back to the willingly naked arms of Jordan – the cunt-faced, man-stealing, bitch monster from hell. Actually, to say she was from hell was probably giving her too much credit. There had to be worse places.

"What are you doing here?" I finally asked, because my mouth couldn't seem to stop itself from forming words that shouldn't have been spoken.

The asshat took his big, brown eyes off me and turned a charming grin on Clea instead as he extended a hand to her. "Austin Mercer, we had an appointment."

I was too stunned to do anything, and Clea mimicked my response with her fish out of water look, until the asshole spoke again.

"It's good to know we're in the clear with your rabies test, but um, maybe your friend should go have it done too?" He pointed his thumb in my general direction. As if.

"What?" I growled while standing up because staying seated

ANNE STORM

while angry was impossible. Then I said the first thing that came to mind. The one thing that I'd wanted to say to the man since I rolled up to his house and watched him entertain his mostly naked fuck buddy. "Fuck you, Austin!" Movement out of the corner of my eye drew my attention back to my best friend, whose office we were all standing in and embarrassment swamped me. Shit. The asshole was here on business, and I might have just screwed that up for her.

"I'm sorry, Clea. I didn't..." My face burned with a mixture of fury and mortification.

"Becs, can you leave us so that we can get down to business and we'll talk later?"

"Sure. Yeah." I backed away from them, afraid to turn around and let him out of my sight for some reason. It was official. I was crazy. "Sorry," I mouthed to Clea before finally turning tail and running away, like I should have done before I ever opened my stupid, traitorous mouth. Hopefully, he wouldn't hold my shit against Clea, and she wouldn't lose out on much-needed business because of me.

Despite making an ass out of myself, I couldn't make myself leave Clea's building. It was like my brain stopped firing on all its cylinders or something. Why in the hell couldn't I get my damn legs to work? I made it as far as the bathroom in the hallway and then stayed there until I heard Clea's secretary call out her good-byes to the man who I'd been hiding from.

I needed to know what he was there for and how much inter-action my best friend might have with my asshole ex. Truthfully, I wanted to tell her that she couldn't take his business. That would be wildly inappropriate of me though. Instead, I made my way back to Clea's office so I could at least get a few answers.

"What did that asshole want?"

"He wanted me to supply a party full of models and locals for an image rebuild at the bar he and his brothers purchased."

The Mercer brothers went into the bar business? I wondered

how long it would take for Clea to finish her part of the job and move on from dealing with them – with him in specific.

"What happened with him anyway? You never did say."

"I didn't want you to think it was your fault," I waved my hand at her as if to sweep it all under the proverbial rug where she wouldn't ask any questions.

"Um, no, we're not doing that." Clea stared at me and when I didn't speak, she tacked on, "You really need to tell me now."

"Your blind date was supposed to be his brother."

"The party where I met the asshole? The whole reason I hate Cupid!"

I laughed at her apt description. "You loved Cupid for years for that accidental fixup," I reminded her.

"Well, I was stupid." I laughed again, because I'd told her exactly that numerous times until she drew a line in the sand of our friendship and told me I had to stop accusing Jeff of things I couldn't prove.

"So, that guy who just walked out of my office was your boyfriend-"

I cut her off. "Friends with benefits is more like it." My eyes itched with the need to cry. I thought we had been more than that. If you were truly dating someone, with all the boyfriend/girlfriend labels, you were supposed to at least respect them enough to tell them when you're over, not just move on in front of a window where you know they'll see to spite them. All this time, I'd referred to Jordan as his fuck buddy, but that should have been my title all along. She had more of his heart than I ever had.

"Okay, well I remember you wanting to be more than just that with him. He dumped you because I never met up with his brother at that party?" Clea asked.

"Saying that he dumped me would be putting it mildly." Clea stared, sort of horror-stricken at me. I wondered if she could see the heartbreak. It felt like the whole world should be able to see

55

the devastation that still seeped out of my pores. "He completely ghosted me," I admitted, feeling utterly defeated all over again.

"I haven't talked to him since that night. When he saw you with someone else, he was angry, said that I'd promised not to screw his brother over if I set shit up because he wasn't in a healthy enough place to take it well." I shrugged my shoulders as I thought back to that time.

"As if his brother's mental health was my responsibility or that I could control you, that dumbass diaper-wearing Cupid, or anything else that happened that night." I certainly had zero control over Jordan or the fact that she was at his place, strutting around in her underwear that night.

"Becs, I'm so sorry. You were so excited about your Texas guy."

"Nope!" I halted Clea's progress with her apology. "You're not putting *his* bullshit on your shoulders. He thought I was responsible and ghosted me for it. That's on him and no one else. As far as I see it, he did me a favor, since his response was to bail and ghost me for things I couldn't control. Imagine if he'd gotten me pregnant and did that? Good riddance," I added at the end as I swiped my hands back and forth together, as if ridding them of unwanted dust. If only it had been that easy to rid myself of him and all my memories of our time together.

"Sorry," I heard that all-too-familiar voice mumble from near the door. "I think my phone slipped out of my pocket."

I stood, glanced down and found the phone that had been stuffed into the crack of the chair, next to where my thigh had been when I was seated. I wanted to pick the damn thing up and throw it at the man, accuse him of not knowing how to use the damn thing anyway, but I didn't. Instead, I moved to stand by the wall of windows that lined one side of Clea's office. It was the best I could do to keep myself in check.

I knew it was rude, that I hadn't just handed the man his phone, considering I'd been sitting on the damn thing. My emotions were too heightened to face him, or my best friend for that matter. The itching in my eyes from earlier turned into burning dampness as tears threatened to spill free.

"Thanks," I barely registered his one-word response. I didn't know if it was because he found the phone, something Clea said, or the fact that I moved so far away that he was thankful for.

I took in a deep breath and willed the tears to wait until I got back to the privacy of my own home. "You okay?" Clea whispered in my ear before wrapping my body in her arms.

"That was only slightly embarrassing."

"Moreso for him."

"Yeah, right," I huffed.

"Well, if you had seen him, you'd understand. His shoulders were hunched like this." She demonstrated his stance and while I appreciated what she attempted to do, none of it mattered. "And the tips of his ears were red as freaking cherries," she went on to say.

I giggled about that, but not for the reason Clea thought. No doubt, he remembered the night he shared with Jordan because of everything that happened. Who knows? Maybe the asshole popped a boner while thinking about his bestie in her lingerie and was embarrassed because he thought Clea noticed it. Either way, I wasn't about to let on that there was more to everything.

"His ears only turn red like that when he's really embarrassed, so I guess you weren't lying to make me feel better," I suggested.

"Nope. But I think you were lying to me, and maybe yourself, about how serious things were getting with him before he ghosted you."

"Doesn't matter. It's all in the past now."

That was the truth of the matter and one I needed a good long cry about. I thought I was long done crying over that relationship and certainly that man, since he didn't deserve my tears. The bastards wouldn't listen and threatened to spring up again.

"Clea, I'm sure you have work to do, with a new client and all, so I should get going."

"If it's going to hurt you, I can call and tell him that I can't honor our contract."

"No, you can't. You have a contract and not honoring it will lose you more than just the Mercer's business. I'm fine. I promise."

I so was not fine, but she didn't need to know that.

CHAPTER SEVEN

THE HADN'T BEEN A GOOD WAY TO GET OUT OF GOING TO THE party with Clea. Not even the possibility of the Mercer brothers' anger over my being there stopped my best friend from demanding that I go with her. The only excuse she would accept was if I told her that I couldn't go because it made me too uncomfortable. If I admitted to that, I'd have to fess up to why I felt that way and tell her the whole sordid tale.

I still didn't know why I kept it to myself, even six years after the fact. Every time the thought of unburdening myself of what happened cropped up, I buried it even deeper inside where all the hurt still festered. The truth was, I couldn't go through it again.

It didn't feel right to tell my stupid tale, and the whole damn thing just felt so unbelievable anyway. I grew angry with myself for still being upset about any of it. Admitting my story to Clea would make it ten times worse that I couldn't just get over it. Austin and I hadn't been together that long. Including the time when we first dated and the time leading up to the party, it was from Halloween until Valentine's Day. That was nothing in the big scheme of things, especially with six years separating the last time we spoke as a couple.

I had been lost in thought when we made our way to the club, so it was surprising to look up and see the huge line of people waiting to get inside. Luckily, we were able to bypass them and went straight to the employee section of the lot that had been roped off.

"Wow! I guess everyone hates Cupid as much as you do," I commented before faking a laugh in a sad attempt to ease the tension I felt at being on *his* turf. It didn't work for me, but Clea seemed to buy it as the real deal, so there was that.

"I guess so. I think this is a better turnout than we had hoped for. It seems like word of mouth spread and maybe we better get someone out here with a clipboard and have people pre-sign their photo release forms."

"You're the boss!"

"No, Becs, your Texas guys are the bosses. I'm just here to help them out tonight."

They weren't my anything, but I couldn't snap at Clea on her opening night. "I prefer to think of you as the boss. It makes it easier to go into a place that belongs to him."

"You don't have to be here," she reminded me. It wasn't the first time. Every excuse I made, that was the answer she gave, or something similar.

"Hush, come on, I hear this place is giving away drinks tonight."

We waited for freaking ever at the back door for someone to come let us in, and to my absolute horror, the last person I expected to see – though I don't know why – was the one to pop her head out the door.

"Hey! Come on in, Clea. I'm pretty sure we have everything set up per your instructions, but I'm guessing that you want to double-check before they start letting bodies through the door."

I wanted to wipe that smirk right off her stupid, whorish mouth. My hand twitched with the need for violence as I remembered the last time that I saw the bitch and the fact that she gloated about fucking any thought of me right out of Austin's mind.

Jordan and Clea were conversing, but I couldn't understand a word of what was being said because anger made my pulse thrum heavily inside my ears, blocking out all other sound. Eventually, I got tired of staring at her smug face as she pretended that I wasn't standing right there with my best friend.

"Where are your bosses?" I asked. She eyed me with contempt before turning to Clea again and answering her, like she had been the one to ask the question.

"They're in the office going over some staffing stuff." She walked away then but threw a glance back over her shoulder. "Feel free to find me if you need anything, Clea." The distinction that only Clea was offered the hospitality wasn't missed by me, and I didn't think it blew past my friend's notice either.

"What was that about?"

I sighed and turned to Clea. Keeping my secrets buried was turning out to be harder than I thought, especially when I was constantly confronted by them. "They used to date."

"Who used to date?"

"Austin and Jordan. They dated before he started seeing me back then." It didn't seem like much of a stretch to call what they had been doing dating, since he'd had more respect and love for her than he ever did for me. Clea's eyes narrowed as her attention swung back and forth between me and where Jordan had retreated deeper into the club.

"Before or during?" She attempted to clarify.

"Maybe one day, when I'm at the bottom of a bottle of tequila, I'll tell you all about it."

"You don't drink tequila because of that one night."

"Exactly."

The night Clea referenced had been two days after the Valentine's Day of Doom. He never called, and even after what I saw through his living room window, if he had called and explained, I might have taken him back. Knowing how weak I was to even think that made it worse, and that was why the tequila came out and stayed out until the very last drop. A few hours later, the whole world started to spin, matching the way my life had flown apart. Clea had come to check on me and found me in a puddle of my own tequila-drenched vomit.

Alcohol poisoning was a bitch. Just the smell of tequila was enough to trigger my gag reflex since that night. All thoughts of tequila induced illness left as the motherfucker, who started everyone's downfall, made a reappearance in an unexpected way. Clea tripped over something and would have faceplanted in the concrete if someone hadn't caught her. I realized it was Houston, the man who should have been by her side at the frat house six years ago instead of Jeff, who caught my best friend before she could hit the ground.

When I looked down, it was to see that Clea had tripped over Cupid's fucking bow and the little thingy that held the arrows. Clea thought she hated Cupid, but I had a hate-on for the guy too. He ruined everything. Absolutely everything. Then again, who was to say that the night wouldn't have gone to shit the minute we left that party. The plan had been for Houston to take Clea home and for me to leave with Austin. We were going to head back to his apartment. I wondered if naked Jordan would have been there waiting for us to arrive.

I put my rogue thoughts on the backburner as some woman tried and failed to pick a fight with Clea, who was not about to take her shit. Luckily for my bestie, the better Mercer brother had her back the whole time, despite the bitch-a-saurus-rex being his ex-girlfriend.

"We work together," the woman argued when Houston continued to take Clea's side. I'd missed most of their conversation because I was on my own personal tailspin down memory lane. I shouldn't have come to this damn opening night soiree.

"If you don't want that to change, then I suggest you get your shit together and stop this." Houston explained before glancing around for anyone who might help. "Someone get her out of here and make sure she doesn't come back tonight."

"Gladly!" Two voices chorused in the background. When I looked behind me, it was to see Austin and Jordan grinning at one another like they'd both just won the best "jinx" prize ever and it wouldn't be a coke. Knowing their history, they'd probably celebrate their oneness with a quick lap dance or maybe just a hard fuck in the office later.

Once everyone dispersed, I was left standing there as the male bartender handed me a drink. I lifted the thing to my lips, not knowing what it was, and took a sip. The strong bitter taste didn't even faze me the way it should have.

"Well, you took that like a champ," the man teased. "I honestly didn't think you could handle it, but it looked like you needed a strong drink, and I heard your friend say you don't do tequila."

"Thanks," I muttered before slamming the rest of the glass back and sitting it on the bar. Jordan and Austin were standing not twenty feet from me, and they were together, watching as security removed the woman from the premises. I wanted to throw up whatever the nice bartender had made for me.

"Becs!" A man called out. I turned slowly, unfortunately in the direction where Austin's presence couldn't be ignored. Austin's eyes met mine as Jordan's turned away. Cory, Clea's videographer for the night, and the man who had just called out to me, strolled up with a cocky grin on his face. "Is tonight my lucky night?"

"I don't know, Cory, is it?"

"I'm just waiting on you to say yes to a date. That's all I need. Give me one shot and you'll have me walking down the aisle and worshipping at your feet for the rest of our lives."

I laughed at the kid. He wasn't really a kid, but he was a few years younger than my twenty-seven which was why I kept turning him down. He was sweet and could make me laugh, but flirting was where I drew the line.

"That's a bit of a stretch, don't you think? From one date to marriage, just like that?"

"Nah! The way I figure it is that I've been in lust with you so long we might as well call it unrequited love at this point," he said with complete confidence.

It just so happened I knew a little something about unrequited love, which was how I knew Cory was simply teasing me.

"Uh-huh."

"Okay, new approach, what if I said that I could be content with a date and maybe a one-night stand?"

"Did you ask me to agree to a one-nighter with you? And you did it with a straight face too. That was good," I teased.

"Either good or I'm serious," he muttered.

"Cory, Cory, Cory," I started to say.

"Nooooo!" He interrupted by drawing out the word before I could say anything more than his name on repeat. "And she shoots me down again, ladies and gentlemen!" He offered up loudly to anyone who would listen. "How will I ever live without you?" He asked while dramatically clutching his chest.

"You're a fucking nut."

Cory winked at me. "Takes one to know one, sweet cheeks."

"If you value your family jewels, you'll never call me that again."

His hand moved from over his heart and straight down to his balls. That was the typical path for most men I knew. They thought they were leading with their heart, turned out that it was the balls leading the show all along.

"You wound me, Becs."

"Not yet, I haven't." It was my turn to wink at Cory.

"Looks like our fearless leader is over there," he nodded toward Clea, who stood exceptionally close to Houston as they spoke. That could have been because the music was loud, but I didn't think so. Six years ago, I knew they'd be perfect for one another. Seeing their chemistry in action only proved that I'd been right.

"Come on, let's go see what she has in store for us tonight."

We got to Clea about the same time Houston started to walk away, and while I liked to think that Austin was completely out of my mind, it felt as though someone was staring a hole in my back. Whether that was Austin, Jordan, or both while they talked about me, literally behind my back, I had no clue. There was no way I'd look either. I didn't want to know. It was more like I couldn't handle knowing.

"Hey," I called out to Clea and giggled as she jumped after being startled.

"Hey." Clea smiled at me as she muttered the greeting, but there was a sparkle in her eyes that I didn't miss, despite the way she tried to appear all nonchalant.

"You have that look in your eye."

"What look would that be?"

"The one where you can't take your eyes off a certain Mercer brother."

"Am I an idiot for even thinking of going there this soon?"

I snatched my bestie's arm and slung her around to face me instead of watching Houston's ass as he walked away. Cory had wandered off somewhere instead of sticking by my side, so my advice to Clea was frank and unfiltered.

"The only idiot was your ex. You are a catch and I hate that you're second guessing your own possible happiness because he blew it." Hmm, maybe that was a poor choice of words because I think him being blown, or otherwise sticking his dick where it didn't belong, was why they hadn't worked out. "I guess maybe he got blown and that was the problem," I amended for her since she couldn't read my mind.

"If that was the problem, he wouldn't have so many baby mommas lining up for paternity tests," Clea snorted out a laugh at her own joke at Jeff's expense. For some odd reason, I felt like a proud momma.

"Yeah, you're ready for this," I told her while glaring down at my feet. Being happy for my friend finally getting a re-do on that shitty night six years ago didn't preclude me from feeling the burden that it would never happen for me.

"What makes you say that?"

"You can joke about what that asshole did without falling to pieces. That means you'll be fine."

I scanned the crowd, wondering what I could do to help, to keep my mind off everything. Staying busy meant staying sane, in my world. While my assessment was underway, my eyes drifted to where Austin and Jordan stood, side-by-side behind the bar. They seemed to be having an intense conversation in between filling orders. They would go to their separate ends and meet in the middle again while making drinks and grabbing beers. Their mouths moved almost imperceptibly, but the body language spoke volumes. She constantly pressed into the space between them while he would back away and relax until she pressed again. The only time that little dance wasn't happening between them was when they had to walk away to take more orders.

Yeah, okay, I only noticed all that because I hadn't been assessing what was needed of me. My heart and mind were lost to anything but the two people who worked so hard to break my heart the last time I dared to celebrate the dreaded V-Day.

"You ever going to fill me in on what happened there?" Clea asked me, after cluing into my all too obvious obsession.

"Oh, look, isn't that your videographer trying to flag you down?"

Cory had come back from wherever he'd disappeared to before. If it wouldn't give him the wrong idea, I'd kiss him for creating the best distraction ever to get my friend off my ass about Austin and Jordan. She already had her hooks in, so I'd have to explain things to her eventually. There was no way I could even attempt to do that while we were on his turf, with that bitch watching as my eyes sprung a leak. No, the best friend explanations would have to wait for another day and definitely another place.

I avoided everyone after that by keeping myself busy cleaning up after assholes who set their empties down on tables or railings even though there was a trashcan not five feet from where they left their garbage. I trashed the unattended empties along with some not-so-empty containers, too. Seriously? Did people not understand how easily an unwatched drink could be dosed with something? They couldn't complain about me doing them a favor and throwing away their unwatched drinks. I'd probably saved at least one person tonight from a terrible outcome.

My fingers twitched to pick up the empty glasses and return them to the bar, but there was no way I would willingly go over there unless Clea called specifically needed me. Maybe not even then. It would probably take a whole act of God to get me near Jordan and Austin's space. It wasn't that I was a coward. Seeing the two of them interacting all night was like having salt rubbed in a wound though. It didn't need to happen up close where I might overhear something that would make me sick on the spot.

One of the waitresses passed by me and I grabbed her. "Hey, I'm helping tonight. Is there somewhere I can take all the empties, like to the back where a dishwasher is or something, rather than the bar?"

"Oh, yeah. They should have told you." The woman turned and pointed to the swinging door that led to the back where I assumed the offices were earlier. "Just go through the door and veer left toward the washing station. Mikey is back there taking care of the dishes and the boys stock the bar again once their clean." She started to walk off and turned back. "Thanks so much for doing that. Stopping to pick up the empties kills my tips."

"No worries," I announced as she walked away. Getting paid wasn't on my agenda. I needed to stay occupied and as far away from the bar as possible. That was the goal until Clea eventually said we could leave for the night. My best friend didn't even realize how much she owed me for coming tonight to help. Then again, she really owed me nothing because this was a job for her and it was going well, which meant her business was bound to take off into a new stratosphere. Anyone who could turn around the reputation of Ned's Nest in one night was a damn hero to businesses.

The rest of the night, I ran empty glasses back to the dishwashers, kept up with dumping people's garbage into the cans, and then informed the dishwashers when they also needed to go empty the trashcans in the club, since they were too heavy for me to take out on my own. Otherwise, I did everything possible to avoid being near the bar. All in all, I felt useful and only once or twice, maybe a half dozen times did my eyes wander over to see Austin, Jordan, or both behind the bar. Every single time required a quick trip to the dishwashing station or to the bathroom I discovered in the back that had no line to wait in.

No one saw my eyes grow misty. They certainly didn't see the one time I cried over my own stupidity. Nope. Not a single witness in sight beyond my own reflection.

My feet hurt and I was exhausted physically and emotionally by the time last call hit. I redoubled my efforts to get glasses back to the dishwashers so they could get out at a decent time.

"Meet me at the bar, I'm just going to finalize everything with Austin and Houston, then we can leave," Clea told me in passing.

"Headed to the bathroom first, then I'll meet you there."

It would be the one time during the night when I wouldn't mind going near the bar because it meant being able to leave hell on Earth. Seriously, no friendship is worth having to watch your one and only love – ex-boyfriend or not – and his friend, fuck buddy, girlfriend, or whatever the hell she was to him these days as they frolicked and played behind the bar all night.

That probably wasn't fair. The bar stayed slammed from

opening until last call, so I was sure they didn't do much frolicking, but in my mind, that's all they were doing because this night had been my own personal living hell. I loved Clea to death, but never again.

After returning from the bathroom for the last time, I meandered up behind Clea as she mentioned my name. "I drove Becs here. I need to give her a ride home."

"I can take Becs home." I thought the world had opened up and swallowed me inside when I realized it was Austin who offered me the ride. A quick glimpse of Jordan showed that she was none too happy with his quick act of chivalry. I must have missed something though because I didn't understand why it was necessary.

"Why would you take me home?"

Houston was the one who answered. "I asked Clea to come home with me when we're done closing down."

I glanced between Houston and Clea, regretting what I was about to say before the words were out of my damn mouth. It couldn't hurt any worse than the rest of the night, could it? Yeah, I didn't believe that for a second. Still, I was a glutton for punishment, or at the very least for my best friend's happiness since I couldn't have my own.

"I don't live that far. It doesn't matter who drops me off. You should go with Houston. It was a big night and I'm sure you both want to celebrate."

Clea leaned in and hugged me tight. "I owe you."

If only she knew the price tag was in the priceless range. Still, I did get the tiniest bit of satisfaction when I watched Jordan throw a towel before she huffily grabbed her bag from beneath the counter and took off like a stomping toddler who just had her crayons stolen. I supposed that was a fair enough analogy, since she probably thought I would steal her man again. As if I'd put my heart in jeopardy all over again for a man who had no problem stomping on it with silence.

Austin watched her go too, and I was surprised when he didn't attempt to stop the bitch or call her back to explain that he was just doing a favor for his brother. Then again, he'd never been known for his communication skills, so I wasn't sure why any of it surprised me, beyond his offer to give me a ride. Clea leaned over toward my ear one more time.

"Be careful."

"Aren't I always?" I gave enough of a sarcastic response to let her know that I was perfectly cool and unaffected. In other words, I sold my friend a bunch of bullshit.

"No, that's why I warned you."

A genuine laugh burst free of my body without my permission. It was probably the exhaustion laughing. She wasn't wrong though. Not being careful and listening to my gut is what got me in trouble with my heart in the first place.

"Whatever. I'm too tired to not be careful."

CHAPTER EIGHT

"I HOPE YOU DON'T MIND, BUT I HAVE TO MAKE SURE EVERYTHING gets cleaned up before we can leave. I haven't seen Dallas since the beginning of the night, Houston just took off with Clea, and…" Austin glanced in the direction Jordan had stormed off earlier. "Well, we're short-handed."

"No worries. I kept up with taking the empties to the dishwashers all night, made them take care of overflowing trash as I saw it, and picked up any garbage lying around, too."

Austin stared at me for a solid minute before he managed to shift his focus and really assess the state of the emptying club. I think it was the first time he noticed that most of the closing work had already been alleviated. "Why did you do that?"

I scoffed at him. "This was Clea's big night. Why did you think I came along?" Before he could answer, I stopped him. "She needed tonight to be a success. It didn't matter who owned the business she was helping, so I came along and did my part. I would do anything to make sure she is happy and successful. I'm not a photographer or videographer. I certainly don't fit the part as a model, so I did the job no one else seemed inclined to do all night. I kept the place looking good. I'm tiny, so no one even noticed me. It was like your bar had a house elf running around taking care of the little things."

Austin stared, as if he'd never seen me before. "Word of advice, hire someone to do that job on busy nights. Your servers lose out on tips when they have to run the floor for garbage, dirty dishes, and then take everything to the dishwashing station in the back. By the time they get back to the floor, people are angry because they couldn't find their server to help them, and their tips go down. Then, your staff won't be happy enough to stick around."

Austin continued to stand there and stare at me, so I pulled my smartass remarks out to shield myself from looking at him too long. "You might want to write that down. It's solid advice."

"Noted."

"Do you have a cleaning rag back there or something, so I can wipe the tables down?"

"Sure." Austin tossed me a white, damp towel and I turned immediately to get busy cleaning so we could get the hell out of... well... hell.

Once the bar was cleaned, chairs put up on the tables, and everyone was out, Austin wandered through the place locking everything up until it was just the two of us standing at the back-door. He peeked his head out there first and looked around.

"Okay, hop on out, it's safe. I have to set the alarm and then we'll head out."

I did as the man asked and left to stand just outside the door to wait for him. Two minutes later, he came out and locked the deadbolt with a key before he turned to me and nodded to his newer model pickup truck.

"That's me."

"Great. I don't live far from here." We got into his truck, and I immediately noticed the hair elastic that hung from his gearshift. Under normal circumstances, I wouldn't have thought anything of it since the man had a mother and two sisters who he was close to. After seeing that he and Jordan were still close as well, and in fact worked together, I imagined it was hers and wanted to vomit. Instead, I gave Austin my address and turned to watch the dark scenery out the window. Unfortunately for me, night-time meant that I saw more reflection in the window, than scenery. I saw enough to know that Austin kept looking my way, whether to get my attention or because he couldn't believe how incredibly unlucky he had been to be stuck with me, I didn't know.

Clearly, he loved his brother as much as I loved Clea, since he volunteered to be my driver for the night. "Becs." His gentle voice was almost startling in the quiet of the truck cab. He hadn't even turned the stereo on.

"Hmm?"

For the longest time, he didn't respond. I thought maybe he hadn't heard me at first, so I turned to see him grinding his teeth together in apparent agitation.

"Look if this is a problem for you, I'm close enough. I can walk the rest of the way."

"No, the fuck you can't. Do you know what time it is?" He asked just as an inadvertent yawn hit me. I glanced at the dash anyway. It was almost four in the morning.

I shrugged my shoulders at him. "What's your problem then? I realize you were just doing Houston a favor by letting him have his night with Clea that Jeff robbed him of six years ago. Me too, buddy. There's my place up ahead. It's almost over. Then, you can go back to pretending I don't exist. I'll even ask the powers that be to make sure you are still crowned hide and seek champion of the decade. It takes great skill to drop off the face of the earth and remain unseen for six years."

Oops, I think a little bit of my angry sarcasm may have slipped out.

"Yeah, well then I think we tied, since I don't seem to recall you picking up a phone or showing up at my place like you said you would." I laughed and finally turned to look at the man as he pulled the truck next to the curb in front of my apartment.

"That's where you're wrong." I unbuckled as I spoke and turned to open the truck door when he slammed the auto lock down. I glared back over at him.

"What am I wrong about?" He waggled a completely different phone in my face than he had back then. "Different phone, same number though."

"I showed up," I blurted out. "I was there."

"You were where?"

"Outside of your house that night. It took me a little longer to get there because I was dealing with Clea for being a bad friend and leaving me behind. Plus, she just left the party with that douchebag and didn't know if she would be safe with him. Sometimes, I think that woman thinks there aren't any bad people at all in the world."

Austin stared at me, jaw agape, as I continued to prattle on. "So, I was late by about thirty minutes. Unfortunately for me, that made me right on time to see the show you had set up for me by the time I got there."

"What show?" He asked, though his words came out slowly, as if they'd been dipped in molasses.

"The show your girlfriend put on for you for Valentine's Day."

"My girlfriend never showed up," he countered.

"No? That's not possible because I saw it all through your living room window. I hope you and your brother grew up some and bought curtains at some point. I watched you sitting there, sprawled out in your chair with your beer and your lap dance partner doing her little strip tease. Though, I have to say, a good strip tease usually requires a few more layers."

"You had it all wrong," he tried to deny.

"Really? So, I guess that means I missed the part where you got up, pushed her coat back over her scantily clad body, and threw her ass out before things went further?"

"Nothing went further."

"You didn't kick her out or ask her to get dressed though, did you?"

"What?"

"I sat there, with my fucking heart breaking, for fifteen minutes before I could get myself together well enough to drive home that night. Not once, in all that time, did you get up and escort her out, or even throw a fucking blanket at her. You also didn't bother to call and warn me that she showed up, or what I might see when I got there. So, I did what I was supposed to do, and assumed I was meant to see her parading around naked in front of your living room windows while you sat back and eagerly watched."

"There was no show. You weren't meant to see anything because she should have never been there that night."

"Oh, was she scheduled for the following night?"

"No, that's not what I meant."

"Sure, whatever." I laughed at him. "It's funny, because Jordan had no problem telling me all about how you spent Valentine's night together, how you believed the bullshit lies she told you about me that night, and how you didn't even miss me because she'd kept you too busy fucking her to even think of me."

"What the fuck?" He roared into the cab of the truck. "When exactly did she tell you all that?"

"About two weeks after I stopped hearing from you. It was during that first warm day just before March." I rolled my eyes to emphasize how fucking cliché it had all been before launching into the details.

"I was sitting on the lawn at school, soaking up the sun, hoping to feel warmth again. She plopped down and told me all about how the two had been together since that night. Your girlfriend also took great pride in explaining how you took her word about some off-the-fucking-wall revenge scheme that I supposedly perpetrated and that you never even cared to hear my side of things. I do believe she hit the nail on the head there." I shook my head at him, disgusted all over again.

"Wasn't that my one steadfast rule for agreeing to a second chance with you? You were supposed to ask me, and not just believe any bullshit she spouted to you, like she did to all your other relationship attempts? Well, there was that rule, plus the one where you weren't supposed to be fucking your best friend behind my back. I watched you breaking one of those rules and she told me all about the other.

I flicked the lock button on my side because childproof locks only existed in the back seat and then I slid out of his truck and headed to my apartment. It was sad that I didn't live in a place where I could leave my door unlocked while I was away. It was frustrating to try to unlock a door while my hands shook with anger, heartbreak, and whatever other emotions had been pushed to the forefront thanks to the night from hell. Never again. I would never again leave home on the dreaded V-Day. It was the absolute worst.

"Stop," Austin ordered as he placed his hand over mine and took the keys from me. It didn't take long for him to get the door unlocked. He ushered us inside and then leaned back against the door while he locked the thing, as if he was afraid that I would push him out. He was right to think that.

"We need to talk this out."

"No. The time to talk this out was six years ago, when you were too busy being entertained by mostly naked Jordan. You took the time, that was meant for us to talk things out, to listen to your other girlfriend weave some story about me while she stood in front of you in her underwear. That was more important than checking to see if I even got home safely. You remember, right?" I asked. "The Valentine's Day frat party, where everyone left me stranded to walk by myself across campus back to the apartment I shared with my best friend."

His eyes closed and his head dropped. It must not have

occurred to him before that they all basically abandoned me that night. My boyfriend and my best friend both.

"You said you were late because you were yelling at Clea," he muttered and shook his head. "Dammit, Becs. I wasn't thinking clearly that night. We didn't meet you at the door because Dallas caused fucking chaos before the two of you showed up."

"Well, bully for him. He caused chaos after we showed up, too. Unfortunately for me, I took the blame for the crap he caused."

"I know, and for what it's worth, I'm sorry. The first time I realized that Dallas was even involved with what happened to push your friend into someone else's arms was when I heard you and Clea talking in her office."

"Funny thing, if you'd ever bothered to come ask me what happened, I could have told you all that six damn years ago."

"Would you have spoken to me after seeing Jordan at my place like that?"

"That's the difference between you and me. I would have listened to you. That doesn't mean you would have liked the outcome because even if you had come to me that night, or the next day, the same question would have plagued me. Why didn't you kick her out immediately, especially when you thought I was on my way there?"

He shook his head. "I don't know. She kept talking and I listened while I waited. Part of me thought I didn't have anything to hide, since I hadn't arranged for her to be there, and that if you showed up, you would see it for the desperate act it was on her part."

"The problem with that theory is that I would also see that you would allow her to get away with doing it."

"I didn't do anything with her."

"So, it would have been okay for me to have some dude over at my house, a real version of Clarence for example, and have him stripped down to his boxer briefs where everything was on display including most of his package because the boxer briefs were lace and mostly opaque? You would have been okay showing up to my place and seeing him there like that, knowing I was apparently enjoying the view enough that I never once asked him to cover up, put clothes on, or gee, I don't know, maybe get the fuck out of my house with that disrespectful shit?"

"You were late,"

"So that was an excuse to ogle your supposedly ex-fuck buddy?"

"No. Would you let me get this out?" The animalistic growl that came after his question did more to shut me up than his demand did. It was clear the man was frustrated. "You were late, didn't call, and yeah, I was angry because shit didn't go well for my brother. It felt like my fault that his night became a disaster."

"No, that's not right. You felt like it was *my* fault," I interjected. "You blamed me long before you even left that party."

"Partly, but it was mine for listening to your hairbrained scheme to hook my brother up with your best friend." I nodded but didn't say anything because I already figured that was the case long ago.

"Jordan must have been at the party. She claimed to have been there with my sister, Victoria. They supposedly heard you and your friend talking about how you were going to get back at me and show me what humiliation felt like."

"I already know this," I explained because I didn't feel like rehashing the lies that Jordan had told him. The fact remained that he sucked them up like Gospel and believed the shit she dished out to him without ever speaking to me.

"Yeah, well, the believable part was when you never showed up to my place, called, or even texted me. That was something she claimed to overhear that night. You planned to ghost me."

"So, you decided to listen to her and ghost me instead?"

"You never showed up!" He yelled!

"I told you that I did! Why in the hell would I go into that house after seeing her parading around in nothing but skimpy lingerie while you looked for all the world like you were enjoying the show. Fifteen minutes I sat right outside your house, Austin. You must have noticed my headlights when I pulled up, and maybe even when I took off again, because I had to back up a bit that night before I could pull out."

He shook his head. "I never noticed headlights that night."

"No, I guess not, since your fuck buddy was busy shoving her own headlights in your face."

I laughed then and turned my back to him to keep the asshole from seeing the way my eyes had grown wet again. Damn the never-ending hellscape night!

"You expected me to call or text after you sent me to walk home alone at night, didn't check on me, and when I did show up to your house, you had the woman who caused problems for us before standing in front of you in her bra and panties. Would you have called or texted if the rolls were reversed?"

"Would you have called or texted if Clea told you she over-heard that conversation and then I didn't show or call or anything?"

"Yes! I would have because we promised each other that we would not believe random shit from previous jealousy-motivated fuck buddies without speaking to one another first!" He was quiet for a minute, and I turned to face him again.

"Let me ask you a question, Austin." He nodded, so I launched into it. "I didn't see Jordan's car outside, so I assume she got a ride to your place. Probably so that she could put on that show in front of the window for me, or possibly so I would come catch the two of you in the act."

"Your question?"

"Did you make sure Jordan got home safely from your house?"

He appeared stunned by the question for a few minutes before he finally nodded. "After Houston got up and found her sleeping on the couch, he told me I needed to get her out of there and make sure to get the key back that we didn't realize she still had."

"So, she slept there?"

"Yes, she fell asleep on the couch while I sat up waiting for you to call or show up and prove her wrong."

"It's funny how I was the bad guy who had to prove your girlfriend wrong."

"You were my girlfriend."

"It didn't look like that when I was sitting outside your window watching the two of you. You took her word and ran with it. I fucking told you that you would do just that when you asked me for a second chance. It was why I made you promise to come to me first if she ever tried to feed you a story about me. You swore you wouldn't let her manipulate you that way."

My frustration hit its peak as I shook my head, trying to rid myself of the dark feelings that plagued me along with the memories of that night and the weeks that followed. "I can't keep going in these circles with you. It really is pointless anyway, since all this happened six fucking years ago, Austin. You and Jordan are still two peas in a pod from what I saw tonight. Why are you even here?"

His shoulders slumped forward, and he mumbled something to himself that I couldn't hear before his eyes lifted to meet mine again. "We are only friends. She works at the club. That's it."

The disbelieving smirk on my face was enough to tell him I didn't believe that one bit. "So, in the six years since I saw you last, you never picked up with being her fuck buddy again?"

The tips of his ears immediately heated to a very noticeable red tone and there was no way for him to hide the guilty look either. "We just scratched an itch together sometimes after things fell apart between us, and very rarely at that."

My laughter was something that should have been bottled and used as a weapon against every clueless bastard who ever bothered to speak.

"My, my, my. You do not bother to learn from your mistakes at all, do you? I already knew that about you, considering the conversation we never had before you were steam-rolled by your girlfriend into believing I was some evil-plotting vengeful banshee out to get you. I don't even know how that seemed plausible to you, but whatever." I turned and walked to my kitchen to grab a water to take to bed with me. "I've heard about all I have the energy for, considering we're ancient history anyway. The door is behind you, please see your way out."

The stupid bottles of water were pushed all the way to the back of the fridge, so I had to lean in to be able to get ahold of one. When I pulled back and stood up, a warm body was directly behind mine. Austin's hands grabbed my hips and held me firmly in place.

"It didn't feel like we were ancient history when I saw you again in Clea's office," he admitted. There was no way I'd agree to that. "When I saw you tonight-"

I turned in his embrace and craned my head back to look up at him. "When you saw me tonight, you ignored me and spent the night talking and flirting with Jordan, so don't try to feed me some bullshit about how you couldn't take your eyes off me."

"Apparently, you couldn't take your eyes off me all night, since you seem to think you saw so much." I rolled my eyes because there wasn't much I could say by way of denial since I had told on myself about watching him. "The truth is, Jordan and I were arguing most of the night."

"I really don't give a shit about your lover's quarrels, Austin."

"You should, since we were arguing about you."

"Not sure why either of you would bother. She won whatever game she was playing a long time ago and you gave her the win. The two of you continued with your fucked up relationship since then, so that's like a win-win for both of you guys. There was nothing to argue about."

"Becs," he pleaded. I shook my head and tried to wiggle out of his grip, but the bastard was unrelenting and pushed forward so I was trapped between his incredibly strong body and the refrigerator door.

"Why are you here? Doing this..." I wasn't proud of the fact that anyone saw me whine like a baby, but exhaustion really had kicked in hard. "Working all night in my own personal hellscape was beyond exhausting, please, leave me alone so I can go get some sleep."

"Why was it your personal hellscape?" He pushed.

I pushed back, physically. My hands landed with one on his firm pectoral and the other on his freaking washboard abs. In my dreams of Karmic balance, the bastard had a beer belly, flabby arms, and he'd gone bald. Unfortunately, even Karma was not on my side. What had I ever done to deserve the life I'd been given?

When Austin didn't budge, I did the only thing left to do. My dignity hit an all-time low as the tears, that threatened to wreck me all night, finally made their true appearance along with accompanying gut-wrenching sobs. I leaned forward so that my forehead rested on the middle of Austin's chest and let loose the deluge of six-years' worth of pent-up emotions. Later, the blame for my emotional breakdown would fall on the sheer exhaustion I faced after being awake for almost twenty-four hours.

Austin held me there, as I completely soaked his shirt with my salty tears, until my legs gave out. Then, he picked me up and carried me to the bedroom and laid me down on my unmade bed. I couldn't move beyond the tiny little hiccups caused by the endless sob-fest.

It didn't even register what he was doing, when the man started to pull the shoes off my feet, the dress I wore soon followed, and I was stripped down to just my panties and bra. If I hadn't been so fucking wiped out, there probably would have been a dark joke in there about how Austin seemed to like his women stripped down to their underwear, crazy, and vulnerable.

Instead, I closed my eyes and drifted off into the dark oblivion of a much-needed sleep.

In my dream, there was a man's body wrapped around mine, emitting warmth that made me snuggle closer. February was still cold as shit and my heat was set at a balmy sixty-four degrees to save on the electric bill. I was rarely home and when I was, it was to sleep. I enjoyed snuggling under cozy blankets, so normally it seemed perfect to keep the temperature that low. Dream me devised other ways to stay nice and toasty. Too bad dream me and real me couldn't get together and make it happen in the waking world.

Sure, relationships scared the crap out of me, especially considering how my last attempt at a relationship ended. Still, that didn't mean I didn't get lonely and crave the touch of another person. I snuggled even closer, completely done in by the masculine aroma that damn near obliterated my senses. It was something dark and spicy mixed with the perfect amount of enticingly yummy pheromones. Whatever it was, dream dude's scent tripped my trigger and transformed my lulled, cozy self into a horny lust hound in a matter of seconds.

My body itched to get closer even though his arms were wrapped around me, our legs seemed to be tangled together, and my lips were petting his slightly hairy chest. Okay, in reality, I was kissing my dream dude's chest while attempting to wiggle even closer. The bulge that greeted my efforts signified that either me being wrapped in his arms, or the wiggling I'd been doing, was having the same effect on him.

Either way, sleepy, dreamtime me was ready to take full advantage. I wanted my dream guy to ravage me before we both woke up and poofed away into naughty dreamland again. If I wasn't going to get dick in real life, might as well enjoy the fruits of my very active imagination.

"You better mean it," the very male voice rumbled from above me as I fished his exceptionally hard cock out of his boxer briefs.

There really was no time to undress. This was a dream after all. Our clothes would magically fall off at some point anyway. That was the best part about dreams. Less work. More enjoyment.

"Mmm." The sleepy moan that escaped from my slightly parted mouth, as the man of my literal dreams slipped his fingers inside my panties, should have been enough stimulation to wake me fully. Instead, I luxuriated in the way it felt when he then swiped those same fingers up my slickened slit before pinching hold of my clit and driving me absolutely wild.

"Oh God!" I groaned the words deep from my throat as he quickly pulled my panties aside and rolled us in one fell swoop, so I was lying on my back as he hovered above me. After gaging that my body was ready for him, my wonderful dream lover didn't hesitate to shove himself deep inside me.

To my surprise, considering the dream state I was in, it hurt quite a bit. Sex had not been on the menu for nearly a year, despite a few hot and steamy make out sessions and a little oral play from a date six months previous. The discomfort at finally having a man inside me again would have been expected, if it was happening in real life and not a dream. For the first time, I opened my eyes and realized I knew the chest of the man who thrust into me with wild abandon.

"Austin?" While I questioned whether it was really him or dream him in my groggy, just waking state of mind, his name sounded more like a moan of encouragement. He took it exactly that way, considering his thrusts drove harder into my body as those talented hands of his glided along my fiery skin, grabbing, holding, exploring, and my favorite of all, pinching in all the right places. The man always knew just when to apply the pressure to make me combust.

Sunlight slipped through the slightly parted curtains and caught me in the eye as I threw my head back in orgasmic bliss. Unfortunately, the unexpected light chilled the feeling almost as quickly as it had begun. I tapped on Austin's chest to get him to stop and hop off me because I couldn't get my voice to work. The shock of waking up to sex with him for the first time in six years sort of fried my synapses.

"Please, don't let this be happening," I mumbled to myself. "No, no, no!" I groaned as I tapped his chest again only to realize he was already at the point of no return.

"Fuck! Becs, you always felt like heaven and home to me."

I didn't think it was possible for a person's heart to shatter more than once in a lifetime, but that was what happened as I lie there in shock, digesting the words he'd just given me. Ones I wished he had come close to six years ago before everything came crashing down. No, they weren't the three little words every girl seemingly longed to hear. They were more poignant to me. To be someone's home, their anchor, was far more than simple love or lust cloaked as love. Feeling like you were someone's home was everything.

That was what I'd always felt for Austin. It was the whole reason I'd given him another chance after that fateful date where Jordan happened to be at the movies when they let out. Come to think of it, I would bet money Jordan placed herself there on purpose that night. Not that it mattered now.

"You need to get off," I finally managed to verbalize.

"I just did, beautiful."

"Ugh," I groaned. "Get off me," I replied forcefully. "I need to go to the bathroom. You just came inside me without a condom."

"I'm sure it'll be fine. You're on the pill."

"No, I'm not. I was on the pill six fucking years ago. I stopped taking them, for almost a year now, since they were causing debilitating migraines."

"Shit!" He jumped up so fast, he should have won some kind of Olympic award.

And the gold medal for quickest man out of a woman's body and bed goes to...

"I don't even understand how that even happened. What in

the hell are you still doing in my apartment?" I asked while jumping up and running for the bathroom. A brisk waddle was the more apt description, considering my thighs were clamped shut to avoid leakage before I could get to the toilet and empty myself out. Sex was wonderful, but there were some gross aspects too. The cleanup afterward was always an iffy thing. Sometimes, the cleanup could be just as sexy as the act itself, if done right with a partner who cared. This was not one of those times.

"After your emotional breakdown, I stuck around to make sure you were okay. I guess I fell asleep."

"In my bed without your clothes on?" I asked through the bathroom door.

"I kept my underwear on. It's not my fault I woke up to you pulling my dick out of them this morning." There was a pause before he corrected himself. "Afternoon."

I heard shuffling from the other room as I cleaned up quickly and grabbed my robe off the hook on the bathroom door. Thankfully, I'd put it back where it belonged the last time that I'd used it.

When I opened the door, Austin was hopping on one foot while stuffing his other one into the dark denim pants he'd worn the night before. He glanced at the digital clock beside the bed again.

"Shit," the man muttered.

"Late for something?"

"Actually, yes. I was supposed to meet with the crew from last night to go over how everything went, so we could train on what to do or not do when we officially open."

"It was kind of an asshole move to make that a mandatory meeting the day after the longest night in history."

"It only felt that long to you," he countered.

Well, if that wasn't a slap in the face, I don't know what was.

Then again, the confession that the night was like my own personal hellscape did hang in the air between us.

"I didn't mean it like that. Most of my employees have been working clubs and bars for years. They're used to the late work hours and the physical labor that goes with it."

"Sure," I agreed, even though it sounded like a bullshit line to me. "Can we just forget that my dream got out of hand, and we ended up doing that?" I pointed to the rumpled mess of a bed.

"No can do, Trouble," he responded.

I narrowed my eyes on Austin. "Do not call me that."

The bastard smirked. "If I didn't have to run to work, we would continue our conversation where we left off last night."

"No, thank you."

"We're going to talk about it until we both come to terms with what happened. And that," he pointed to the bed, "definitely happened and I won't forget it anytime soon." He grabbed his jacket off the chair that sat in the corner near the door. "Gotta run, but we'll talk later."

I stared longingly at my laptop as he took off. Maybe a trip to Europe could be in the budget? No, that wouldn't work because I didn't have a passport. Suddenly, that seemed like poor planning on my part. Then again, I figured I'd be too broke to travel for the foreseeable future anyway. There had to be an alternative. I'd gone six fucking years without ever running into the man, or his lying whore-friend, around town. There had to be a way to go back to the status quo I'd grown used to.

CHAPTER NINE

THE KNOCK ON MY DOOR AS I GOT OUT OF THE SHOWER WAS unexpected. The fact that it took me all day to get up and shower because I didn't want to wash away Austin's scent from my body was ridiculous.

"What are you doing here?" I asked as Austin pushed through the door the minute that I opened it.

"I told you earlier that we were going to finish our conversation."

"Funny, I'm pretty sure I told you there was nothing to finish. We covered everything last night."

"Nah, not everything Becs. There was something pretty damn important that I think we both left off."

"What was that exactly?"

"The fact that neither of us wanted it to be over back then. We had an amazing connection. What happened last night is proof that it never died."

I chuckled at him because it had to be a joke. "Seriously? What happened last night was proof that I had a sexy dream and started to act it out in my sleep, and you took advantage of that."

"Whoa, wait a minute, I didn't take advantage of you," he defended.

"I'm not accusing you of anything inappropriate. I started everything. All I'm saying is that if I hadn't been so exhausted and emotionally rung out, none of that would have happened."

"The fact that you were emotionally rung out speaks volumes, Becs. It means you still have feelings for me."

"No, it means I have regrets and repressed feelings of loss. I never grieved the end of our relationship until last night because I packed it all up and stuffed it in a neat little box inside my brain with all my memories of you."

"I remember doing something similar," Austin admitted. "That doesn't change things. All those old feelings are still there, whether it's because we never dealt with them or we should still be together, is the thing we need to work through."

My earlier chuckle turned into a full-fledged laugh. There was no way he could be serious. The asshole admitted to going back to being fuck buddies with his future wife.

"Did you sleep with, and I'm clarifying here when I say fuck, have oral sex, finger, or otherwise engage physically with Jordan that night?"

"No, I swear to you that I didn't. Houston was there almost the whole time. He saw that she was sleeping on the couch, and I was sitting up in the chair waiting on you to call when he got ready to leave. She woke up a few minutes after he left the house, and I took her straight back to her house."

"Okay, then how long was it before you started back to your fuck buddy situation with her?"

"Please, don't go there. It has no bearing on what happened between us."

"How long?"

"A couple weeks. I thought I could fuck your memory away and she was there. For the record, it didn't work."

"A couple weeks?" I questioned as I remembered what

happened two weeks after that fateful Valentine's Party. "No wonder she was so smug that day," I muttered to myself.

"What are you talking about?"

"The day Jordan came to find me on campus was exactly two weeks after the Valentine's Day party," I explained. That was the day she told me all about how you didn't even miss me because the two of you were fucking, and how you believed everything she told you that night. So, there you go. You slept with her to get me out of your system, and she came straight to me to remind me of what I lost and whose arms you fell back into."

"Jesus fucking Christ," he groaned. "I'm so sorry. I didn't think-"

I cut him off. "That seems to be the way of things with you where she's concerned. You don't think, but she always has a plan and everyone around you gets hurt. Not you though, because she soothes away your ache before you can even feel the loss."

I could see the disbelief in his eyes. He still didn't think she had it in her to be so calculating as to run everyone in his life off to keep him all to herself. That was the crux of the problem back then and nothing had changed.

"You don't plan on fixing your Jordan problem. I don't plan on dealing with it for you, so this," I stated as I waved my hand back and forth between the two of us, "can never happen again."

Austin sighed. "Becs, she's not a problem. I swear it to you. We've talked about all that shit; the expectations and she's even dated other people over the years too."

"Real people, who you've met?"

"Yes," he rolled his eyes as he answered though, which pissed me off. "I've met a few of them."

Something told me there was more to that story than I would ever get from him, but it was a drastic change from the dynamic they had years earlier where Jordan never dated anyone else.

"It's been six years, don't you think if I really wanted to be with Jordan, I would be?"

I shrugged my shoulders. "You are though. You hang out, work together, and she still has plans to be with you, whether you think she does or not."

"I don't want to be in a romantic relationship with her. That will never happen because she's not who I want. What the hell do I have to do to convince you of that?"

"That's just it, Austin, you can't. You tried before, and you failed. You failed me, anyway. It was her test that you passed. It was Jordan who you chose."

"I didn't choose her."

"In her mind, you did, and that's all that matters."

"What about in your mind?"

"You left me that night and never considered my safety. You never called, texted, met up with me, came to see if I even made it home okay. What if I had been in the hospital after being attacked? How do you think I would have felt to wake up and find out you weren't there?"

"That didn't happen."

"It could have! You would have never known because you didn't fucking care to check. The irony is, you took the time to make sure nearly naked Jordan got home safe and sound. You can claim that you never wanted a romantic relationship with her, and that you did with me, but you treated her with more respect and care than I ever saw." He seemed completely taken aback by that statement, as if he'd never thought of it that way. Maybe that was the case since he had blinders on where his little BFF was concerned.

"Dammit, Austin, I don't want to keep having this argument. You will never see things for what they are because you're too blinded by her. It always comes down to HER." I yelled that last bit because it made me so angry to think about how easily I was forgotten while he coddled that conniving fucking bitch.

"If only you understood, she says the same damn thing about

you," he admitted as he shook his head, clearly at a loss about what to do.

"Well, then, there's your easy fix. She's the more important person in your life. I'm just a footnote. Go make her happy."

I opened my front door and held my hand out for him to follow the gesture out of my apartment. He didn't budge, though he also wouldn't look me in the eye. His gaze stayed trained on his feet for a long time before I got frustrated and snapped the door shut. It was fucking February and cold as hell outside. Truthfully, I couldn't afford to lose the little heat I had inside my apartment while he remained stubbornly glued to my floor.

"Go out with me," he requested before his eyes finally moved to meet mine.

"No."

Becs, please? I'm begging here. We're different people than we were before. Older. Wiser. Go out with me."

"When was the last time you slept with Jordan?"

I could see by the way his temper flared, and the asshole worked to keep it under control, that it must have been recent. "I don't see how that is any of your business."

"Oh, but it is. See, I like to learn from history. Remember when we went out before and I found out in an awkward, embarrassing run-in after our date that you never bothered to break things off with your girlfriend?"

"She was never my girlfriend."

"You treated your fuck buddy better than you ever treated me, so I think she won the girlfriend distinction by default. The only person who was your disposable fuck buddy was me."

"Fuck! I can't win with you, can I?"

"You could answer the damn question and we'll go from there." I didn't think he'd do it. The Austin I knew before wouldn't be honest about things.

"We haven't had sex since before the new year, but we messed around a bit the day before I saw you in Clea's office," he admitted. "Dallas walked in and interrupted before anything could go further that time." It both shocked and disgusted me.

I nodded my head. "Well, then the answer remains a solid no from me."

"I haven't touched her since I saw you again, and you still won't give us a shot?"

"Do you hear yourself? I can't be with a man who has a permanent fallback girl on standby. You will never press to work on things with me. The moment things get hard, or there's a miscommunication, you'll ditch out again because you don't have to work for anything when she's there to catch your lazy ass."

"You and I had sex last night and I'm here trying to work things out with you today, despite the fact that Jordan was angry and threatened to quit her job at the club if I started seeing you again." He threw that sentiment at me in anger but somehow missed how knowing that would only solidify my resolve to stay away from him.

I laughed. "Your precious Jordan threatened to quit working for you, if you dated me again, and you don't see that there's a problem? I don't want to do this again, Aus. I can't. Did you miss the part where I fucking soaked your shirt with my tears and snot last night? Do you think I want to sign up to keep going through that when it's taken me six years to…"

"To what? You haven't gotten over me. I know because I couldn't get over you either, Becs. It was supposed to be us. I know it was. I talked to my dad about you all those years ago and you know what he said?" I shook my head. "He told me that I sounded just like he did when he started dating my mom."

"Everyone gets excited about new relationships." I attempted to blow him off.

"That wasn't it. I knew beyond a shadow of a doubt that you were the one for me. I saw our future together."

"But you were so quick to just throw it all away."

"I thought you had done that."

"If I was truly your one, you would have come for me."

"I nearly did."

"Nearly?" I laughed. "That sounds so promising."

"When I was about to leave, Victoria and Jordan showed up and when Vic asked where I was headed looking so nice, since I dressed in a suit to go beg your forgiveness, I told them where I was headed."

"Let me guess, they talked you out of it."

"Not in so many words. They said they'd just come back from dinner, and you were there kissing another man. Apparently, it looked romantic and there were roses on the table."

I laughed so hard it was a wonder I didn't pee my pants. "Newsflash, asshole, I didn't date anyone for almost two years after you ghosted me. When I did finally start seeing people, I wouldn't call it dating because I never took them seriously. Once again though, you took Jordan's word and ran with it."

"No, I took Victoria's."

"Then there's something wrong with a sister who would rather her brother be with a manipulative, crazy woman than with someone who he thought was the one."

"Yeah, well, I'm going to have words with Vic now that I know. She was the one who was supposedly at the Valentine's Party and overheard you talking about the plan to humiliate me."

"Your sister told you that?"

He stared at me blankly for a minute before he shook his head. "Maybe your whole family has a Jordan problem then."

"What can I do to convince you to give us another try?"

"Can you rewrite history?" I asked in all seriousness because I didn't think there was a possibility of anything between us otherwise.

He took the time to look me over from head to toe then. "Were you about to go somewhere?"

"No, I just finally grabbed a shower and was about to figure out what to make for dinner."

"How about I call for delivery? Whatever you want, we'll eat here and talk. I won't even suggest that we call it a date, just two friends catching up on the six years they've missed."

"I don't think that's a good idea," I told him as my stomach growled.

"Sounds like it is," he teased.

"Fine, but I'm going to grab something warmer to wear. I'll be right back."

"Why is it so damn chilly inside your apartment, anyway? Is your heat broken?"

"Something like that," I murmured before trotting off to go put on my sweats. There was no point in tempting fate by trying to look appealing. Besides, it might turn him off to see me in some manly castoff clothing. It wasn't from a past boyfriend or anything, but my old roommate, Gavin stayed here for six months, which was just long enough to skip out on two months' worth of rent. I locked him out and kept his shit, which wasn't much, to be honest. I think the only reason he had a room with me was because he needed a beard since he hadn't come out of the closet yet.

Clearly, no man in my life had ever been worth trusting, not even the gay ones. Once I was finished getting dressed, I reluctantly went back to my living room where Austin was staring at the wall. No, that wasn't right. He was staring at the thermostat on the wall.

"Why in the hell do you have this thing set so low? I know you get cold easily."

I shrugged my shoulders. "Did you order something?"

"Chinese from the place a couple blocks over. I figured I couldn't go wrong with that and ordered a little bit of everything."

"Okay, let me know how much it is and I'll pay when it gets here." My stomach sank at the prospect, especially since I had no clue what a 'little bit of everything' would come to. The place he ordered from wasn't exactly the cheapest delivery in town.

"No. I already pre-paid, so you don't have to worry about that. Now, what's up with your heating situation? It seems to work just fine."

"I'm only usually here at night to sleep anyway, so I keep it set low. It saves on energy and makes for good snuggly, under-the-covers sleeping."

"So, I discovered last night," he teased.

"Well, you'll have to adjust your own thermostat because there won't be a repeat of that."

Austin moved to go sit on my couch and I followed. His eyes narrowed as he tracked my movements and took in the clothing I wore.

"What in the hell are you wearing?"

"Oh, Gavin left these when he moved out." I shrugged. The plan was to keep things vague, so he thought that I had been living with another man at some point. That should drive home the "I moved on" vibe.

"Gavin, huh?"

"That's what I said."

"Would you by chance be talking about Gavin Bryant?"

My jaw dropped. "How in the hell could you possibly know that?"

Austin laughed as he pointed at the sweatshirt. It was from USC, as in University of South Carolina not the one in California. "Gavin worked for me briefly, when he was trying to afford the rent of his place with his boyfriend and the place where he told his family he lived with some chick. Only, his boyfriend got mad and delivered an ultimatum. Gavin raved for a month about you locking him out and keeping his shit."

"He hadn't paid his part of the rent in two months. I don't care if he was living somewhere else, I needed a roommate to help with the bills, not someone taking up space like my apartment was a free storage unit."

"I guess I can see your point there. Still, that doesn't explain why you're wearing his clothes."

"They're comfy and as you pointed out, it feels a little chilly in here when I'm not sleeping under the covers."

"The thermostat works, you know. Just crank the heat up and wear something normal."

I sighed. Austin always was clueless as to how the other half lived. The other half being the poor people of the world. I worked hard, but barely got paid for all my hard work, or at least that's how it felt by the time I paid my household bills, student loans, and that one other thing that kept me in debt.

"Did you want to watch something?" I asked and pointed to the television. "I have Netflix." The clarification was so he wouldn't be expecting cable channels, but the asshole took it the wrong way.

"Did you just invite me to Netflix and chill? I thought that was outdated these days."

My eye roll was epic and should have made the record books. "I meant that's pretty much all I have to watch, since I don't have time for a lot of television anyway."

Austin's brow furrowed and he looked about ready to ask me a question, that I probably didn't want to answer, when there was a knock on the door.

"I'll get it. Why don't you go grab us some plates and stuff so we can dish things out."

That, I could do. I had everything ready on the coffee table by the time Austin came back from the door with the food. "It smells wonderful," I said as my mouth watered in anticipation.

"Becs?"

I glanced up to see Austin was watching me. "What?"

"What do you do for a living?"

"I teach art and history classes at Whitmore Elementary." I

also waitressed three nights a week and usually on the weekends, if I could pick up a shift, to help make up the difference in what was needed. He didn't need to know that.

"So, why are you concerned about money?"

"I have student loans to pay off and other debts I'm working on." He also didn't need to know that I'd been helping my parents out since my dad lost his job. There was no way in hell that I would move back home to save money. My parents hadn't been the best. They did the minimum required by law to raise me when I came along unexpectedly, and then sent me out on my way as soon as they were legally able. They never looked back either, except to ask for help when my father was laid off.

They helped as much as they could with my college tuition, so it was like I owed them for going above and beyond at least a little bit in my life. At least, that's the line I got when I tried to explain that I didn't have a lot left over thanks to my student loans. In truth, my parents barely coughed up $1,500 per year to help with college, which was why I had so many loans to begin with. The money they'd given me barely covered books and fees.

Thankfully, my father recently found a new job, but I still kept the extra money I'd been sending them to the side just in case it didn't work out and they came at me with another guilt trip to help again.

"Let's eat before everything gets cold," I finally said when he wouldn't stop staring at me.

"You know, if you need help, all you have to do is ask."

I glanced over at Austin just as I was about to put a fork full of steamed broccoli in my mouth. I set the loaded fork back down on my plate and smiled sweetly. "No offense meant here, but you are the last person on this planet that I would go to for help."

"Why is that?"

"Beside the fact that we're strangers?"

"We're not strangers, Becs. We've just been estranged for a while."

"You didn't even know what I do for a living five minutes ago. Do you even know if I have siblings or parents who are alive?" I asked to prove my point because I've never talked much about my parents and didn't recall telling him a thing about them before. He swallowed and continued to stare, knowing that he didn't have those answers.

"You knew a college girl who was just about to go start her life, and barely at that, because you were too selfish to really get to know me, and too preoccupied with the other people in your life to ask the simple questions."

Austin sat there with a look of deep concentration on his face as if he were diving through every conversation that we ever had in his memory.

"Did you know that we met on my birthday?"

His head snapped back up and his eyes seemed almost glassy as they met mine. "We met at a Halloween party," he reminded me.

"October 30th is my birthday. It fell on a Saturday that year and no one wants to attend a Halloween party on Sunday and be too hung over for class the next day. Well, that's not true, but they held it on Saturday anyway. It was my twenty-first birthday."

"Why didn't you tell me?"

"Why would I?" I shrugged it off. "We just met, and I didn't want anyone treating me weird that night. Plus, birthdays were never something my family celebrated." That wasn't strictly true. My parents celebrated one another's birthdays every year with special dates. I got a card, sometimes with money in it, and a pat on the head. Kind of a 'good job on surviving another year, kid' acknowledgment.

"See Austin, we don't know one another that well."

"When is my birthday?"

"March 12th, I rattled off."

"You knew my birthday."

"Yes, because it was coming up soon, and I was trying to plan something for you." Again, he focused inward as if trying to recall something.

"You asked when it was, didn't you?" I nodded. "And at no point in that conversation did I ask when yours was?"

It was my turn to think back. The shake of my head made his shoulders slump before I could remember why he hadn't asked. "You got a phone call, and it distracted you because you didn't seem inclined to speak to whoever it was while I was sitting there." Jordan had been the only reason I could think of for why he wouldn't have spoken to someone in front of me, so it had soured the rest of the evening, whether he knew that was why or not.

"I remember now. It was Jordan and I didn't want you upset that she called during one of our dates again."

"Like I said, too occupied with other, more important people, to get to know me."

"I swear to you, it wasn't like that."

"If it had been one of your male friends, you wouldn't even have answered that call while we were out. That's a fact because I watched you decline calls from them and even from your brothers before when we were on dates. You never once declined a call from her, though. That was the first time I put two and two together about whose calls you were answering, since I'd seen the screen the other times to know who you were ignoring."

"You don't understand. Jordan was upset with me back then because she didn't think it was fair that she had to leave town. Then, when she came back, it pissed her off that she couldn't just come over to the apartment and hang out the way she used to. I was dealing with her emotional shit because I felt like it was me who caused it."

"That's just it, Austin. I warned you it would happen before we ever tried to have a relationship. You promised it wouldn't because you guys were taking a break, but it never really stopped with her. You were always at her mercy, and she never let you forget it for a second. We were on a date, getting to know one another, and you made her the priority when you took that call. It will always be that way. There will always be an excuse, even if you don't realize that's what you're doing. She will always be your first and last choice while I get lost somewhere in the middle. I've lived my entire life being someone's afterthought, I won't throw myself into dating someone who will make me an afterthought for the rest of it, too."

"If Jordan was a man, would you feel the same way, that I was prioritizing her over you if I accepted a phone call when I knew she was upset?"

"If Jordan was a man who you had slept with, yes."

"If it was just a platonic buddy?" He asked, clearly exasperated that I'd insinuated a sexual relationship with a fictional man, instead of getting his meaning. I got it, but I was making a point that he needed to grasp.

"No, because like I said, you didn't answer those calls, so I would have assumed it was important."

"It was important, Becs. Jordan was going through a lot, and I was the reason life was hard on her."

I laughed at him. "The 'a lot' Jordan was going through was having your dick unavailable to her and you breaking her heart by dating someone else. That made it entirely inappropriate for you to answer her phone calls while we were on a date. It could have waited. It's not like you couldn't see who was calling."

"You're right. I'm sorry. Back then, I was in a horrible position because my family was on my ass about what I'd done to make Jordan so sad and why I had to be so heartless toward her. She was falling apart, too. Then there was you who demanded that I cut her out completely."

"Whoa! I never made that demand."

"Didn't you?"

"No, Austin, I didn't. I told you that your actions would have consequences and I didn't know if I could handle them.

The fact that your family was pressuring you about her, like I feared they would, and you hid it from me just proved that things could have never worked out. You cannot be fuck buddies with someone who expects everything from you. It doesn't end well, especially in your situation where your families were intrinsically linked the way they were. Imagine if we had continued dating and you took me home to meet your family. How would I have been received? Would someone have invited Jordan to that event? I bet Victoria would have, since they're close enough that your sister lied for her about seeing me on a date."

"My dad would have loved you, and he was your champion all along, telling my mom and sisters that who I loved was my choice and that Jordan had never been a choice that I wanted to make in that way." He chuckled at the memory.

"I thought my mom would give him the silent treatment forever over that until they had a talk about things privately and then she came around. It wasn't like she ever pressured me to marry the girl, but she was always happy to see us at the house together or upset when Jordan complained that I was ignoring her. My dad must have said something to my mom about our conversation because that's when she stopped getting involved when Jordan came to her. It was too late by then because I lost you anyway."

Silence hung heavily in the room after that as I sat contemplating everything. My appetite fled the moment Jordan's name came up again, so eventually I stood and started closing up the containers and picking up our dishes. I didn't bother to ask if Austin was done. Our dinner was over, he had seen all the ways it couldn't work between us, so all that was left was for him to leave.

When I came back from carrying the dishes into the kitchen, Austin was sitting there staring at his phone. I could see that it was Jordan calling once again, but to my complete surprise, instead of answering it, he put his phone on silent and tucked it back into his pocket.

"You could have answered that," I told him. He startled and turned to see me standing there between the living room and kitchen.

"I may have been an idiot when I was younger, but that doesn't make me unteachable."

"Well, that specific issue only applied when we were dating. We're not, so feel free to pick up any and all calls. Actually, while this has been illuminating," I moved to grab the bagged up left-over food and hand it to him, "I think it's time for you to go. This is my last night off before I have to get back to work, so I'd like to curl up under my covers and read a good book to destress."

"What if I want to do exactly that with you?"

I quirked an eyebrow up in question. "Did you bring your own reading material?" I asked sarcastically.

"Kind of," he muttered and moved to stand directly in front of me. That dark spicy scent of his hit me immediately, stoking fires inside my body that had no business being lit. "I love to read you," the infuriating man said as he drew closer.

"You have a bad habit of reading me wrong. This was me dismissing you for the night, so I could be alone with my book."

"No, I don't think that's what you really want, and I know it's not what I want."

"Austin, what if I told you that it's what I need?"

He stopped dead in his tracks and his features sobered from the lusty haze that he'd worn only a moment before.

"Then I'll respect your needs for the night because I don't want to do anything that will make you think I'm not completely serious about giving us another shot. I'll be back though, Becs. I gave up last time when things looked bleak. That was my mistake, not going after you, and it's the biggest regret of my life."

He turned and left my apartment, making sure to twist the lock on his way out. The food still sat on the coffee table, so I managed to pack it away, throw the deadbolt on my door, and then I hid under my covers and cried for all the missed opportunities we'd lost out on because of his crazy relationship with his stupid life-long best friend. One day, he'd see that their friendship was something that had been tragically and irreparably warped. Until that day, I didn't think there could really be anything healthy between us.

Then again, he hadn't answered her phone call because he was with me. That was different than before. Maybe, it could work this time.

CHAPTER TEN

GOING BACK TO WORK, AFTER A TIRESOME WEEKEND, ABSOLUTELY sucked. The relaxing with a good book that I meant to do the night before never happened because my recent conversations with Austin were stuck on replay in my head instead.

"Ms. Robinson," Clara called out to me with her hand wiggling in the air as she twisted and squirmed in her seat. My assistant called out sick that day, so there wasn't anyone to watch the class while I escorted her to the bathroom. Dammit. "I need to go," she insisted.

"Everyone line up," I huffed. Teaching the youngest kids at the school was usually the best part of my day, since they were so enthusiastic and unburdened by doubt. The problem was all the extra crap I had to deal with when it came to them, like bathroom breaks that took up the majority of a class period when I had to wrangle all the littles to the bathroom without the help of an assistant. Luckily, I only had fifteen children this class period, so it shouldn't be too difficult.

"Ms. Robinson, I don't know if I can make it that long," Clara whined.

"It'll be okay, Clara," Tommy Ross assured her as his friend

Brandon punched him in the arm. "What? You peed your pants last week and everyone laughed. Do you want that to happen to someone else?" He asked his friend. I loved that children their age attempted to whisper, but it never quite worked out for them.

The other children giggled as I opened my classroom door and almost ran face-to-chest into someone who had been standing outside.

"Sorry, I'll be right with you. We have a slight emergency here," I told the person as I backed him up out of the way and started to guide the line of children around him.

"Who is that?"

"Ms. Robinson, do we have a special guest?"

"Is he a painter?"

"He doesn't even have any paint."

"Aren't we supposed to be quiet in the hallways?" I asked before turning around to see who they were talking about. I was shocked to find Austin standing there grinning widely.

"Shit," I mumbled.

"That's a bad word," Clara informed me.

"Oh, don't worry, I'll wash my mouth out with soap when we get to the bathroom."

"Ew, that's gross."

"My mom did that to me one time when I said the F-U-C-K word."

"You're not supposed to spell it either, Jack," I warned him much to the amusement of all the other children.

"Are you going to wash Jack's mouth out with soap, too?"

"No, I think we can forgive this one small mistake, as long as no one else makes it. Two at a time, kids. Clara and Monique go on into the bathroom. Tommy and Brandon, go to the boy's side."

Four little children peeled off from the line and all but ran inside. Clara wasn't the only one in need of a bathroom break. That meant their teacher didn't take them before she brought them to my class, like she was supposed to. As per usual. She was a young math teacher and didn't think I had a 'real' teaching job. Whatever the hell that meant.

I took a moment to glance back down toward my classroom door to see that Austin had helped himself inside. I had no clue why he showed up to my job or what to do about it. Once all the children had their chance to go potty, we marched back to the classroom to find Austin making himself at home while sitting in my chair at my desk.

"What are you doing here?" I whispered once I was close enough that the children wouldn't hear me.

"I came to see when you got a lunch break, and the woman at the front office sent me on back. She said you had a planning period next, then lunch, and that you didn't need to be here the rest of the day because there was some kind of field trip, so your other classes won't be around."

"Crap, I forgot about the field trip."

"Even better, that makes me the bearer of good news."

"Do you want a gold star?"

"Can I get a gold star?" Tommy asked. I hadn't even seen the sneaky shit approach my desk. I glanced around to see that all the children were watching Austin and me.

"No, Tommy, you need to go back to your seat and get to work on your project." Then I projected my voice. "Remember, we'll be sharing your projects with your parents at the spring showcase! We all want to make the best clay pots we can, right?"

"I don't like it when they're squishy," Clara informed me.

"I already baked them, so they aren't squishy anymore. Now, they're ready to paint."

"My mom baked a cake lesterday," Billy Seaport mentioned while replacing the 'y' with an 'l' again. Speech therapy had not worked wonders for him just yet. Before I could ask why his mom baking a cake was important, Billy licked his clay pot that looked more like an upside-down version of what his classmates attempted to make. It would have been cool if he'd done it that way on purpose.

"Billy, your pot is not edible, please stop licking it."

"But you baked it, and mom baked a cake." He scrunched his nose in distaste, just as I finally got his point. "Tastes like dirt. My mom should teach you how to makes them taste better."

Austin cracked up laughing, unable to help himself. That only encouraged my students to start showing off for him.

"Look Mister, I made the bestest pot."

"Best pot," I corrected. Too bad for me, I forgot how quickly littles would compete for the 'best' slot. I'd only been correcting her English, not reinforcing the idea that hers was indeed the best. Austin was throwing me off my teaching game.

"In another environment, that might have been an inviting notion," Austin cracked quietly to which I rolled my eyes.

"I thought mine was the bestess?" Grady called out.

David chimed in right along with him. "Nope. Ms. Robson loves mine better. She saids it has clean lines." Dammit, the kid brutalized my name again.

"How can it be clean when it's made of dirt?" Grady asked him in all seriousness.

"Who are you?" Clara asked as she twirled her hair around her finger and batted her eyes at the man who was old enough to be her father. That little hussy almost peed her pants a few minutes ago, and she was flirting with my man. Oh hell no. I did not just think that. I wanted to smack myself. Austin wasn't my anything.

"My name is Austin. I'm a friend of Becs," he started to say until Clara interrupted him.

"Who is Becs?" She asked while looking around at the other girls in the class, as if a new student had appeared, and she somehow hadn't noticed.

He turned wide eyes on me.

"Mr. Austin meant to say he is a friend of mine."

"You're not Becs. You're Ms. Robinson."

"And you are very astute, Clara." She grinned as I told her that, but then seemed puzzled.

"What does astute mean?"

"Smart," Austin and I answered at the same time. Clara beamed at him for complimenting her.

"Clara, you're supposed to be painting your pot."

She poked her lip out, flounced around, and stalked to her table like I'd personally told her that Santa and the Easter bunny were both as made up as the tooth fairy. Kids were the worst sometimes.

"When is class over?"

I glanced up at the clock. "Another fifteen minutes."

"Great, I'll wait outside for you, in the staff parking lot. As soon as you're done here, we can go grab some lunch." I started to protest, but Austin held his hand up. "I don't want to hear any excuses about you having to go do something. Remember, the lady in the office informed me that you're out of here after this class, and you just admitted that you forgot all about it, so that means you couldn't possibly have any plans today."

Dammit!

"Fine, I'll see you in twenty minutes in the parking lot."

TWENTY MINUTES LATER, I made my way out to the employee parking lot to find Austin leaning against his truck while waiting for me. It wasn't exactly a warm day to be hanging around outside.

"You know, you could have waited inside your truck with the heat running," I said to him.

"Yeah, but that would have made it easier for you to slip by me unnoticed."

"I'm twenty-seven years old, Austin. I think I've outgrown the hide and seek stage of life. Besides, you know where I live, so trying to ditch you here would be a moot point, wouldn't it?"

"Probably. Why don't you hop in, and I'll take us somewhere for lunch, then bring you back for your car afterward."

"Why are we going out to lunch?"

"We have unfinished business," he said as he hopped in the driver's side and waited on me to join him. There was no point in denying the man, since he'd spent nearly an hour waiting to take me to lunch anyway.

"Fine, but lunch and then we're done."

"Okay, for today."

If my eyes could roll any harder, someone would probably get hurt. "I don't understand why you're trying so hard. It's obvious that this won't work out between us. It didn't before, what makes you think it will this time?"

"We've both learned a few things since the last time. Plus, I'm determined to fix a mistake that should have never been able to spiral so far out of my control."

"What mistake was that?"

"The one where I lost you," he admitted without any hesitation.

I stopped questioning things after that as he drove us to the highway and away from town. A smart woman would have inquired about our destination, but I'd already proven my lack of intelligence by getting in the car with the man. An hour later, we pulled up outside a quaint little restaurant two towns over.

"Are we having a top-secret lunch no one can know about?" It seemed weird to me that we would go so far away to eat together.

"Truthfully, I figured the chances of us running into people we know, who might ruin this for us, was less if we headed out of town."

The only 'people' I could think of who might try to ruin a lunch date, would be Jordan. "Are you hiding me from your girlfriend?"

"I don't have a girlfriend."

"Okay, from your fuck buddy then."

"Don't have one of those either," he grinned at me as he pulled my door open and helped me out.

"The woman who has been your best friend and you've had sex with?"

"She isn't an issue, Becs. I promise that she knows what's going on between us and won't step in the way this time. I was more concerned with one of my brothers popping up out of the woodwork to create havoc."

That made me laugh because Dallas certainly had done a number on all of us, Houston and Clea included. "Okay, fine. Let's go eat lunch. I'm actually starved because I didn't get a chance to grab breakfast before heading to school this morning."

"How did I not know you wanted to be a teacher?"

I smiled warmly at Austin. "I wanted to be an artist, but I managed to throw teaching into the works because if the art thing didn't work out, I wanted to encourage other people to try. Honestly, my original plan was to work with much older kids, but it's hard to get those gigs. They're almost always locked down by tenured teachers who busted their asses to keep their programs afloat every time someone tried to cut funding for the arts."

"So, you're both a noble and desperate teacher?" His eyes crinkled at the corners with the teasing laughter that followed as we were seated in the rustic space. The interior of the restaurant looked like a mountain cabin straight out of a ski lodge adventure.

"I suppose so," I agreed before peeking at the menu. "I've never been here before."

"Me either, let's hope my internet search and the reviews didn't lead us astray."

"If the aroma in this place is anything to go by, my mouth is already watering."

"Yeah, mine too," Austin agreed as he stared at me. I ignored it and continued to look at the menu. It took a lot more focus than it should have to make a selection since I could feel his eyes on me practically the whole time.

"What can I get for you today?" Our waiter asked when he came back to the table to deliver the drinks we'd ordered.

I gave my order easily, but Austin's ears pinked at the tips as he grinned at the man. "Can I be honest?" He asked him almost conspiratorially.

"Sure."

"I was too distracted to look at the menu. Is there something that you would suggest?"

The waiter turned to look at me immediately before he bounced his gaze right back to Austin. "I get it, man. The Mountain Lion is my favorite meal. Steak however you want it, loaded baked potato, our house greens, and a side salad."

That was the cutest thing about the menu. The names of the meals were that of animals that might be found in the area. The men agreed on what Austin would eat while I glanced around and took in the ambiance.

"This place is really cool," I stated, truly impressed that Austin thought to bring me somewhere that was so unique as opposed to a chain place that didn't have a lot of character. "You might want to do your brother a solid, and mention it to him, because Clea would fall all over herself to dine somewhere like this."

"Maybe, whenever they decide to come back up for air. Those two have been inseparable ever since the launch party for the bar."

"How are things going with the bar?"

"Well, we haven't officially opened, since that was just a party that we were throwing to get the promotional materials that we needed out of the way. The phones have been ringing off the hook lately though."

"That has to feel good." His excitement was palpable, so it went without saying.

"It does. It's been a long time coming. Houston and I have been talking about this for a long time."

"And Dallas," I added for him.

"No, Dallas was a last-minute addition because he somehow managed to save up an ungodly amount of money over the years."

"As weird as it is to say this, I can kind of see that. I think your brother hides a lot of who he is behind the immature bullshit he pulls."

"Houston and I are beginning to think that as well. Especially after Dallas offered us the capital that we needed to get the Tippler's Lounge up and running. He only wanted to be a silent partner until we paid him back. Truthfully, he didn't even want us to pay him back, said it was a gift, but we both refused."

"I hear male pride is a bitch that way."

"While I can't speak for Houston, taking a handout to get started in life didn't feel right."

"I bet it felt worse knowing it came from your younger brother who everyone thinks is a royal screwup."

Austin laughed. "I'm not saying that's true…"

"But you're also not saying it isn't," I finished for him as we both had a good chuckle at his expense. "Everyone is entitled to their secrets."

Austin grew serious then and reached over to take hold of my hand. "I don't want there to be secrets between us."

"There isn't an 'us' here."

"I think we both want there to be. I know you have your reasons for shying away from anything to do with me. I didn't handle things the right way before. We both know that. I never successfully dated anyone before you came along."

"You didn't successfully date me either, just to be clear."

"No, I didn't. Part of that was because I hadn't been invested with anyone else before and didn't learn those lessons with them first. I know that sounds ridiculous, and really what I'm trying to say is that I've grown and learned a few things since then."

I wasn't sure how to take what he was trying to explain. Did he learn lessons because of what went wrong between us before, or because he tried seriously dating other women in the past six years? That was something I didn't even want to think about.

"I'd really love it if we could try dating again. We can start off slow, keep the lines of communication open, and see where things go. I'm not married, dating anyone, and I don't have a current fuck buddy either."

"I don't have any of this in my life either." I waited until our eyes met before I added the last bit because it was important. "I also don't have a jealous, opposite sex best friend, and former fuck buddy, who might cause problems."

"While I don't really want to bring her into our lunch, I'll say this much, she knows. I explained that we were going to give it a real try this time if I could convince you to do it. She agreed to back off and-"

"This sounds a lot like what I heard before," I interrupted to say, because honestly, there was no point in listening to the same song and dance that didn't turn out the last time.

Austin sat quietly staring at me across the table as the waiter came to deliver our food. My body was hungry while my mind, or maybe it was my heart, felt differently. I stared down at the loaded bacon and cheesy potato soup that I'd ordered. It was one of my favorite comfort foods, so when I saw it on the menu, I knew that's what I'd order. It smelled divine.

"Becs, I never want to go through the loss of you again, and don't want to put you through that either. I was hoping that transparency, and understanding what happened before, would be the steppingstones to get us started on a more solid footing than we had last go round."

"Austin." I dragged his name out with the same reluctance as I felt toward trying to date him again. Agreeing to do so was dangerous. My heart couldn't take another rejection. It also couldn't handle being the least important person in someone's life again. My parents had one another, Clea had Houston now. I didn't begrudge my best friend that because I never felt discarded when she was with Jeff, but then again, she never seemed as happy with Jeff as the few times I'd seen her with Houston.

I knew it from the start that those two were perfect for one another. While I felt put on the back burner for the time being, I knew eventually they're relationship would settle into a more comfortable position where we'd always remain best friends and extremely important to each other. Houston needed to be her priority, and that was as it should be. I wasn't certain that I'd get the same experience from dating his brother. Sadly, history already taught me that lesson and it was hard to overlook the probability of a repeat performance.

"I'm only asking for a trial period, until you feel you can trust me."

"Fine."

"But?"

I shook my head. "No, there's no stipulations this time. You already know where I stand on everything, that never changed for me."

"I was the idiot who didn't listen the first time around."

I shrugged because what could I say? It was true. He knew exactly what he had to do the first time, well technically the second, that we dated, and he failed. Whether six years apart would make a difference this time, I wasn't sure, but we would see. Either my heart would make it through intact or it wouldn't. Life was short and getting shorter though, and I didn't want to keep denying myself the potential for happiness with someone I felt an immense, almost otherworldly connection with.

"Lunch is on me," he commented as he tipped his fork in the direction of my steamy soup bowl. "You didn't have to do that soup and salad thing that women do."

I laughed at his incorrect assumption. "This is part of the 'getting to know me' thing you didn't do before. Loaded potato soup, potato leek soup, pretty much any kind of hot gooey potatoey goodness on a cold day is one of my favorite things. It's my comfort food. It's also very rich, so there's no way I'll be able to eat anything else when I'm done with this bowl. No matter how much I'll crave a second."

Austin chuckled at my explanation. "Well, maybe we'll have to grab you one to go then. You can take it home to your freezer-like apartment."

"Oh, hush. My apartment is not that cold. In the summer, most people would kill to be able to keep their places that temperature."

I wanted to get lost in his smile and run my hands across his thickly stubbled jawline. He must not have shaved for a couple days, because if he waited one more, he'd have a full beard instead of the neatly manicured look he seemed to wear since I first saw him again. It did lovely things for his appearance, that much was for sure. Clea told me he looked like a lumberjack in a business suit the day he showed up at her office. I had to agree with her assessment.

"What are you thinking about over there?"

"Trees."

"Trees?" He asked and it was hard to tell whether he thought my answer was amusing or worrisome.

"Yep, and how you would look while hanging out shirtless in the forest, chopping those trees down."

"Not that I'm complaining about you wanting to see me shirtless, but what the hell, Becs?"

He had decided on amused, and I loved the way it warmed his dark eyes and made his smile seem so much more vibrant. I shrugged my shoulders at him as I relished another spoonful of my soup.

"Look around, I was going with the vibe of the place," I

explained my new fetish away, rather than throw my best friend under the bus. It went without saying that her new boyfriend probably wouldn't want to hear about how she thought he looked like a suited-up lumberjack, ruggedly handsome, or anything else. Knowing the Mercer boys as little as I did, there was one thing that no one could miss. They were a bit competitive with one another. It would be something Austin would gloat to his brother about.

"Well, don't freak out if I bring an axe to the bedroom one day. It'll be strictly for roleplaying purposes."

I squirmed in my seat and tucked into my soup rather than grabbing Austin's hand and running as fast as possible straight to the hardware store and then the nearest hotel. He must have seen the flash of heat in my eyes before I lowered them because the man sucked in a harsh breath.

"Jesus, Becs, you're killing me right now. Take your time with the soup or I might embarrass myself when I have to stand up."

"There's nothing embarrassing about you," I disagreed. When my eyes lifted to meet his, they were full of humor and heat, two of my favorite things on a man. Austin Mercer was trouble and unfortunately, he was just my type.

CHAPTER ELEVEN

TO MY SURPRISE, AND DESPITE THE HEAT WE'D EXPERIENCED AT lunch, Austin dropped me off at my apartment with the promise to 'see me soon'.

He didn't text or call that night and neither did I. It took a few hours of digesting what happened at lunch to really let it settle in that I'd agreed to date Austin again. Was I a complete moron? Probably. There was just that certain something about him that was irresistible to me. The man was everything I ever wanted in a partner. He would have been absolutely perfect if not for the best friend/fuck buddy situation that followed him around like a shadow.

That left me wondering what exactly I needed to do about the situation. They worked together, and would no doubt be closing down the bar with one another more often than not. Could I handle it if he came home late? We didn't even live together, so how would I even know? The constant worry about what they might be doing together in the backroom, or after hours, or... Yep, I was going to drive myself insane with worry.

Either I had to let the past go, and trust that Austin would be up front and honest with me, or I had to let the man go for good and admit that there was no way to properly handle his relationship with Jordan. Since he admitted that they continued their fuck buddy arrangement over the six years since our last non-breakup, breakup, that made things infinitely harder to navigate than before. Instead of two years of on and off sexual activity, I was faced with them having almost a decade's worth of a sexual arrangement and even longer as close family friends.

I fell asleep that night with a tummy full of the extra order of soup Austin insisted that I take home with me. My mind was full of questions, and they translated into a rough sleep and multitude of nightmares where I lost Austin over and over again to the woman who had been at the root of everything.

When I got to school the next day, Louise in the front office stopped me. "Wait! Rebecca, you have a delivery here."

"A delivery?" I tried to think of any supplies that might have been ordered for my classroom, but sadly the last grant I applied for had been denied. It went to the rival school across town instead because they were deemed more in need then the school I worked for. That sucked because their school was notorious for funding the arts programs while mine was not. The school I worked for funded sports programs, often to the detriment of the arts.

"Here you go," she hefted a large bouquet of flowers in a beautiful pink crystal vase onto her desk. "I left them sitting on the floor, so you'd be surprised when you first saw them. Are they from that handsome young man who came to see you yesterday?"

Louise was a nosy old bat, but she was sweet too, so I couldn't very well tell her to mind her own fucking business. "I don't know who they're from."

"The card said, Austin," she informed me with a nod of her head, as if she'd done me a favor by reading my private message.

"Why did you read my card?" I snapped, unable to hold back my irritation. I had a thing about privacy and the fact that I didn't like mine violated.

She huffed out an indignant sound before sputtering her answer. "W-well, I had to know in case you asked."

"For future reference, I won't ask you, I'll just read the card myself. Thank you," I added at the last even if it did come out sounded a bit vitriolic. Then I took my flowers down to my classroom and pulled the card out of the damn envelop it was tucked into for privacy's sake. Louise could kiss my ass. It wasn't like it was a simple card where the message was easily seen without prying. She had ripped the seal on the envelope open.

BECS,
DINNER TONIGHT AND I WON'T BE DROPPING YOU OFF
ALONE THIS TIME.
XO,
AUSTIN

Crap, and Louise had read the damn thing. A nice chat with Austin about not delivering messages like that to my work was in order.

Thanks to the flowers that mocked me every time I looked at my desk, the day dragged on at a snail's pace. Every kind of paint, paste, and marker you could think of ended up on my clothes or hands by the end of the day. It was like the kids were feeding off my impatience and thwarted my every effort to get out of the school in a timely manner and to be able to go home and get ready quickly. The stupid card didn't give a time that he would be picking me up, just that he would.

♥

ONCE I GOT HOME, the shower was my first destination. There was no way I'd go anywhere, with anyone, while covered in paint, glue, and other questionably sticky things. Damn fifth graders were worse than the Kindergarteners, especially since they made most of their messes on purpose.

The flower arrangement sat on my dresser, so every time I passed by to grab clothes, get dressed, or just double-check in the mirror that I looked okay for the 432nd time since getting home from work, I would smile at the damn thing.

They weren't your conventional "I love you" bouquet of red roses. It was a wild mix, full of color, that I totally appreciated, especially since I was an art teacher. Calling myself an artist had ended abruptly after I received my degree from college and realized that selling art was extremely hit or miss and boiled down to luck or who you knew in the business that could give you a leg up. The most successful seemed to have a healthy dose of both.

It probably didn't help that I didn't have a focus in any one medium. I enjoyed them all. Sketching was something to clear my mind, painting was for when I was in the mood to really pay attention to detail, and clay was when I needed the therapy of making something with my hands that required that I got messy and just let go.

No one seemed to appreciate that I actually used all the mediums for some of my projects, since I would sketch them out, then form them out of clay, and paint in the end. My apartment wasn't conducive to having a pottery wheel, kiln, or anything else on site either. So, that killed my abilities a bit as I was relegated to doing that kind of work on school premises and only if I thought I wouldn't get caught.

The knock on my door made me pack my financial woes away, since that was really what kept me from being able to produce the art I wanted. When I opened the door, it was to Austin, standing there looking absolutely amazing. He wore dark wash jeans that hung down over black boots, a navy-blue button up shirt with a black t-shirt underneath it. His facial hair was trimmed close but had definitely become a full beard overnight instead of the usual well-groomed sexy stubble. His eyes flashed with interest as he gave me the same once-over that I had just given him.

"Hey Trouble," he greeted me as his eyes wandered around the underwhelming space of my apartment. "Did you get my flowers?"

"Obviously, or I'd be dressed in my old roommate's sweats while trying to figure out what to do for dinner before I crash tonight."

Austin grinned. "It's a good thing I rescued you from your mundane existence then, huh?"

My eyes rolled of their own accord. I swear, they had a mind of their own. "They're in my bedroom," I finally answered his unasked question about where the arrangement he sent might be. The man didn't even hesitate as he sauntered through my apartment and went to see them for himself.

"Better than the picture," he said to himself as I finally caught up.

"Help yourself," I muttered.

He turned a gorgeous grin on me that would have made me agree to skip dinner altogether, if only he'd asked. Instead, he pulled me in for a steamy kiss with his arms wrapped around my waist before he quickly took a step back.

"Just wanted to make sure that you got what I wanted you to have. Sometimes, they show you a picture and what they deliver is entirely different."

"Send a lot of flowers to women, do ya?" It was meant as a joke, but he stopped me cold.

"Not unless they're my mom or sisters."

"Oh," I murmured.

"Yeah, well, we should probably get going. I'm sure you're starved after dealing with those kids all day. How many classes did you have to pause to take a field trip to the bathroom?"

I laughed at his, most accurate, assessment of my job. "My

assistant showed up today, so thankfully, I didn't have to take the field trips of yesterday."

"That's good. Do you normally have an assistant?"

"I'd say about fifty percent of the time. She's supposed to be dedicated to my class, but if one of the others doesn't show, they'll pull her to cover for a 'real' class over mine. You know, since the kids aren't missing anything important if my whole classroom has to take a field trip to the bathrooms."

"That's fucked up."

"That's arts in the schools."

"Well, it sucks."

"Preaching to the choir, Austin," I informed him as he helped me into my coat and then led me out of my apartment. I turned to lock up, but the man grabbed my keys and did the job for me. After making sure the door was firmly locked, he escorted me out to his truck with the palm of his hand rested firmly on my lower back. My brain was in sensory overload because he smelled deliciously dark again and his warmth bled through my clothing, or maybe that was my imagination. Either way, it felt good to be beside Austin, on our way to another date. Hope filled my chest that this time would be different. My heart fluttered at the prospect of finally being able to have the man of my dreams all to myself. Well, to myself as much as any adult couple gets one another to themselves. I wasn't completely delusional. Yet.

"I have a confession to make," Austin said as he tucked me into his truck and then moved around to get in on the driver's side.

"Okay," I replied hesitantly, not sure if I should be ready to bolt out of the vehicle or not.

"I spent forever racking my brain trying to remember what your favorite food was, and I couldn't think if you'd ever told me."

Memories assailed me of our time together, snippets of

conversation here and there, but I don't think he'd ever asked. I shook my head in response. "Nope, don't think it ever came up."

"How could that not come up?" He asked, almost as if it was a question for himself and not me to answer.

"Don't know. For the record, I'm not picky and you saw my favorite the other day."

"Potato soup is your favorite food?"

"It's my favorite comfort food. Don't judge me."

"Not judging. Okay, is there anything you won't eat?"

"My stomach doesn't agree with super spicy, but I don't have any allergies or anything, and I'm a fairly adventurous eater."

"I know the perfect place then."

We ended up at an upscale looking restaurant with a sleek, modern design. The name didn't seem to match the vibe until we went inside, and I realized why it had the moniker it did. Teasers, while sounding like a strip club, was all about giving its patrons a sampling of foods. It was kind of like one of those fondu places without the fondu. Actually, there were dipping sauces too, so it was kind of like that.

"This is crazy cool," I told Austin as we both took in the different menu selections that were samples based on theme or an overall general sampler with a little bit of everything.

"I say we go all in and get The Whole Shebang." I giggled because that was literally the name of the sampler platter with a little bit of every theme included.

"That works for me." I grinned at him as he placed our order. "You find the best places to go out to eat," I informed him, as if he didn't already know.

"Again, we have an internet search to thank for this one. I didn't even know it was here."

It was a small space in the heart of our growing town and probably didn't get as much attention as it deserved here, but depending on how things went with our platter, I hoped they were here to stay. It was just the type of place we needed to go from smallish bumpkin community to a moderately sized city with a little culture. Since our town was in the growing pain stages, it was a wait and see mentality with what would stick and what wouldn't.

Our dinner was spectacular and surprisingly filling. Sure, each item was basically only a couple bites each, but after testing all of them, I found myself pleasantly stuffed, but not overfull in the way that makes you feel gross.

"That was so good," I gushed to Austin for what was probably the tenth time as we climbed back inside his car, and each sat back and digested for a minute.

"It really was. Maybe I should let the internet make all my culinary decisions for me from now on."

"I am not opposed. You're two for two now."

"The food wasn't the only thing that made the night memorable, Becs."

"Yeah? Was it the sleek design of the place?" The teasing was meant to lighten the mood from the serious that seemed to be impending.

"Well, that was nice enough, but getting to know you better is something I should have done years ago. I think we got caught up in all the physical back then and forgot to do the 'getting to know you part'. Not that we didn't do a little of that, too," he quickly back peddled.

"I know what you mean. No need to get your knickers in a twist."

"My knickers in a twist? What century do you live in, or better yet, what country?"

"Eh, it's an expression somewhere, just roll with it."

"You are something else," he admitted after he finally started the car.

"So, where to now?"

"Now, we're going to your place and ending the night in a way we can both enjoy while working off all those calories."

"I thought you just said that we spent too much time on the physical before and not enough on getting to know one another?" I almost couldn't hold back my laughter.

Austin bit into his lower lip as he backed up before he shifted his attention back to me. "This time, we're going to try the well-rounded approach. We just did *getting to know you 101*. Next stop is *getting reacquainted with our bodies*. It's a level three course though, so it might get a little more intense."

"Hmm, and here was me thinking I was all done with class-work for the day."

"I promise, it will all be worth it."

"Well, then I guess you'll have to prove it to me."

CHAPTER TWELVE

I COULDN'T BELIEVE IT HAD BEEN TWO WEEKS SINCE THE Valentine's Day from hell. Every single day during those two weeks, Austin and I called, texted, or hung out on dates chosen for us by the internet searches he did.

Tonight's date was the best of them all, even though it wasn't the greatest restaurant of the six we had tried together in the four-county radius we'd ventured to. It was the best because he took me to see the Immersive Van Gough Exhibit after dinner. I hadn't even known one of the showings was coming so close to us.

"I can't believe you got us tickets to this," I gushed, not for the first time that night.

"Why not? You're an artist, I thought this would be right up your alley."

"It totally is. I'm just…" I twirled and took in the painting that had come to life all around us, which meant sunflowers were literally everywhere. "This is heaven. I've died and gone to artist heaven."

Austin pulled me close to his body, so my back was to his front and his arms remained wrapped around my mid-section.

"I'm glad you like it so much," he whispered against my neck before he placed a kiss there.

I turned in his arms and slipped up onto my tip toes. "I love it," I murmured before planting a kiss on his lips. He opened immediately and deepened what was supposed to be a chaste 'thank you' kiss. The man nearly melted me on the spot. The only thing that could have made the night more perfect was if a bed had appeared in the middle of the floor and Austin and I could make love surrounded by Starry Night, which was my favorite of Van Gough's pieces. It might have been too commercial for other artists to claim it as their favorite, but I didn't care about how popular or not a piece was. If it spoke to me, then it just did.

"Eww, why does that man have his tongue in her mouth?" A kid squealed from off to our left.

"This is a public event," the mother hissed at us. "Go be inappropriate somewhere private."

"Like she's never been inappropriate when she has that many kids trailing behind her," Austin stated, clearly annoyed with the woman, who heard his retort and huffily stomped off with her five leash-bound kids being pulled in her wake.

I laughed at his take on things. "You're probably not wrong, but we should keep things PG-rated until we get out of here," I explained as I glanced around to see that there weren't really that many people with kids out and about.

"She probably should have brought them to a matinee showing," he suggested.

"Yeah, but maybe she had to work."

"Stop looking on the bright side for other people," he teased. "You're supposed to be angry that we couldn't have a full-on make out session in the middle of the sunflowers."

"I was actually daydreaming of doing quite a lot more while surrounded by Starry Night."

"Oh, you dirty girl, I'm going to make that dream of yours come true one day."

The crazy thing was, I just bet he would pull it off, too. Austin was all about finding the things that made me happy and giving them to me. Not material things, either, which proved he did know me better than he let on. He offered up experiences he thought I'd love instead. Obviously, the man was determined to make me fall head over heels in love with him and I was well on my way to doing just that. The Austin of six years ago had nothing on this guy and I had been completely infatuated back then.

"You should take me home tonight," I suggested while pushing my body even closer to his. "We can always just pretend there was a blackout at the event that we took advantage of."

"I like the way you think, Trouble. Are you sure you've seen enough?"

"This has been the best night ever, Austin. Thank you, and yes, I've seen enough. Now, I just want to go home and be close to you."

When we passed my place and pulled up at a house, that I assumed was his, I gave Austin a quizzical look. "I don't mind going to your place all the time, but I want you to feel just as comfortable here, too. Besides, I have plans for you tonight and that double bed you have isn't going to cut it."

I laughed. "Trust me, if I had the spare room, it would have been upgraded to a larger size long ago."

"Well, there's no need now. I just so happen to have a king-sized bed that I've been dying to wake up with you in."

My heart hammered away in my chest as he helped me out of the car and into his house for the first time. It was a two-story stone and wood construction, which made me smile. The first restaurant he had taken me to, the one that looked like a mountain retreat or ski lodge, was a larger scale version of his house.

"I love your home, but it looks like it belongs in another place and time."

"Yeah, I know. I'm sure my neighbors complain about it not

matching their cookie-cutter bullshit, but I don't care. I like what I like."

"I love that you don't bow down to other people's expectations and do things your own way."

He grinned at me as we walked into an open concept space that housed a giant fireplace in the back corner with a large, gray leather sectional placed strategically in front of it to soak up the ambiance. The kitchen and dining area were open to everything as well, and to the left was a gorgeous wood beamed staircase with stone steps that matched the outside of the house perfectly.

"That staircase alone is a masterpiece," I commented.

"Glad you like it because we're going up. I'll give you the grand tour of the whole place in the morning. You'll appreciate it more with the light streaming in, anyway."

"I appreciate it enough now, even in the dim lighting, but I'll take your word for it."

We ascended the masterpiece of a staircase and immediately I fell in love with the large loft area that was open to the full width of the first floor from the front to rear of the house. The fireplace along with the full expanse of the living room, and a bit of the dining area and entryway was visible. The kitchen and anything else that came beneath where we stood and back weren't visible, obviously.

There appeared to be a hallway, or maybe another, smaller staircase on the opposite side of the loft from where we stood. It seemed to stretch in the opposite direction as the one we'd come up. "What is down there?" I asked for clarification.

"There's a smaller stairwell that leads down near the backdoor in the kitchen, in case of emergencies," Austin whispered in my ear.

"I can't wait to see this place in the daylight," I murmured.

"I know, and you will." He tugged gently on my hand to get me moving again. "Let's go, so I can show you what my bedroom looks like in the dark."

I giggled as he pulled me along down a wide hallway in front of the main stairs we'd just come up. We passed one door on the left and there were several lining the right side, but we ended up ducking into the second one on the left before I could really see much else.

My clothes were peeled off by overeager hands before we even made it to the grand bed with the large wooden posts that had to be at least six and a half feet high at each corner. I really couldn't wait to see the bed in the full light of day, too. That would not stop me from putting it to full use until then.

As my bare back rested against his still-shirt-clad front, Austin grabbed my breasts with each hand, and it felt like a perfect fit as his fingers wrapped around and held their weight.

"Fuck, Trouble. I wish we had the light show of that art exhibit here right now, to paint your gorgeous skin in beautiful stars." He leaned down and licked my neck before nipping just below my ear as he squeezed my breasts roughly in his hands again.

"Close your eyes and picture being back there. We were trapped after closing but figured out how to turn everything on."

"Wouldn't security notice?"

"Nah, they were too busy dealing with the ninjas trying to steal the show."

"Ah! A clever distraction. Good thinking."

One of his hands dipped down into my panties, the only clothing that still adorned my body. "I would touch you like this," Austin slid a finger down the crease of my sex until he could dip the digit inside me and swirl it around in my increasing wetness.

"Anyone could come back at any time, though," I breathed the words out in heavy, aroused pants.

"We better make time our bitch then, and make the most of it," he countered as the man turned me to face him and then pushed me onto the edge of his bed. "We're going to become one with those stars as I fuck you," he insisted.

"Make me feel them," I challenged as I arched my back and leaned up to nip at his beard covered jawline.

Austin pulled back only long enough to disrobe, then he crawled up my body and groaned against the base of my throat while placing the sweetest fucking open mouth kiss there. "I can't wait," his strained voice vibrated against my skin to emphasize his warning as he slid inside me.

"Oh, Austin," I moaned his name the minute he slid so deep I could feel his pubic bone grind down against my clit and upper mound.

He picked one of my thighs up and lifted a little higher, using the crook of his arm to rest inside the groove of my leg, which opened me a little wider so his hips could hammer home without hinderance. His other hand slicked my hair back from my face as Austin stared down into my eyes. There was just enough moonlight coming from somewhere that I could make out his hungry look before he dipped down and kissed me completely fucking stupid.

Austin worked me through three incredible orgasms before succumbing to his own and tucking us both into the middle of his bed.

The post-sex haze and the incredibly comfy mattress lulled me into an easy sleep, but it only felt like my eyes had been closed mere minutes when something, or someone, banged on the front door like they were SWAT coming through the solid-wood construction with one of those battering ram thingamajigs.

"It's probably Dallas being an ass as usual. You would think he didn't have his own place to go at night," Austin muttered as he quickly pulled on some sweatpants that made his butt look bitable as fuck.

I sat up, wondering if the wild Mercer brother would storm the upstairs, and decided that it was better to be prepared for Dallas than not. I grabbed Austin's button up that he'd worn earlier and put it on before I heard voices raise downstairs. That was most definitely not Dallas.

Quickly, I slipped my pants and shoes back on and then hunted down my cell phone and the small cross-body purse I'd brought with me on my date. Then, I headed for the stairs and stood at the top where I could just peek down into the lower level without being spotted, thanks to the shadows the beams formed in the low lighting.

Austin stood, shirtless with only his sweatpants on as he faced off with a very angry Jordan.

"Do you really think it's okay to have me work your shift so you can go galivanting off with the whore who keeps causing trouble in our friendship? She doesn't want me around you, so you drop me, and worse, think it's okay to make me work your shift while I have to imagine all night what you're getting up to with her?" The woman sounded desperate and slightly unhinged as she all but screamed her questions at Austin.

"It's not like that, and you know it, Jordan."

"Oh, no I don't. I'm sick of her ass coming into your life and pushing me out. The last time you two got together, I had to leave town for you, so that she wouldn't see me. Now, I'm working your shifts for the same damn reason."

"I was right to ask you to leave back then. You proved that by the stunt you pulled showing up to my place in your underwear on Valentine's Day. My girlfriend saw you that night and never bothered to come to the door again. You can't tell me you didn't arrange that on purpose."

I didn't miss the smug look on her face from where I was standing, so I know there was no way Austin could have missed it unless he'd suddenly gone blind or somehow managed to have the conversation with his eyes closed – just in case she was dressed inappropriately again. If that was the case, kudos to him. Then again, she was wearing her work uniform from the bar, so he could look all he wanted, as long as his next move was to throw her ass out the door.

"I don't think it's amusing," he growled at her.

"Well, too fucking bad, Austin! I've been in love with you my whole life. Do you think I find it amusing that I'm working extra shifts so you can go play with some whore you have a temporary infatuation with?"

"Keep your voice down," Austin warned as he glanced at the stairs, but not high enough to notice that I was hiding there in the shadows watching them.

"What. The. Fuck. Austin?" Jordan all but yelled. "Did you bring your whore to this house?" She snipped. "You promised you wouldn't do that. This is our space."

On that note, I'd heard enough. Considering we always went back to my place, tonight being the only exception, something about what she said rang true.

"Jordan, this is my house, and I can…"

"We picked everything for this house together, including the bed you probably have that bitch tucked up in."

It was a miracle that I didn't get sick right then and there. I didn't wait to go back and change out of my shirt. Instead, I hauled ass across the loft to the back set of stairs that Austin told me earlier led to the kitchen and backdoor. Once I was there, I took the stairs so fast, there was a real danger I might fall and kill myself on the way down. As soon as I got to the backdoor, I unlocked it quietly and flung the damn thing open. Austin had a security alarm on the house, but I was betting that he hadn't reengaged it with Jordan still in the house, considering he was probably trying to get rid of her before I found out it was her banging down the door earlier.

I supposed her urgency made sense. She always thought she had a claim on Austin, but after hearing she helped pick every-thing in his house out with him, that claim obviously extended to his house as well. Again, I thought my dinner from earlier might resurface as the bile began to rise in my throat.

I managed to get three blocks away from Austin's house, before my hands stopped shaking so hard that I was finally able to summon an Uber driver to come get me. Once I did, it took another fifteen minutes for him to show up. Truthfully, it was a miracle that there was one on duty, considering it was around four in the morning.

As soon as I opened the door of the Toyota Prius that showed up, the music, which sounded suspiciously like Hello Dolly, dropped to an inaudible level. For that, I was thankful.

"Says here we're headed to..." the man called out to me before reading off my address.

"That's correct."

He looked at me in the rearview mirror for a minute. "Bad hookup?" He asked being far too nosy for my liking.

"Can you just drive, please?"

"Sure," he huffed, obviously angry I wouldn't share my drama with him. Up until that moment, I didn't realize that I'd been crying at all. Damn Austin Mercer and for real, fuck his bestie straight to hell too. Unfortunately, my bastard of a driver liked to wake up with show tunes blasting on his car stereo.

As if I'd pissed off Karma herself, my night ended with the tone-deaf driver attempting to sing the show tunes, loudly, the whole way to my apartment. The minute I got myself free from his car, there was no holding back the sickness that followed.

I purged my stomach of anything that hadn't already been processed from the night before and then some extra bile just for funsies. My landlord would probably have a huge hissy fit when he saw the mess at the curb in front of our building. With any luck, I'd be firmly ensconced inside before he realized it was there and could blame me.

Once I was safely tucked away in my apartment, I counted down the minutes, until Austin realized I left his house. I truly expected him to come chasing after me, a phone call, or at the very least a text checking to make sure I was okay.

After the first hour, I figured he was still trying to deal with the Jordan situation, and I picked my phone up to send him a text, since not communicating after a Jordan incident before was what killed us.

> Becs: I made it home safe and sound. I tried but couldn't stick around for front row seats about all the ways you and Jordan had built a home together. You never should have taken me there if that was the case. We can talk about it, later, but Austin, we might be at a very significant crossroads. That talk needs to happen sooner than later.

There. I sounded mature, not entirely angry, and willing to work on things despite having my heart chopped to pieces by their conversation. I took my shoes and pants off and laid down on my bed with my phone clutched in my hand and the ringer turned all the way up, so I wouldn't miss any calls from him.

As I watched the clock, another hour passed.

No calls.

No texts.

And certainly, no knocks on my door.

It felt like history was repeating itself, only I'd done the right thing this time and opened communication between us. So, why wasn't he communicating?

I bargained with Karma, explaining that the Uber driver had been payment for anything that could have been past due on my account. I even tried to tell her I would take on Austin's karma, if it meant we could have a simple conversation and I was no longer left in limbo.

Karma ignored me. Not that I truly expected a response from an ideal that had been personified.

When another hour ticked by, I thought maybe Austin was

angry with me for leaving without a word and decided to sleep on it before coming to see me. At some point, my eyes drifted shut against my will and my body shut down. It probably had something to do with the mental and emotional drain of sobbing for the past two hours.

Sleep didn't claim me for long. It was around nine in the morning when my blurry eyes tried to focus on my phone only to see that there were still no calls or texts. I needed my best friend. It was time to come clean to her about how stupid I'd been. She would talk me off the emotional ledge, maybe tell me I'd simply hit my head and imagined the past two weeks with the one who got away. Then, things could get back to normal.

I reluctantly peeled Austin's shirt from my body, though it was evidence that proved I wasn't having some crazy weeks-long delusion. Then I hopped in the shower and attempted to wash the previous night away. What had been the greatest night of my life, turned into another nightmare instead.

The worst part was, I knew this would happen so long as things remained in limbo where Jordan had been concerned. We hadn't talked about her. We had avoided his house altogether until tonight, and now I knew why. At least, what Jordan wanted me to think about why his house had been off limits. I wouldn't take anything she said for gospel, until Austin and I spoke.

I managed to get all the way downstairs, into my car, and over to Clea's house without actually thinking. It was like my brain was on autopilot, trying to get to the one person who might help me make sense of everything.

Only, she wasn't there. I assumed she was at the other Texas boy's house. Hopefully, things went better for her. As I sat there, wondering what to do, a text pinged my phone. I grabbed the damn thing so fast that it dropped, and I ended up having to get out of my damn car to search under the seat for it. Once I had it back in hand, I glanced down and was disappointed to see that it was my best friend, not my boyfriend.

Yes, I was at her house, looking for comfort, but there was still a stubborn part inside my heart that refused to believe history was truly repeating itself. I had hoped it would be him.

> Clea: How was your night? I got food poisoning, tell you about it when I see you.

That sounded so normal. Why couldn't I have gotten food poisoning at dinner and then we wouldn't have had a fabulous night together, so there would have been no reason for it to fall apart in the end. Denial was a bitch, because then I thought about what would have happened if I'd gone home alone, sick while Austin went back to his place and Jordan showed up. Would the night have ended in more than an argument between them? For that matter, did it? I still hadn't heard a thing from Austin, but she'd been there with him when I left. Maybe she still was.

Was I that easily replaced when push came to shove, and Jordan was the one doing the pushing? It felt like it in the bright light of day. I glanced down at the text my best friend sent because I needed something to ground me and keep me from going down the 'what if' rabbit hole of my relationship.

> Clea: How was your night? I got food poisoning, tell you about it when I see you.

Nope. It hadn't changed. Still just a message from Clea about food poisoning.

> Becs: Will you be home after lunch? I stopped by, but I'm guessing you're at lover man's place.

> Clea: I can leave now if you need me.

> Becs: No, I'll see you for lunch.

Clea: Okay, see you then, but I'll probably just be on a liquid diet, so no need to bring food for both of us.

Becs: No need for food then. Gotcha.

There was no way I'd have an appetite either, so I guess we both had our own illnesses to attend. Clea had her food poisoning, and I had my heartbreak. I didn't wish this feeling on anyone, so trading places was out of the question, but I wished that food poisoning was all I had to deal with. My heart ached for that to be what ailed me instead of what was happening.

By the time my pseudo lunch rolled around with Clea, I decided to keep things vague. Dallas had apparently warned Houston and my best friend that something had gone down involving me being at Austin's place as a hookup and Jordan showing up and throwing a fit.

I don't know why I lied to her, maybe it was because I wasn't ready to deal with everything just yet. Part of it was because I couldn't handle the pity or lectures about how I should have known better. Not that Clea would lecture so much as pity my situation. Truthfully, there was no way to admit that I'd spent the past two weeks falling for Austin all over again, only to have the past repeat itself. There was nothing my friend could do to help me with that, so I sugarcoated things. I told her we basically had a one-night stand and that it was ruined by Jordan.

"Did he at least text you or call to make sure you got home safely?" She asked me, when I explained that Jordan was saying some shitty things about me being there in the house they'd built together. It was understandable that I ran. My bestie would have done the same thing and we both knew it so there was no reason for her to voice that part.

"No, and he's the one that drove me to his house." I left out what the rest of our night had been like, because if she heard about it, she would know. She would know how fucking heart-sore I was and then try to hug me, at which point I would fall to pieces on her.

"I walked three blocks from his place before I could even call for an Uber to come get me. Then, I had to wait there for the guy to show up, and to top off my miserable morning he was playing show tunes on the stereo."

"What do you have against show tunes? You like musicals."

"Sure, when the people singing them can actually sing, but you didn't let me get to the part where my driver thought it was a ride and a show. He was singing along at the top of his lungs, and it wasn't pretty. It wasn't even ugly, Clea. It was so awful that I think a little bit of my brain might have leaked out of my ears in an attempt to escape."

Clea tried to make me feel better by telling me the story about her bad Thai food incident and shitting herself in front of Houston. It worked to take my mind off my own sorrow for a bit and the way she told her own story made me laugh so hard my stomach was in stitches but the time I got everything back under control.

"I'm sorry. At least Houston was understanding and also sick, so he really knew what you were going through."

"Yeah, there is that." She giggled and then pulled me into that hug I'd been dreading. "I'm sorry that you don't have that, too. I know you had hoped…"

Her response was bad enough that I was glad I hadn't told her the whole story. I couldn't handle Clea crying with me over a man who only set out to hurt me time and again, thanks to his too-close ties to his best friend.

"Hope is a bitch that I wish I could meet one day, just so I could punch her in the face," I admitted. Violent? Yes. I considered it a necessary form of therapy to give Hope a face that looked a lot like Jordan's and then mentally punch it until it pancaked into a flat, blob of disgusting goo to match her personality.

"Remind me to screen new people for you from now on, just in case."

"You know what I mean." The breath I let out felt like it might be my last. My body actually ached with it as if everything might fall apart and fly away into nothing. I felt like me being happy with Austin looked like those sunflowers in the immersive display we saw the night before. Being without him was to look at a poster copy of the original painting. It was still okay to see but lacked the luster and inspiration of the other. How in the hell was I supposed to go back to the life I was living before he barged in and demanded another shot from me?

"Maybe it's time to give up on him completely. I know you've dated, but there hasn't been anyone serious since Austin." She was talking about since the Austin incident of six years ago, not the most recent one. Obviously, since that only ended the night before. No, it was this morning. Same day. It hadn't even been twenty-four hours.

"I don't know, Clea. Maybe, I'm meant to be alone."

"No one is meant to be alone for life, Becs. Just because one guy was a complete tool and didn't know how to drop his child-hood bestie, fuck buddy, or whatever the hell she is to him, that doesn't mean the rest of them are like that."

Not a single molecule in my body wanted to find out if there was a better man out there for me. Not because I was holding out hope that Austin would come through for me this time, but because I would never put myself through this potential heartache again. Never.

*LINK TO BONUS Chapter 12 - Austin's POV

CHAPTER THIRTEEN

AFTER MY NON-LUNCH, LUNCH DATE WITH CLEA, I WENT BACK home to my apartment and sat there on the couch staring at the wall. It was the weekend. I'd planned to spend the bulk of it with Austin before everything imploded. Saying that we imploded sounded better than intimating we'd blown up, because there hadn't been any explosive charge from either of us to end every-thing. Our relationship just quietly ripped itself apart from the inside out while I sat there in the dark literally and figuratively.

He hadn't ever called or even texted me back to check in with me, give me a head's up about what was going on in his mind, or with Jordan. There was nothing. The nothing made the ache grow by the minute. I always thought people who needed closure were stupid, but having been in a relationship, twice now, where closure was never granted, I understood. If someone died, at least you knew there was a reason for that finality. If they broke up with you, but didn't give a reason, you at least had the fact that they told you it was over. The not knowing killed. The fact that Dallas had sent Clea to check on me was a bitter pill to swallow because he knew what happened, which meant that Austin spoke to someone about it. That someone just wasn't me.

Whoever the asshole was who came up with the concept for the stages of grief was an idiot. I cycled through the stages at least twice before lunchtime and a few more times before the dinner that I never ate.

"How could you do this to me again?" I screamed at my walls when it all became too much to deal with. He wasn't there for me to yell at, and as much as I wanted to go to his house and scream that in his face, I couldn't handle seeing him cozying up to Jordan in the place they'd apparently built together.

And wasn't that just a kick to the pants too? How could he take me there? How could he parade me around the house he'd made with her, the home they'd made together. He made love to me in the bed they'd probably shared hundreds of times, and that thought sent me running from the couch to the bathroom again. I really should have been smart and put a puke bucket by the couch.

The next morning started with my wearing Austin's shirt. The same one I'd worn when I ran out of his house. It smelled like him, and I wasn't ready to give that up just yet. In fact, his beautifully dark and spicy scent sent me spiraling and I fired off another text.

> Becs: We promised we wouldn't end up this way again. Please, talk to me. I don't know what happened between you and Jordan after I left, but I at least deserve to hear it from you instead of sitting here with my imagination.

I hit send before I could chicken out. Then, regret hit, and I threw my phone as far from me as possible. Granted, that wasn't very far considering the size of my apartment, and I was lucky that the damn thing hadn't broken.

By lunchtime, the shirt came off and my old roommate's sweats were put on instead. Fuck Austin. Fuck his shirt. His scent. Fuck everything about him!

I cried after that, for about an hour, before I finally gave in and went to eat something because even in my grief and rage driven depression, I knew that sustenance was necessary to survival. There was only a blip of a moment where survival wasn't an option because it hurt too much, but that was quickly bashed away because no man was worth my life. Not even Austin. Especially not Austin.

My entire Sunday was more of the same back and forth between raging out at an imaginary Mr. Fucking Texas, because we were back to that, since he'd proven that the more grown-up version of Austin Mercer hadn't been any better after all. Then, I would go back to crying jags that left my face swollen, eyes puffy, and my head pounding. The worst part was, I couldn't even drown myself in a bottle of tequila because I'd been there and done that the last time we went through a breakup where I wasn't even worth a conversation to end things.

No amount of convincing myself that he wasn't worth all my emotional outbursts helped either. You can't reason with a broken heart when it needs to cry, scream, and purge the love from its system.

My phone still sat across the room where I'd thrown it the day before. The battery died at some point but charging it hadn't been an option because it meant obsessing over him calling or texting to put me out of my misery. Deep down inside, I knew that wasn't going to happen, so I left the damn thing where I'd thrown it.

On Monday, I emailed in sick to work from my laptop. It was the first time in all the years I'd worked there that I did so. If anyone deserved a sick day, it was me. Guilt riddled me because I felt like me missing a day was a disappointment to the kids who enjoyed my class and saw it as their only escape from the boring classes that were always deemed more important. I knew how they felt, because I'd once been them and my art class was the one thing that got me through the rest of the day.

Still, this Becs was no good for them. They were better off missing me for a day than dealing with whatever version of me might show up to class. So, I continued to sulk right up until someone knocked on my door that evening.

My stupid little heart got herself worked up that Austin had finally come to his senses and came to beg my forgiveness. My head knew better and was proven correct when Clea's voice called out through the door.

"Becs, open up, or I'm using my key and I'll feel really bad if you're in there boning some hot dude instead of just feeling sorry for yourself!"

I heard the muffled sound of a male speaking before Clea's voice came through again. "I don't know whether that's chivalrous or gross," she said. It must have been my neighbor who talked to her. He was a semi-decent looking pervert, but one who never took things too far, thankfully.

"I'll pass that on to her," she told the person, then she shouted into the door again and banged her fists on it. "Your neighbor just offered to get under you. You need to open up before everyone in the building starts making an attempt at helping you get over someone."

I slid over to the door and pulled the damn thing open. Clea wasn't kidding, her next step would have been to use my key and then I would have felt worse at having her see me unable to even open my own damn door.

Did I mention that I was wearing Austin's shirt again? There should have been a moment, when Clea eyed me, where I felt embarrassed over that fact, but I didn't. Like the good friend that she was, she didn't call me out on it either. Instead, she crinkled her nose at me in disgust.

Fair. I hadn't showered since the other day and applying deodorant hadn't been a thought either.

"Okay, first thing, you're getting a shower. Then, we're going to a movie to get lost in someone else's drama for a while."

"How is that going to make me feel better?"

"One – you'll be clean. Two – you need to get out of this house. Three – we are not letting the asshole win!"

"Fine!" I spun around, slowly to stave off the wave of dizziness that not eating much more than a cracker and a half bowl of soup in days caused. Before I entered the bathroom, I laid down my one rule. "No romantic comedies, though. Fuck love!"

"Yeah! Fuck love!" Clea shouted back at me.

It almost made me laugh because I knew she didn't mean it for herself but was trying to commiserate with me anyway.

"Shut up, you liar!" I yelled back to her. Then I got a shower, shaved my previously stinky pits. Twice. It was weird how fast the hair grew there. My legs and bikini area remained unshaven though because who the hell did I have to impress anymore? No one, that's who.

I dressed in a simple jeans and t-shirt with a hoodie thrown on top for good measure because it was still much cooler outside in the evenings, even though we had a pretty balmy warm front move into the area at some point. I only knew that because my heat hadn't kicked on as much, which meant the outside temps must have been higher than the sixty-five threshold my thermostat was still set at.

I'd stopped setting emergency money aside for my parents. In fact, I quit my second job as a waitress that I'd used to come up with the money to help them out, too. That was why I had the entire last weekend off in anticipation of spending it with... Nope. Wasn't even going to think his stupid name. His mom was probably dropped on her head as a baby to name her kids after a state that she never even lived in. Maybe that was why she ended up dropping him on *his* head, too. There had to be some brain damage involved in his decision-making abilities. Had to.

I slipped my feet into a pair of furry on the inside, suede on the outside boots and made my way out to find Clea texting away on her phone. When she saw that I was ready, she stood and tucked her phone away.

"Okay, let's get out of here," she ordered. The dubious look I threw at my door forced her hand, and she came to tug me out of the apartment before turning and locking my door, so I didn't have easy access to get back in. I also didn't have my keys with me, which sucked because it left me at Clea's mercy. There would be no bailing out early.

Once we arrived at the theater, we chose an action flick. It was sure to have a bit of romance, but everyone knew that the action hero never had the same love interest in the sequel, so I would just remind myself of that when it looked like they might be falling for one another. Clea ordered a tub of buttered popcorn, and two large drinks. I almost reminded her about the Reece's Pieces, but decided I wasn't really in the mood for the sweet to go with the bitter I felt inside.

The lights were still up when we made our way into the theater. Honestly, I wished they hadn't been because wallowing in a dark space while pretending to pay attention to the previews and then the movie sounded like the best idea. Too much time in the bright lights without a distraction meant that Clea might say the wrong thing and trigger another sob-fest. No one needed to see me sob and scream at myself like a lunatic.

We managed to find our seats just in time to turn around and be smacked in the face – not literally – with the reason for my misery. It was as bad as I feared and worse all at once. He'd left me for her. I'd imagined it with so many different scenarios, but honestly thought it couldn't be possible. There had to be another reason why he ghosted me after the best two weeks of my life.

The reason was locked in a sensual kiss with him three rows up from where I stood, having not yet been able to take my seat because my eyes had locked on the living embodiment of the nightmares that had kept me awake for the past three days.

I glanced down as their lips broke apart and she tried to feed him whatever was in her hands. He turned away slightly, and she huffed.

"I dumped the candy in, just the way you like it," she cooed to him before he leaned over and kissed her again. She dumped the candy in? I glanced down and couldn't be sure from the distance, but it looked like Reece's Pieces were floating around in their shared bucket of popcorn. He'd shown her my way to eat popcorn at the movies. It felt like even more of a betrayal that he'd shared that with her. Never mind the kiss, that felt like a violation. He had blatantly shared something of mine – something I turned into ours – with her.

This was why leaving the house had been a horrible idea. I didn't think I'd ever do it again. Briefly, I wondered if anyone would care if I dumped our popcorn on the floor, so that I had the bucket to use to vomit in. I would imagine they'd rather clean a popcorn mess than my nasty stomach bile off the carpeted floor.

Clea must have clued into what had me frozen in place, because she announced, rather loudly, and much to my dismay, "What a fucking douche!"

The couple broke apart and turned to see who made that announcement and why. Jordan looked extremely pleased with herself when she noticed who was standing there. I don't know what Austin's reaction was because I couldn't bring myself to look. It would be even more devastating to see his reaction and have it be less than heartbreak. Then again, the fact that he was at the movies, kissing another woman, made it more than clear that he was not experiencing the same level of heartbreak that I'd been going through for days.

That thought managed to unglue my feet from the floor and I took off out of the theater at breakneck speed. There was no honor in sitting through a movie and pretending that seeing them there together didn't hurt me. I couldn't do it anyway. Nothing about my feelings for Austin had ever been pretend.

"Becs!" I heard Austin call out from behind me, but I ignored it. Actually, I used his voice to motivate me to move faster than before. Clea could find her own way home. I'd take an Uber or something. Unfortunately, I remembered that I'd have to wait for my best friend because she hadn't let me take my keys or wallet with me. That meant I had no way to get home or to get into my apartment once I got there. Despite my neighbor's kind offer to get under him and forget my troubles, that wasn't an option that was open for me in my state of heartbreak and desperation.

I managed to dump my popcorn and drink into the trash, mostly so they couldn't be used as weapons. No way did I want to go to jail for assault by popcorn. That would just be embarrassing on top of the pathetic mess my life had already become.

"Becs!" I heard Austin call again, and he sounded far too close, but I couldn't stop and allow him anywhere near me. I'd wanted closure days ago, and now I had it. There was no longer any need for a conversation.

"Go on home, Becs, I'll get a ride there in a minute," Clea called out to me. I moved around the corner, out of sight, to wait for her. She must have forgotten that she was my ride here and all that nonsense about me not having keys or money. Still, she stopped to stall Austin so I could get away, and I would owe her for that one day when I was capable of paying her back.

"You are the biggest asshole I have ever met," my best friend said. Obviously, that was not directed at me.

"You don't know him!" Someone else defended. Clearly, it was Jordan, since she was the only bitch who was dumb enough to do so and put up with his wishy-washy crap after all these years of dealing with it. As far as I was concerned, they deserved one another and could rot in hell together.

"You – shut the fuck up. I'm not speaking to you right now," my best friend snapped at the whore. Go Clea! If I were in a better place, I'd probably do a little cheer in the hallway. Unfortunately, I was depression's bitch, so that wouldn't be happening anytime soon.

"My best friend didn't deserve what you did to her all those years ago, and don't you dare try to claim that it was in solidarity for your brother. I'd bet good fucking money that a certain woman was in your ear, giving you that bad fucking advice because she didn't want to lose you."

Way to call it exactly how it was, Clea. And I hadn't even confided in her what went down all those years ago, not the whole truth of the matter anyway.

"My friend didn't deserve you playing more games with her again the other night either." I cringed at that because Clea really did think it was a one and done between he and I that night. The done part being all his fault, of course. Still, it probably seemed weird to Austin to hear her talk about it like it was one night, not weeks of us being together.

"I wasn't playing games with anyone," Austin denied her accusations, as if he had any room to do so, considering how we'd found him at the movies living his best life with his lips wrapped around those of his supposed best friend.

"Really, Austin? So, you slept with her, then your childhood fuck buddy showed up and you missed the fact that Becs even left your house. When you did realize, you couldn't be bothered to check on her, to let her know what happened, or at least let her down easily?"

Oh Clea! I loved my friend, but her recap was breaking my heart all over again.

"Instead, you ghosted her again, and after I finally convinced her to shower and leave the house to help heal her heart, what happens? We walked in on you right as fucking rain, sucking face with the woman who is always at the goddamn center of you brushing my bestie off like she's the dirt under your shoes! Grow the fuck up, Austin, and leave Becs alone. She deserves a real man who can make her happy, not a little boy who doesn't know how to fucking decide between his past and his future."

I don't know if what Clea had to say left Austin as stunned as it left me, or if Jordan held him back from chasing after her to get to me, but when Clea rounded the corner, she was alone. Part of me was once again equal parts disappointed and resigned. Did my heart really think he'd try harder than he had? What a silly organ. Maybe they did transplants for defective proverbial hearts the same way they did for the part that kept your blood pumping through your body.

Clea came up short when she saw me slumped there against the wall, then she wrapped herself around me, as if to shield me from prying eyes. "You didn't have to wait," she whispered.

"Yeah, I kind of did. You made me leave the house without keys or money."

"Shit! Sorry, Becs. I'm so sorry," she whispered again to reiterate the point. I didn't think the second sorry was really about leaving me stranded and more about how her plan backfired and I had to see the cause of my pain out enjoying his best life with another woman.

Life sucked that way.

"Thanks for having my back," I muttered to her.

"I will always have your back, that's what real besties do," she promised. That was the lesson Austin never learned about his supposed best friend. She didn't have his back, she continually stabbed him in it and then smiled sweetly like nothing was amiss, and he believed the lies she fed him hook, line, and sinker every time.

Clea squeezed me tighter before she finally managed to get us to her car. "Oh, Becs," she hissed when she saw my face. "One day, you're going to tell me all about it because I really don't believe all this is over a one-night stand, even if you did have prior history."

I didn't say anything as I swiped the sleeve of my hoodie

under my nose to keep the snot from trailing down my face with my tears. When I glanced up and past where Clea stood, opening her car door for me, I saw Austin standing there watching us with his phone to his ear. Jordan stood a couple paces away from him looking angrier and angrier by the second.

Served the wench right to have her night ruined the way she'd been ruining mine for years.

On the way home, Clea answered her ringing phone via the Bluetooth in her car. "Hello?"

"Hey sweet Clea," Houston called over the speakers. His voice sounded so much like Austin's that it sent shivers up my spine and made me want to cry again.

"Hello, handsome. What can I do for you?"

"My brother just called me," he mentioned casually, though I didn't think the call was all that casual and I wished he'd waited until I was no longer in the car with his girlfriend before they had whatever conversation was about to take place.

Clea winked at me. "Oh yeah? Which one?"

I snorted in an attempt to hold back what amounted to sarcastic laughter. We both knew exactly which brother would have called him recently and why. Actually, I wasn't sure why he'd call Houston, unless it was to tattle to him that his girlfriend broke up his date night and said mean things to him. I really did owe my best friend a lot. I wished I'd been the one to say mean, angry, horrible things I'd never be able to take back in a million years.

"I think you know the one. The biggest asshole of the bunch."

"Well," Clea hedged. "A week ago, I would have said Dallas deserved that title, but this week, I'm going to assume you're talking about Austin."

"That would be the one."

"Are you calling to fuss at me for yelling at him and Jordan?" She asked. I could hear the trepidation in her voice and worried that I'd inadvertently caused problems for her with the man of her dreams. That was something I didn't want, even if it meant I'd have to hear about him from time-to-time as a result of Austin being Clea's brother-in-law one day. While things might not have worked out for me, I had no doubt that Clea and Houston would go the distance, as long as my bullshit didn't just pop a hole in their happy bubble.

"Nope," Houston told her quickly, obviously having heard the same bit of fear in her voice. "Just wanted to check and make sure you and Becs were okay."

"Seriously?" I asked, shocked beyond belief that Houston would give a shit about how I was doing after his brother decimated my heart.

"I'm sorry that my brother hasn't managed to get his head out of his ass and act like the man he's supposed to be. So, yeah, I'm serious when I say that checking on you was a priority."

"I'll be okay," I managed to say before I turned my head to stare out the window. Tears threatened to fall again, and I didn't want to openly sob with him on the line.

"I know you will be," he agreed. It was a lie. I lied and he knew it and was lying to me, too. "Will you be staying with Becs the rest of the night, Clea?" He asked.

"I think that's for the best, handsome."

"If you need anything, I will be happy to play delivery driver and then leave you both to it. From what I hear, you didn't even get to eat your popcorn at the movies. How about I bring some by, with some ice cream, and…"

"How are you so perfect?" Clea's sweet question cut off Houston's offer and made me want to vomit again. Just a few days ago, I'd thought the same about Austin when he'd taken me to the Van Gough exhibit. If only I'd known then that he was about to ruin the artist for me, for all time.

"…help," Houston said, though I hadn't caught the rest of what he'd told Clea. It didn't matter anyway. Someone laughed in the background and Houston added, "You forget, I have sisters. I know what they needed when they felt the same way."

"We'll be at my place in case someone tries to find Becs at hers," Clea proclaimed, which was unwelcome news to me. "And thank you for being amazing." She hung up then and I settled back for the rest of the ride, not even bothering to disagree about our destination because I didn't think it would matter.

CHAPTER FOURTEEN

APRIL WAS THREE DAYS AWAY. SCHOOL LET OUT FOR SUMMER IN two months, and the countdown had already begun. There was no way I'd be able to sit around and do nothing for the summer. There were a couple of summer camps in the area for kids, but the positions for arts and crafts director didn't exactly pay well. Still, it was something to do to pass the time, so I'd applied and started working on some cool week-and month-long plans for each, just in case I managed to snag one of the positions.

If I had unlimited funds, I would have already booked one of those huts over the water in Fiji for the summer. Even a week to get away from everyone and everything would be nice. Since I'd helped my parents out for the majority of the year, my savings had completely depleted so even a trip to the lake for a week was out of the question, never mind some exotic giveaway where I could watch the fish swim underneath my floor.

My phone pinged as I got home from work.

Clea: Can you come over?

I glanced at my couch longingly, but knew I'd spent far too

much time there over the past three or so weeks. My heart tripped over itself at the thought. Three weeks post my last date with Austin didn't feel much better than three days. My only saving grace was that there had been no more accidental run-ins with him or the bitch he was with.

> Becs: You need me now? I can bring food, too.

> Clea: No food. Just hurry over if you can.

Well, that didn't sound great. I didn't even bother to change out of my paint-stained t-shirt and instead took off immediately to Clea's place. My early, post-work dinner so I could be in bed by eight could wait. Yeah, I was that person with absolutely no life, so bedtime started to come earlier and earlier for me. I figured once the depression went away, I'd have more energy anyway.

When I got to Clea's place, the first thing I noticed was her frantic pacing and wringing of her hands. She was worried about something, and I couldn't tell if she had bad news to pass along or if the worry was her own. What if she told me that Jordan and Austin had run off to get married? How in the hell would I handle not falling apart in front of her? No, I didn't think that was it, especially when I glanced at her counter and saw what looked like twenty different boxes of...

"I thought you got your period already, and you guys were in the clear about the broken condom thing?"

"Becs!" Clea whined to me. "I only spotted for like two days. That's not normal for me. What if I was wrong and I really am pregnant?"

I wanted to laugh because she looked adorable all panicked the way she was. Not that I found it funny that she was clearly going over the edge, but Clea never lost her cool, so it was amusing to see the role reversal.

"Okay, but you haven't had any symptoms, other than one light period."

"So?"

"So?" I teased the way she sounded with her one-word question. "Why all the tests?"

"I'm nervous. What if I'm one of those women who just never knows she's pregnant and then the next thing you know, I'm walking down the snack food aisle in the grocery store," she glanced up at me with a knowing look, "to satisfy my cravings, and bam! It looks like I'm pissing myself, except my water just broke."

I chuckled at the mental image my bestie painted. "You have such a good imagination that maybe you should think about writing books instead of doing marketing for authors."

"You're an asshole. It could happen."

"Prom babies happen because those girls are in denial. You might be sort of stacked in the boob and butt department, but I think you'd notice if your tiny waist started expanding enough to fit a whole baby."

"I just want to be sure," she pleaded with me, as if I was some sort of pregnancy crystal ball there to tell her what twenty tests couldn't.

"Fine." I grabbed a test out of the pile and headed to the bathroom. "Since we're stupidly taking pregnancy tests for no good reason, I'll take one with you. Solidarity my bestie!"

Clea giggled, which had been my intention. Then she went to the ensuite bathroom in her bedroom, and I took the one that was meant for guests to use. We reconverged with the tests and put them down on the counter after Clea neatly placed several layers of paper towels down.

Neither one of us seemed inclined to look down for results, so we talked instead.

"I'm only home like fifty percent of the time now. It's weird, like we're time-sharing houses or something, though I can tell that Houston prefers when we're at his place."

"Why is that?"

"I guess because I lived here with Jeff and had planned to make this our home once we were married." She shrugged her shoulders, as if it was a silly concept.

I didn't have the heart to tell her that I completely understood where he was coming from having been faced with that same reality once before. At least in her case, she hadn't gone straight back to Jeff's arms and broken up with Houston by not speaking to him. That was a cruel twist of fate that I didn't wish on anyone.

"What about you? Did you ever take your neighbor up on his offer? He's kind of cute. Anyone else catch your eye?" She prattled on with her questions and I shook my head to each one. The only date I'd been on lately was the one with my couch after work, where I did mindless things to keep wandering thoughts about what Austin was up to with Jordan from crushing my soul. I didn't think my friend needed to hear that, though.

"My only dates have been the gym with you every morning. I have to go to bed early just to be able to keep up after getting ready to meet you at ungodly o'clock in the morning." Clea gave me a quick smile that didn't quite reach her eyes.

"I guess it was silly to have you take one of these with me, since you hadn't seen anyone for months before Austin, and then that was only one time."

It felt like she was attempting to pry again. The one time she spoke of, with some guy I went out with about six months before Austin crashed back into my life, hadn't even ended in sex because the guy had been strictly against going down on me while demanding that I do it for him. It was a sex non-starter and I'd kicked him to the curb before he even managed to pull his pants back up.

Clea was like a dog with a bone though, and her focus wasn't even on that 'one time' with the dude from last August. She knew there had been more to Austin and me than the one-night roll in the hay I'd admitted to. I couldn't talk about it. What was the point? Reliving the most wonderful two weeks of my life and then heartbreak that followed would only set me backwards.

I thought I heard the doorknob jiggle but then Clea's timer went off on her phone indicating it was time to look at our results. We both picked our test sticks up. I hadn't seen Clea's reaction because I was too busy staring at the test in my own hands. It couldn't be. I felt faint all of a sudden and needed to sit down but couldn't make my body work. Instead, I just stood there and stared at the test until Clea snatched it away from me.

"No," I cried. There was no way this could have happened.

"Marry me!" I turned on a dime, having mistaken Houston's voice for Austin's. Dammit why did they have to be so alike? Why did Jordan always have to ruin things? If it hadn't been for her, I might have been taking this stupid test with my boyfriend and he might have been the one shouting out an impromptu marriage proposal. Instead, I'd be raising my baby alone. Oh God! Even worse, he would want split custody and his whore would help him raise our baby. I felt so sick at the thought. She'd already taken him from me, and now she'd get the chance to steal my child, too.

I didn't hear Clea when she agreed to the proposal, but I did when she said, "Oh, shit! No, Houston."

"No, you won't marry me?"

"No. I mean, yeah. I mean, this isn't mine!"

My best friend had been waving my peed-on pregnancy test all about like it was the most sanitary thing in the world. It didn't bother me. I worked with kindergarteners and saw worse on a daily basis. Clea was a different story though, when she realized what she was doing, it would give her a good case of the gross willies.

I snatched the test back out of her hands and took a step away from the couple who were staring at me.

"Is it Austin's?" Houston asked. I stared at him without answer, pleading with my eyes not to say that name again. It was bad enough that he sounded like the man who had knocked me up. And that was when I hit my breaking point. I crumpled to the kitchen floor and became a sobbing mess despite the fact that there were people to witness it.

"Dammit," I heard Houston mutter.

"Don't tell him," I managed to choke out.

"Don't ask me to keep something like that a secret," he fired back.

"I'll tell him, but..."

"Tell him. Decide what you're going to do together, but Becs, do it soon because I won't lie or keep it from him. He deserves to know."

All I could picture was Jordan holding my baby while staring at me with that smug fucking smirk on her face. It was hard to breathe, like someone turned the oxygen off in the apartment and I was going to asphyxiate on nothingness and despair. It didn't matter that you couldn't have despair if there was nothingness. Logic was not factoring into my panic. Why had I come to Clea's house? I had a standing date with my couch that I should have kept. Dammit. This was the kind of life altering shit that always happened to me when I left my apartment for anything other than work.

"A part of me wants to argue with you about that," I finally cried to Houston. Austin didn't deserve to know after everything he put me through. What if he did the same thing with our child. What if Jordan put her foot down and didn't allow him to bring my baby into her house and so he just stopped showing up and ghosted our child the way he did to me? I would murder them both.

Houston kneeled down and then when that didn't work for

him, he sat beside me and pulled me onto his lap. It only made me cry harder because it was like Austin was holding me, only he smelled all wrong. It wasn't him and it should have been. This was not the life I'd always dreamed of. The wrong man had me wrapped in his arms, and I didn't think I could keep it together anymore even though I carried the biggest reason in the world to get my shit together.

The guilt hit right alongside my sadness. I hadn't even known I was pregnant. Thinking back, I had missed a period, but chalked it up to the depression and weight loss from not having an appetite. Breakups were hell on my body. Correction. Breakups with Austin were hell on my body. I was one of those people who couldn't eat when stressed and depressed, so it meant imminent weight loss. That couldn't be good for the baby I was growing, so already my mothering skills were on par with my own mom's. That sucked. I always thought I'd be a better, far more loving parent.

"I'm sorry he has his head so far up his ass, Becs. I don't know what to say about him. For years, his ass was grumpy because he gave you up."

"Yeah, he looked really grumpy after he ghosted me yet again after sex, only to see him kissing all over Jordan a couple days later. He was really torn up." I pushed off Houston after wiping my snotty face all over his shirt. I'd add that little reaction to my guilt pile later.

Clea left the room as I managed to get back up on my feet. I had my phone out, and dialed Austin's number by the time she got back and handed Houston a different shirt to replace the one I'd just snotted all over.

"I'm going to put it on speakerphone, because I need you guys to be here for me," I admitted. Truthfully, I just wanted a fucking witness to what was about to happen. I wasn't even a little bit surprised when his voicemail kicked in. He hadn't answered any of my texts since the day I left his house, why in the hell had I thought he'd answer his phone? I decided a text was better anyway. He could ignore it like all the others.

> Becs: I need to speak to you. It's important, please call immediately.

I said everything out loud as I typed it in. Honestly, I should have just sent him an "I'm pregnant" text that he could ignore and called it good, but I knew that wouldn't fly with Houston. He basically acted like my own personal Jiminy Cricket.

Almost immediately the delivered and read receipts popped up. "There, he's seen it," I mentioned as I flipped my phone to face Houston and Clea. We all waited. I knew what would happen, or more accurately what wouldn't. They seemed to be growing more impatient with each second that ticked by. I guess they thought he would immediately pick up the phone to see what I wanted. I wasn't sure what part of "he ghosted me" they didn't understand, but at least now they would know what I meant.

After fifteen minutes, Houston grew completely fed up with his brother and pulled his own phone out. He got an immediate response from his brother, which went to show that he was capable. His hands hadn't fallen off. Apparently, Houston wasn't going to have a text argument with Austin though. He dialed the phone instead.

"What?" I heard Austin growl through the phone. "It's my fucking brother, lay off for a minute, J."

My stomach rolled again at hearing that. They were together. Figured.

"You need to get to Clea's place, right now." Houston demanded as I shook my head. No, I did not need him to show up here with her hot on his heels while I had to deliver this news to him.

"I can't fucking leave."

"Get Dallas over there. Put me on speaker," Houston

demanded and waited a minute for his brother to comply. "Jordan?" Houston called out.

"Yeah?" She answered snippily.

"Shit or get off the pot, girl. I'm your boss too and I'm not playing the emotional blackmail games you keep using to keep Austin dangling by your strings. If you don't want to work at the bar, get a new fucking job. Try this bullshit again, and you'll need to look for another job anyway, because I'm sick of it. I will have you replaced if you don't want to work and just want another way to control my brother."

Well, damn. You go, Houston. That was almost worth the price of admission. The price being having to hear that Jordan and Austin were playing happy couples at work. Or not so happy as it seemed that day. Then the price grew steeper as Austin defended the bitch.

"What the fuck, Houston?" He yelled.

"I should be asking you, 'What the fuck?' Austin. That is *our* bar. *Our* business. Stop bringing your personal shit there to fuck things up. If Jordan can't be a grown up about working with you when she's your fuck buddy, then she needs to find a new job. And you need to stop sleeping with employees. Now, get Dallas to cover for you, and get your ass over here. It's fucking important!"

I cringed at the tone Houston used with his brother. That was not going to go over well. The jerk would be in a hell of a mood when he got here and then I was supposed to deliver news that would most likely piss him off even more.

I went to take a seat on the couch, because standing wasn't an option anymore, as all the possible scenarios for how this was about to play out ran through my mind. I hated that Houston had shown up in the middle of us taking those tests. He didn't even give me a minute to process the news for myself before I had to deal with Austin and Jordan drama that ruined everything all over again.

I sat there in silence as Houston and Clea did their own thing. What that thing was, I couldn't tell you because my mind was lost to the endless string of possibilities. Maybe, I could just run away and go live somewhere else and raise my baby where Jordan could never get her nasty bitch hands on him or her. Doing that would mean depriving my little souvenir of knowing family. They wouldn't get to bond with any of the Mercers, Clea, and well my family was pretty much out of the picture anyway unless they needed something from me.

My bet was that my parents would hate the thought that I was pregnant. My priority would be my baby, so if they got in a jam again, I wouldn't be available to bail them out. More than that, I knew deep in my heart that I would hate the idea of having a grandchild as much as they resented having to raise me.

Eventually, there was a knock on the door. I pulled my feet up under me and hugged my legs so that I was a tight ball of scared and angry pregnant woman plopped into the corner of Clea's comfy couch. I'd always liked the thing and wished I could afford something similar. One day, although with a baby to plan for, I might have to keep my too-stiff couch a while longer.

I swiped at the tears that streamed down my cheeks unhindered as his voice registered. "What's going on here?"

That was his voice, not Houston's. I could hear the slight difference now. Odd how just a few short weeks had diminished the sound so that they were indistinguishable until I heard his again.

I hadn't realized until that moment that I still had the pregnancy test clutched in my other hand. So, I threw it at the bastard. "That's what's going on," I insisted as the damn thing bounced off his chest and fell with a clickity-clack to the wooden floor.

I watched as Austin bent down to pick it up and when he got a good look, his eyes immediately rounded out like a cartoon character who realized an Acme bomb was about to blow up on them. He stood there and shook his head back and forth as if he could change the results of the stick he was looking at.

"No," he growled the one-word response. Yeah, I felt the same way, buddy. "You're saying this is mine?" And that insult stung like a motherfucker, considering I wasn't the one jumping from man to man the way he was hopping from Jordan to me and back again.

I shook my head, as if to deny he was the father, but Houston butted his nosy ass in to stop me in my tracks.

"I heard what you told Clea. He's the only person you've been with in six months, at least. Don't lie to him now just because he's being a dick."

"What the fuck?" Austin yelled the question at his brother like it was an accusation, and maybe it was. Houston didn't sound as though he was on his brother's side at all, and Austin had clearly picked up on that fact.

I ignored their bullshit and made my singular statement. "I'm keeping it."

I stood up and walked toward Austin. "This is MY baby. I don't want a thing from you, but your brother was right, you deserved to know about it. So, now you do, and you can go back to your far more important Jordan drama, just like you always do."

"I think this just proved that bullshit needs to come to an end. We'll go get married, and…"

"No, we will not be getting married."

"You're having my kid, we're getting married," Austin demanded. Funny that he and his brother had the same response to seeing a positive pregnancy test. Their parents had clearly instilled a whopping amount of responsibility into them. Too bad he didn't feel that same level of responsibility toward me personally when he started a relationship with me and then didn't have the balls to end it properly before moving on with someone else.

"I refuse to marry you." I thrust my jaw out stubbornly and

crossed my arms in front of my slightly sore chest. Huh, why hadn't I realized my boobs were all tingly and sensitive before?

"What? Why?" Austin asked, clearly shocked by my adamant refusal to marry the asshole.

"Look at you!" I shouted in his face. "You're still playing fuck buddies with the girl who is hell bent on ruining our relationship every single time we take a chance on one another. Not only that, but I even told you about how she came to gloat about everything, and you still couldn't see what she was up to."

"Who said she's even my fuck buddy?"

"We saw you at the movies with your tongue down her throat!" I screamed at him.

"And that automatically translates to me fucking her?" He asked as venom dripped from his words. "And when did she come gloat to you about anything?" He already knew she'd come to tell me that they were having sex again during our little tête-à-tête six years ago.

"It doesn't matter. You chose her then. You chose her this last time, too. I am very clearly not your choice, and never have been, so go live the life you promised her when you were children. I'll live mine, and you don't have to be bothered with us."

"Jesus," Houston murmured from where he stood holding my best friend to his chest as if she had tried to break free and do harm to his brother. "I told you that hole you were digging with Jordan was going to bury you one day." He explained to his clueless brother. He hadn't been the only person to warn Austin about that. I'd done so as well, but since I had a vested interest in a certain outcome my words had fallen on deaf ears.

Houston and Clea took off for her bedroom before anything else could be said. The distraction gave me the ability to take a few paces away from Austin before I turned to look at him again. It fucking hurt. My insides ached with the need to touch him, to have him hold me and tell me that everything would be okay, but I could see the conflict in his eyes.

"I want to be a part of my child's life."

"I don't want Jordan to be a part of it," I told him point blank, even though I knew it was an impossibility and I hated myself for even voicing those words.

"Becs," he started to argue and that did it. Fuck him. Fuck his fuck buddy. Fuck his family. I didn't need anyone. I was so done with his back and forth. The bastard had just asked me to marry him and now, minutes later when I demand that Jordan not be in the picture, he throws a placating tone my way, ready to defend that whore in his life again.

"No. We're done here. It's obvious that she has been, and always will remain, your number one priority. Have fun with that. When the baby's here, we can do a paternity test and all the legal bullshit that's needed. I won't be able to stop you from having my child around her and that fucking kills me. It guts me, Austin, because she already took you from me – twice! Now, she'll get to play house with you and our child, too. It's not fucking fair. I hate you so damn much right now that it's making me sick to even look at your goddamn face!"

He must have been stunned by my sobbing, anger-laden outburst, because I was able to slip past him and out the door. I was in my car and backing out of Clea's driveway before he even popped his head out. He stood there and watched me drive away.

CHAPTER FIFTEEN

IT WAS FUNNY HOW THINGS CHANGED IN THE BLINK OF AN EYE. Austin somehow learned to use the texting feature on his phone to locate my contact information.

> Dickhead Baby Daddy: When are you going for a doc appointment to confirm? I'd like to be there.

I scoffed at that. He'd seen the pregnancy test. Like hell he would accompany me to a lady doctor visit. I knew what they would do on my first visit, besides make me pee in a cup and take my blood. The whole process of pregnancy scared the bejesus out of me, so I'd looked up what to expect at my visit.

They were going to shove a wand up my coochie and peek at the baby I had onboard. Austin didn't get the privilege of ever seeing my lady bits again, let alone watching as a doctor shoved what amounted to a specialized dildo inside me. I took a note out of his book and ignored his text. Then, I sent one to my bestie.

> Becs: Are we still on for tomorrow?

> Clea: I'm so excited!!!!!!

Becs: Whoa there! You might hurt someone with all those exclamation points.

Clea: Ha! Seriously, aren't you excited? You might get to see your baby tomorrow.

Becs: I'm sure it will look like an indecipherable blob, and we'll walk away underwhelmed.

It was true, I'd looked it up and couldn't tell anything from the pictures I'd seen of early sonograms. There was a giant black and white space with more black and white shit mixed throughout. People had doctored their images to circle the blob that was supposed to be the fetus, but I wasn't so sure they knew what they were talking about.

Clea: I bet you lunch tomorrow that you cry like a baby.

Becs: You're on and you owe me dinner too if you cry like a baby, too.

The odds of her crying over a 'cute little black and white blob' were far greater.

Clea: I'll buy you dinner, since you'll be buying lunch because I already know I'll get weepy.

I laughed at her response because most of it was true. I didn't think I'd cry though, since I was going in knowing exactly what to expect.

Clea: Houston asked if Austin got a hold of you.

Becs: Fuck Austin.

Clea: Seriously, I agree, but he is the father. Are you sure he shouldn't be going to this appointment, instead?

Becs: I'd appreciate it if neither of you told him about the appointment. It's not his business. When the baby gets here, then it becomes his business.

Clea: Becs, I'm not so sure...

Becs: I am. Please, drop it. I have first graders up next, and I don't want to accidentally paste their lips shut because I'm angry with you.

Clea: I do understand. Love you. Don't paste the first graders together. Save that for the fifth graders.

Becs: Those little shits are too fast for me. I have to come up with something else for them.

Clea: It's scary that you're going to be a parent.

Becs: Nah. I'm all talk. I love my kids. Well, except that one who took a crap, put it on my desk, and called it butt art.

Clea: I do not envy your job. At all. That's...

She never did say what that was. I assumed she had a case of the dry heaves that kept her from finishing the text and I had to put my phone away since the bell rang.

"Okay, first graders, let's make the best paintings ever for your parents!" I called out enthusiastically to them. For the first time ever, I imagined my child being one of the bright and smiling faces that looked back at me with eager anticipation. I couldn't wait to get my first painting. Then, I wondered if it would go to me or Austin, since there would be two different households for my child. Shit. That was depressing and tears pooled in my eyes.

"Are you okay, Ms. Robinson?" Kaley asked me.

"I'm fine. Something in my eye hurts."

"Probably an eyelash," she offered wisely.

"Nah, it might be one of those crunchy eye buggers," Jake Weller put in.

"Ew, why do you have buggers in your eyeball?" Shayla asked.

"That's a good question for you all to ask during your science class," I informed them. Their teacher hated me, so a little payback for her attitude helped to brighten my day.

⁂

I WAS WEIGHED, blood pressure and temperature taken, peed in a cup, and my blood was drawn, too. I had officially been probed in just about every way you can be for a regular checkup. Then, I was told to put on the stupid paper gown and cover my legs with the even dumber paper blanket. Oh, and it was freezing cold in the office. Even Clea left her jacket on while we waited, and I sat there shivering.

"This is ridiculous, can you hand me my sweatshirt? Luckily, it was one that zipped in front, so I was able to toss it on, on top of my paper gown.

When the doctor came in, she apologized immediately. "I'm so sorry. One of our older nurses had a hot flash, messed with the thermostat, and here we are in the arctic, dealing with extreme temperatures until the heating and air people can come figure out why it's stuck on polar temperature settings. I realize it's the beginning of April, but it hasn't warmed up that much yet," she prattled on.

It had taken a little over a week before they had an opening to schedule me in for an appointment, so March had rolled right into the next month, and I was even more pregnant than before. The exhaustion and slight nausea were proof enough that the test hadn't been wrong, along with my still missing period.

"When was the first day of your last period?"

"The end of January," I answered honestly as Clea stared at me as if I'd lost my mind. "I had a lot on my mind and didn't realize," I explained to my best friend. Considering she had complained about her period being off, I could understand why she was judging me for not realizing the same had been true for me.

"Okay, well it says you took a positive at home pregnancy test."

"Three of them." I'd taken two more after a quick stop at the pharmacy on my way home from Clea's house after taking the first one there.

"Well, our tests concur. Going by your cycle, I'd say you most likely conceived sometime between February tenth and the fifteenth, which makes your due date around November sixth, give or take a few days."

"He took you home from the party," Clea muttered, clearly working out that Austin and I had been together more than once. I nodded my head and stared straight ahead as the doctor got her little machine ready.

"Okay, Rebecca-"

"Becs," I corrected. Only my mother ever called me Rebecca, and I hated the way she said it with such disdain, so I refused to allow anyone else to call me that.

Dr. Danvers smiled placatingly. "Becs, if you could slide down to the bottom of the chair and then put your feet in the stirrups, I think we can take a look at the baby to confirm your due date."

"Perfect," I said as I moved into the awkward position of flashing my most private parts at the doctor. I wondered what it was like for them dealing with pregnant vaginas. Clearly, at some point, I wouldn't be able to bend and see to landscape the lady garden. So, did all women start their pregnancies with a well-groomed downstairs and then over time, the visits became hairier? It wasn't exactly a question I was willing to ask the doctor, but I'd talk to Clea about it when we were done here. Maybe she had some insight. Waxing might be an option.

"Why do you need a condom?" Clea asked.

The doctor smirked at her. "It helps to keep the equipment sterilized," she answered.

"Safe toy sex," I joked at the same time. Clea rolled her eyes at me. "What? I'm nervous and about to be wanded here. Just laugh at my inappropriate joke so we can move on already," I demanded. Both women chuckled, making me feel better immediately.

"I think having you as a patient is going to be a lot of fun," the doctor surmised as she prepped me. "Sorry, it's going to be a bit cold when I insert, thanks to the thermostat issues."

"No problem." I managed to be accommodating, polite, and understanding of the circumstances just before she shoved a damn popsicle inside my vagina. I felt myself shriveling up from the cold as she moved the thing around down there and honestly, if the daggers I glared at her could have done harm, she would have been sliced and diced in under two seconds.

"I know, it's uncomfortable, but should be warmed up in just a minute." Then, Dr. Danvers flipped some switch on the monitor to her left and a whooshing sound filled the room. "You hear that slower beat?" She asked, to which I nodded. "That's *your* heart." She moved the wand a bit, "And that sound, like galloping horses?"

"Yeah?"

"That's *your baby's* heartbeat," she informed me as she pointed to the screen. "You can see it there."

And I did. There wasn't just a blob like in those pictures I saw online. I mean, it still looked like a blob, but it was a blob with a beating heart that I could see. Tears immediately built and then fell down my cheeks.

"I can see its heart beating."

"Oh my Gosh!" Clea moved closer and hugged my side. "I can see it, too. That's so beautiful," she sputtered through her own tears. "You owe me lunch, by the way," she sniffled as she said it, but we both ended up chuckling as she swiped some of my tears away for me.

"This is really happening," I managed to say. Up until that moment, it was more of a theory. Something that might happen, but there really wasn't anything tangible to see yet, unless you counted my slightly larger breasts.

"I can't believe it," I whispered again, reverently that time.

"It looks like we were right on track with the due date, so we'll keep it around November sixth."

"That's not too far from your birthday. If you went early, you might have the baby on the same day," Clea informed me happily, as if stretching my lady bits to painfully intolerable levels was the best present I could hope for. Thinking back on my past birthdays, she might not be wrong.

"Don't hold your breath for that to happen," the doctor interjected. "Most first-time moms go later, rather than early."

"That is not the kind of good news I want to hear, Doc."

She chuckled. "Well, we'll focus on keeping the two of you healthy until your due date approaches, and when he or she is ready to make an entrance into this world, they'll let us know. How's that sound?"

"Like I'm going to have a baby and the first act of being born is that my child has control issues?" I teased. Sort of.

Dr. Danvers laughed again. "I really am going to enjoy having you as a patient. Now, I'll have a prescription for prenatal vitamins waiting on you when you check out, and you'll need to schedule an appointment for four weeks from now."

"Four weeks?" I asked while attempting to sift through all the information I'd read over the past week about doctor visits.

"Yes, unless there is a problem, they'll remain four weeks apart until you're well within the third trimester, then we'll go two weeks, and be down to weekly just before your due date arrives."

"Okay, thank you so much."

"Oh, and I printed these pictures out for you," she offered me a stack of thin, glossy paper that had black and white images on them along with the printed information that included my name, due date, and a bunch of jargon the machine spit out that I didn't understand how to interpret. The big picture on each one was the blob, and thanks to seeing it live, I now knew exactly where my baby's beating heart was situated.

"Thank you," I whispered as the doctor left the room.

"We should probably get you dressed before you get hypothermia," Clea suggested. I handed my photos over to her for safe keeping while I hopped behind the privacy screen and did just that.

After we got back to my apartment, Clea had to run back to work, but wanted to take lunch to Houston on her way. I told her lunch wasn't really something my stomach could handle, but that I would buy her dinner sometime later in the week instead. She understood. I stopped her just before she left and handed over one of the ultrasound images.

"Can you make sure Houston gives that to him?"

"You know I will." She offered a quick smile as she tucked the image into her purse and turned to leave.

Worry had set in on the ride home about what the hell I would do if I was home alone and went into labor. Was I supposed to drive myself to the hospital? In all the movies I'd ever seen, someone else is always there to drive the pregnant woman and grab her bag for her. What about the women who didn't have a partner or other family members to do those things?

So, I sat there alone staring at the ultrasound photos. I was amazed by them but petrified at the same time. My imagination went wild with all sorts of crazy scenarios. What if I was teaching class and went into labor and one of the bugger-picking little kindergarteners had to deliver my baby because no one came when I called out for help? Yes, I realized they were completely ridiculous, wild thoughts. That didn't keep me from worrying over things that were to come in my very near future.

A FEW DAYS after my ultrasound, someone knocked on my door as I sat there on my couch, startled, and wondering who in the hell it could be. Clea was working late, so I knew it wasn't her and therein ended the list of people who would randomly show up at my apartment.

"I know that you're home," a deep voice called through the door. My hand reached out, almost involuntarily, for the handle to let him in, and then stopped in mid-air. I couldn't deal with seeing Austin when I was still trying to come to grips with how to be a single mother, or a single pregnant woman even. Throwing him in the mix in the midst of that was like adding insult to injury.

"Becs," he called out to me. "I need you to hear me out on some things. I never meant to hurt you. Actually, that's a lie. I purposely set out to hurt you by not making contact and explaining, but only so the truth wouldn't do a worse job."

Well fuck you, too buddy! I didn't say it out loud, but I wanted to.

"That night, probably after you left, Jordan told me why she was really there. Pregnant, Becs. She told me she was pregnant, and I knew in that moment that no matter what, I'd lost you.

There was no coming back from that. Jordan would throw down an ultimatum, and she did. She threatened to leave if I stayed with you. As in, take the baby and haul ass."

He paused, as if waiting to let that sink in.

"I don't even know if you're listening, but you need to know all this and you won't answer my texts or calls."

Now, you know how that feels, asshole.

Again, I didn't bother to speak the thought aloud, but he must have imagined that was what I'd say.

"I guess it's deserved, since that's what I put you through. I'm so fucking sorry, Becs. The choice was between you and a child I thought I was having. My parents always drilled in our heads that children come first, no matter what. When she told me she was pregnant, I felt my whole world fall apart because there was no way you'd stay with me through having to coparent with Jordan. Plus, there was no way Jordan would allow that to happen."

I'd wanted to give him basically the same ultimatum. Except, I hadn't. I'd played with the idea, even voiced it briefly, and then lost my shit as I explained just how much his whore of a girl-friend would be taking from me. If he was in our child's life, then she would be too. That was before I knew about her being preg-nant. It was going to gut me, but it was something I'd have to deal with for my baby. My child would have a sibling around the same age. If he hadn't been lying to me about the last time they slept together, then she had to be at least a month or two further along than I was.

"I never asked her to marry me," he admitted.

What the fuck?

"I swear to you, and you can ask my family or anyone else you want, I didn't intend to marry her just because she was pregnant. Jordan asked me to at least try to make things work with her, so our child could grow up with an intact family the way both of us had. That's what you saw at the movies that night. That was the

177

first time I'd been out of the house, and she basically had to threaten me to make it happen."

I so did not believe that. I'd seen them with my own two eyes, and while I hadn't seen who initiated that first kiss, I knew for sure who went in for the second one. It hadn't been Jordan forcing Austin to put his lips on hers.

"The crazy thing is that none of it fucking mattered. She lied."

Imagine that. The lying liar lied.

I rolled my eyes at him through the door, even though he couldn't see me, because he'd been warned time and again that she was lying and manipulating him to keep him around until he finally relented and married her.

"She lied about being pregnant to keep me from kicking her out of my house that night, and to force my hand where you were concerned." Oh shit! The way his voice broke tugged at my heart-strings, but I couldn't afford to offer him my empathy.

"I guess she did it because she knew it was the only way I'd throw you out of my life. The ridiculous thing is, Houston had her investigated because he remembered hearing something Jordan's mom said years ago. That's how we found out that she can't even get pregnant because she had a hysterectomy years ago. I didn't know. She never told me that it was that bad before and then..."

There was a pause in what he was saying, and I could imagine the level of frustration that was building for him. I tried not to care because he had been a cold-hearted coward where I was concerned. He might not have lied to me, but he ignored me and held back the truth that might have given me closure and at least the modicum of dignity that he'd left me for a child, not for her. Still, what did the woman plan on doing when she was supposed to start showing?

"I can't even wrap my head around what kind of damage she did to our friendship, to my family's trust in her, to my relation-ship with you." The last bit was almost inaudible. "I'm so fucking sorry, Becs. I know you kept telling me not to trust her, but I never thought anyone would lie about a pregnancy, especially her. I thought she was telling the truth."

There was another pause and the sounds of rustling on the other side of the door. "Clea took one of your ultrasound pictures to Houston to give to me. She thought I'd need proof that you were really pregnant. I guess she was supposed to deliver the picture to me anyway, but once they found out about Jordan's medical shit, she made sure to point out that your due date was on the top. That's our baby, Becs. I don't want to do this separately."

I sat there, with my back to the door, and cried for the loss of my relationship with him again. Some of the tears were for the shit his supposed best friend had put him through. That was the worst thing I think anyone could have done, aside from trying to kill him, and honestly, an attempt on his life would have probably been more forgivable than the lies she told. I cried for my baby, too because they were an unwitting pawn in her game. My child would never get to grow up in a two-parent household and be embarrassed to watch their mom and dad be so in love with one another. That was all because Jordan had taken the option away with her deplorable lies.

I don't know how long I stayed there, on the floor with my back to the front door. Eventually, I realized that Austin stopped talking and probably walked away at some point. That was for the best because there was a lot to process in what he'd just confessed to me through my front door.

THE FOLLOWING DAY WAS MISERABLE. Clea had gone with Houston to meet his family for the first time, and it sent me into a tailspin. I was happy for my best friend, since she'd obviously snagged herself the best brother of the bunch. Still, there had been a few days in February where I'd thought about how cool it would be for Clea and me to be introduced to the Mercer family at the same time, so it might take the pressure off both of us. Their large, happy family seemed intimidating to both of us who had grown up in less-than-ideal circumstances.

The sky started to grow dark when I finally peeled myself off the couch and away from my pity party for one. I managed to make some soup, and even nibble a few crackers, before I made my way back to the couch. Just as I was about to sit, there was a knock on my door. Clea was with the Mercer family last I checked, and she had sent a message that Austin was there, too. So, I wondered who in the hell could be knocking today. Truthfully, surprise visits were never a good thing.

"It's me, Becs. Open up!" Clea called out.

I rushed to the door and threw it open, wondering if something had gone wrong with the family introductions. Instead of seeing my friend in tears, she stood there with an older woman who had a hesitant smile plastered on her lips.

"Um, hi," I offered by way of greeting as I stepped back and out of the way so they could come in.

"Becs, this is Mrs. Mercer, Houston and Austin's mother."

"Oh." What else could I say? The grandmother of my baby showed up at my door unannounced with my best friend. The little freakout going on inside my body felt a lot bigger than it was.

"I understand this is a surprise visit. If you are at all uncomfortable with me being here, I can come back another time, or you can come to my home whenever you wish." The woman's hand whipped up to her chest and held there as if her heart were troubling her. "I'm sorry. I'm probably messing this up right from the start. What I mean to say is that whatever will make you comfortable, I don't want to pressure you."

"You're here now," I explained as I waved my hand forward,

inviting her inside. "Please, come in. Sorry for the mess, I haven't been feeling very well."

Clea moved into the apartment, but Mrs. Mercer stopped in front of me and wrapped me up in the warmest hug I'd ever felt. I suddenly knew where Houston got it from, considering the way he'd held me the day I found out I was pregnant.

"Don't you worry about a thing, sweetheart. When I first found out I was pregnant with Victoria, she's my oldest, I let myself go completely. All those crazy worries ran through my head, and things were so new with my husband that I was constantly waiting for him to hit the road. It was a mess of a time and then there was the exhaustion and well, I'm sure you know all about that. My point, is that I don't think my house was ever clean for the next decade." She chuckled and Clea added her own laughter to the mix as I smiled at the woman. It was nice of her to try to make me feel better about my cluttered mess of an apartment.

"I hope you don't mind that I asked Clea to bring me by. Things with Austin are contentious, I understand. I'm his mother, and disappointed as can be in both my son and Jordan for the absolute hell they have each put you through. My concern isn't for them right now. It's for you and what our family can do to make things right."

Considering she'd included Jordan and Austin's names together; I wondered if he left my front door yesterday and went crawling right back into the lying tramp's arms? Mrs. Mercer wasn't privy to my wandering mind, but she tipped her head to the side, as if in quiet contemplation anyway.

"Maybe 'making things right' is the wrong choice of words. What can I do to make things easier for you?"

"I appreciate the offer, Mrs. Mercer. I don't think there's anything to be done right now, though."

She nodded her head sagely as I walked to my couch and peeled my throw blanket off and folded it before moving it into a basket beside my couch to get it out of the way. There was nothing to be done about the half-eaten bowl of soup or the sleeve of crackers sitting on my coffee table with an empty bottle of water, a half-full glass of apple juice, and my cell phone. The wadded up, snotty tissues told a story all their own, as did the overflowing bathroom trashcan full of more that sat by the end of my coffee table.

"I'm sure I could get Dallas to record me taking a switch to Austin's backside," the woman assured me before offering up a wink. It at least drew a smile from me.

"I feel like I'm at a disadvantage here because I never knew Austin was dating anyone..." her thought seemed to drop away, but I figured she meant outside of Jordan.

"What would you like to know?" I asked her. My hands shook as I sat down on the chair and allowed Clea and Mrs. Mercer to take the couch together. There was no point in cleaning up my mess since they'd both already seen it.

"Well, how about we start with the basics."

That was open to interpretation, so I started with the most basic of basics. My name. "My name is Rebecca Irene Robinson, though I prefer for people to call me Becs."

"Okay, Becs and what do you do for a living?"

"I teach art classes over at Whitmore Elementary. I was also teaching history to some of the fifth graders, but starting next year, I won't be doing that anymore."

"What? Why not?" Clea asked, worried that I'd been demoted.

"The school board is splitting my time between Whitmore and Jarvis next year." Jarvis was the middle school that housed sixth through eighth grade students. "I'll be at the middle school on Tuesdays and Thursdays and the elementary the other three days of the week."

"That's dumb. Why would they do that?"

"Funding cuts. Neither school had enough funding for a full-time art teacher, so they got together and decided to split it. I lucked out because Tommy Owens, who was teaching at the middle school this year, put in his resignation. He plans to move to be with his fiancé who got a job out of state. Otherwise, we would have been in competition for the same split position."

"Becs!" Clea sighed. "Why didn't you tell me your job was on the line?"

I shrugged. "Seems like all I've had lately is bad news. I thought maybe if I kept it to myself, everything would turn out okay, and it did."

"Oh, Becs."

Mrs. Mercer sat there taking everything in with sadness dripping from her eyes. I could feel the energy she put out, and while it wasn't hostile toward me, I don't think she knew what to do with my sorry-luck lot in life.

"What about your parents? How are they with the recent news?"

"Well, I don't talk to them that much, so they didn't know about my job situation either," I informed her, being purposely obtuse.

She chuckled. "You remind me a little of Dallas."

"Hush your mouth. I do not remind you of Cupid Satan," I told her before remembering that she was the idiot's mother.

Clea couldn't hold back her laughter and Mrs. Mercer joined in. "You know, I was just informed about my son's diaper wearing tendencies this very night. I really thought I'd raised my children better, but turns out, you can do your best and they'll still find ways to embarrass or disappoint. As a mom, you must learn to roll with it. There will be moments of great celebration with them too that make up for the times where you just want to bury them in the backyard."

She patted Clea's thigh. "Despite finding out my youngest son attends parties in diapers, I did learn that I'm getting a new daughter-in-law soon." Then she turned her eyes back to meet mine. "And my first grand baby." The warmth and love in that statement squeezed at my heart. "So, you see, all in one night I got to be disappointed in my son while also finding out there is much to celebrate. That's what being a mother is all about."

I nodded my head and we all sat in awkward silence for a moment, probably picturing Dallas in his diaper, because let's face it that was the craziest part of what she'd found out. Plus, for my part, I didn't want to think about what my pregnancy might mean where this woman was concerned. She seemed happy about it, but I didn't know her, and she was a fan of the Jordan and Austin coupling, so I would have to tread lightly there.

"I don't care if you're with my son, but you need to know that we will consider you family too, Becs. If you need anything, we will be there. I'm speaking for my whole family."

"I appreciate that, but also don't want to make things awkward."

"There is nothing awkward about it. You are the mother of my future grandchild. If you need something, all you have to do is ask. There is no need for you to be in this alone." She glanced back over to Clea. "Though, I know you have a pretty good best friend at your back, I want you to know that our family is there as well. Even if Austin isn't to be trusted by your heart any longer, I hope you'll give the rest of our clan the benefit of the doubt and allow us to be there for you."

"Well, Houston has already had my back, and I worried that it would cause a rift between your sons, so I try to keep to myself."

"Don't you worry about a thing. Whether you believe it or not, I think it would cause a bigger rift if Austin thought his brother was taking his side instead of yours."

We all sat there stewing in that thought for a few more minutes before Mrs. Mercer clapped her hands together excitedly. "Now, I hear that you had pictures of the little one done recently, and I would love it if you could share them with me."

The way she said it made me laugh, as if we'd gone to a

photography studio instead of having a wand shoved in unmentionable places to get images of the fetus I was carrying.

"The pictures they give are nothing like seeing it in person," I stupidly explained to the mother of five as I got up to go get the sonogram pictures. I brought them back and handed them to her. "We saw the heart beating and everything," I leaned in and pointed to the spot. "That's it right there," I announced proudly.

"Oh, would you look at that," the woman sniffed, growing weepy as she looked at my blob with so much love already in her eyes. Dammit, that meant moving away on the sly wouldn't be an option. My little blob would need this woman in his or her life. I had a feeling that I might, too. Since my own mother would never be a font of parenting knowledge to go to in a crisis.

"November sixth," she said wistfully when she noticed my due date. "This Christmas will be an extra special event."

That announcement sent me stumbling all the way back to plop down in my chair completely stunned. How many Christmases would I lose my child to their other family? What about birthdays? Oh, man. I really hadn't imagined the shared custody reality to its fullest yet.

"Becs?" Clea called out to me. "Are you okay?"

"No," I answered truthfully.

"What did I say?" Mrs. Mercer sounded concerned that she'd upset me.

"I think I know," Clea informed her. "You talked about Christmas, and it just hit Becs that she'll have to share the baby with Austin and you guys and that she might not be the one to have them on the holidays."

"Oh dear," Mrs. Mercer huffed. "Don't you go worrying over silly things like that. You will always be invited to our home for the holidays if you choose to attend. If you don't, we will respect your wishes and simply celebrate our holiday on another day. I would never deny you seeing the excitement of a child on Christmas morning."

"It won't matter because your son has a right to experience that, too." I reminded her.

"You're right, of course," she murmured sadly.

"I guess that's something I'll come to terms with eventually," I whispered.

"Are you sure there's no hope of a reconciliation between you and Austin?"

I shook my head. "He didn't just hurt me and leave me in the dark once. This was the second time he's done it. I don't even care that he thought he had a good reason. He could have told me."

"From what I gather, Jordan forbade him from telling you about the pregnancy," she mentioned.

I rolled my eyes. "Of course, she did because she's an evil manipulative witch who knew exactly which buttons to push to make sure I never came back into the picture." I took a breath and then apologized. "I'm sorry. I know she was your best friend's daughter, and I can't imagine someone saying something like that to me about Clea's future daughter. I'd probably want to smack them."

"Under normal circumstances, maybe. Jordan is a grown woman though, and she made some poor choices that led you to feel the way you do. I don't fault you for it. In fact, I want to take her over my knee just the way I'm sure her parents would if they were still alive." Mrs. Mercer shook her head. "I still can't believe she had the audacity to lie to my boy about something so precious, and to ruin his happiness for her own selfish reasons. Her mother did not raise her that way."

"From what Austin has said, I think she did."

"Excuse me?" Mrs. Mercer sputtered, not with attitude but in shock over me calling out her dead best friend's parenting.

"The two of you wanted Austin and Jordan to get married one day," I stated.

"Well, it was a dream that two best friends had."

"I understand that, but whereas you never pressured Austin to do that, I think Jordan's mother did, from what he told me."

Mrs. Mercer sighed. "Unfortunately, I think he's right. Lydia was always very adamant about it happening one day. She even had a wedding book and started planning out their ceremony when they were still in middle school."

"That's not creepy or anything," Clea muttered.

"I assure you, she had only the best intentions, even if she did go a bit overboard."

"Well, if she allowed you to see that much of her going over-board, imagine what Jordan went through," Clea explained.

"Yes, well, I suppose I see your point. Our dreams for them to be together one day should have never even reached their ears. That's something I do regret. It made for a lot of false expectations. While I thought it would be neat, when they were younger, it was clear as they grew older that my son would never see her that way."

"But he did."

"No, he has never been in love with Jordan."

"He still had sex with her, for years," I tossed back, no matter how inappropriate it was to discuss her son's sex life with her.

"That's where he mucked everything up, and I know she pressured him to take that step, too. I overheard those early conversations, and wanted to step in, but that wasn't my place since they were both adults by then. So, I let the chips fall where they may and simply encouraged him to find his happiness and to be careful in the meantime. Sometimes, that's all a mother can do, otherwise we inadvertently end up pushing our children into something they don't want, or to rebel against the very thing we want for them." She shrugged her shoulders. "If only parenting came with a tried-and-true handbook."

Mrs. Mercer stood. "I assure you that nothing Jordan says or does will ever affect how my family treats you from this point forward. I can't speak for what Austin does, but the rest of us would like to welcome you with open arms into the family, and I meant what I said, please don't hesitate to ask for anything you need." She placed a folded piece of paper down on the coffee table next to the nearly depleted box of tissues. "Both mine and my husband's numbers are on that paper along with my youngest daughter, Katy."

She scrunched her nose up as she thought of something and then added, "I left Victoria off because she's going through her own crisis, even though she won't talk to any of us about it, and I don't think she'll be a big support right now."

"Plus, she's good friends with Jordan," I added.

Mrs. Mercer nodded sagely and smiled at me. "Katy and Dallas have always detested Jordan if that makes you feel any better. They saw through her many attempts to trick Austin into settling on her, and they never liked it. I'm not telling you that to ruin a confidence with either of my children or Jordan, but I thought you needed to know that you wouldn't find our home unwelcoming to you. That seemed to be one of Clea's worries for you before our dinner tonight."

"Thank you, I appreciate you being open with me."

"Please, use those numbers and keep us updated."

Clea stood too. "I have to go, since we rode together."

I nodded and saw them both out of my apartment. It had been a lovely gesture for Austin's mother to come meet me and try to set the record straight about where their family stood. It also relieved some the tension I'd felt about them possibly ganging up on me and stealing my baby.

Thankfully, I read in one of the online articles I stumbled across that irrational fears were normal during pregnancy. Hopefully, that was all they'd ever amount to. Still, there was room for worry considering my experience thus far with Austin and his unwavering allegiance toward Jordan.

What if *she* wanted to steal my baby because she can't have one of her own? Maybe Austin would back that play. That didn't sound right, but then again, I'd never expected him to ghost me a second time after begging for a second chance. If only time could be turned back, and he could make an enlightened decision where she was concerned. Then, maybe I'd get my happily ever after with my child's father. I had a feeling I'd fall in love with his family too. I already loved Houston for having my back and treating my best friend as well as he did. Austin's mother was well on her way to becoming one of my favorite people too. If only her son could have kept the number one position and not messed everything up.

CHAPTER SIXTEEN

I READ THROUGH ALL THE TEXTS AGAIN TO TORTURE MYSELF BEFORE starting my day. It had become something of a ritual. As per usual, I talked back to each text, but never responded to the man who sent them.

> Dickhead Baby Daddy: I heard my mom went by to see you, and you let her in to talk. Thanks for that. She was glowing when she got back.

"I didn't do it for you." I stuck my tongue out at my phone just for a little more oomph and childish satisfaction. It seemed to work for the kids I taught.

> Dickhead Baby Daddy: I wish you would have let me in when I stopped by yesterday. I miss your face, Becs. I miss a whole lot more but would give just about anything to see your smile again.

"Guess you should have thought about that before you ghosted me. It's hard to see a ghost."

> Dickhead Baby Daddy: I saw Jordan today. I wanted to be up front with you about that in case it got back to you. We're not even speaking. She came in to get her final check from the bar. If it makes you feel any better, she looked like shit and wouldn't stop apologizing.

"Ha! Like her apologies would ever be directed at me. She was trying to get you back in her good graces again."

> Dickhead Baby Daddy: Dallas saw what I texted you and told me I was a dumbass. I didn't think you'd take that wrong. She was apologizing through me, to you. Said if she'd known you were pregnant, she would have never interfered.

"She's a lying ass liar. I don't believe a word of that, and still don't think the apologies were for me. She's still trying to play you because no doubt your sister has told her about how I still refuse to talk to you. Asshole!"

I'd met Victoria when I accidentally ran into Mrs. Mercer while out at the grocery store. It wasn't one I normally went to, but their deli had advertised the 'world's best potato soup' and I had to go try it out for myself. It wasn't the best. That honor still belonged to the cool place Austin had taken us on our first official date back in February. I'd nearly cried in the store when I remembered that date and that had been when I'd run into Mrs. Mercer and Victoria.

When her mother introduced us, Victoria sneered at me and walked away. I could have sworn she called me a home-wrecker under her breath as she went, but Mrs. Mercer's apologies drowned her daughter out. Clearly, someone was still miffed on behalf of Jordan, even though Jordan was the giant cuntbag in the whole scenario. Or maybe Austin was, since it felt like he played Jordan and me all along. What would Jordan have to complain about, anyway? She had him leaps and bounds longer than I ever had.

> Dickhead Baby Daddy: I woke up wondering how you were doing this morning. I wish you would let me know if there's anything you need or even want.

"Yes, you to leave me the hell alone." My stomach protested that thought, as it always did. What I wanted; I couldn't have though. That would be for time to turn back and Austin to make better, wiser choices. Since that was impossible, I decided to go with another impossibility. If he was no longer in my life, eventually, I'd get over him. It didn't escape my notice that this little game I played every morning wouldn't exist if he was no longer fully in my life, but then again, maybe I wouldn't need the game if that was the case.

> Dickhead Baby Daddy: Has your heart ever ached so badly that you thought maybe you were going to die? Every morning, when I wake up and realize all over again just how badly I messed up, that's what happens.

I never had a response to that one beyond my heart aching in the exact same way.

> Dickhead Baby Daddy: If what I read on online is true, you should have a doctor appointment coming up soon. I'd really like to be there with you. I know you hate me right now, but eventually we're going to have to be able to coparent, at a minimum. I think we should start practicing now. Please, let me be a part of the pregnancy, so I can get to know my son or daughter right along with you. I'm missing so much.

"You aren't missing anything beyond me being sick some-times, my boobs and butt growing, and my emotions being completely out of whack, Austin. If you hadn't been an idiot, you would have been here for all that." The tears always started up when I answered this one because I knew what he was asking was the right thing to do anyway. We did need to learn to work together and that couldn't happen when I was ignoring him.

I didn't have time to go through all the texts he'd sent over the last month, since I was going to be late for my doctor's appointment if I did. Those texts were the highlight reel. The ones to keep me angry and help me move on and try to work my way up to speaking to the man again. It might have sounded counter-productive, but I needed the anger as a shield for when the asshole was around me. Not this appointment, but the one after, would probably involve another ultrasound. That was when I'd invite him along because he did deserve the chance to see his child in person at least once during my pregnancy.

That first time helped me bond with the baby in a whole new way because it made everything real. May was around the corner in a few days. Time was flying by, though I couldn't put my finger on why when each day seemed to drag on from the moment I woke up until the time I finally got in bed. November would be here before we knew it and things needed to be better before the baby arrived.

I finished getting ready and grabbed my keys and purse before heading out and locking up behind myself. Clea wasn't able to join me this time, since she had a bigwig client in who wanted her help with a grand opening like she had done for the Tippler's Lounge. It was a big money client, so I couldn't blame her for dipping out. Still, my nerves kicked up to the ten-thou-sand-mark at having to sit in the ice chamber of doom to wait on the doctor alone. If they hadn't fixed that problem, I might have to look for a different doctor, which would suck.

When I got there, the stupid parking lot was blocked by a

giant delivery truck, so I had to go circle the block, twice, looking for street level parking. When one finally opened up, a block away, I silently cursed every truck driver there ever was for making me late to my appointment, and also making me have to do a mad dash there because I had to pee so bad my eyeballs were practically swimming.

"Becs!" I groaned at the sound of his voice. This was just not my day. "Becs, wait, please!"

"Can't. I'm late thanks to that stupid truck."

"What truck?" Austin asked as he glanced around.

"The one blocking the parking lot I couldn't access." I kept walking toward my destination, determined to make it there before I peed my pants. To hell with being on time for anything else, except the potty.

"Where are you headed?" He asked, so I pointed ahead and when his eyes followed my finger to the sign for the OB/GYN, he grinned. "Can I come with you?"

"No. I was planning on inviting you next time," I ground out through my clenched teeth.

"Sure, you were," he muttered. "Please, Becs! We're already here, just let me come in with you."

"Fine," I huffed as I snatched the door open. Honestly, I didn't have the energy to argue with him because the race to the toilet took precedence.

"Rebecca Robinson," I told the receptionist as I tried to check in.

"Have a seat," she lifted her chin to indicate the lobby seating area.

"Um, listen, I had to walk here because someone blocked off the parking lot and now, I have to pee like you wouldn't believe. If you need a sample from me, then this is the time, otherwise..."

The woman rolled her eyes at me and hit the buzzer to allow me in back. Austin moved to follow. "No. Sit down, I'm just going to pee in a damn cup, and then I'll be right back. You don't need to be there for that."

He huffed, but followed my directions, clearly thinking I was going to leave him high and dry in the lobby. That wasn't the case. He was already there, so we'd make the most of this visit and see how it went.

Once I was done, I headed back to the lobby and took a seat next to Austin who was reading a Parenting magazine.

"Did you find something interesting?"

"Yes," he leaned closer to whisper. "If I don't look completely engrossed in this magazine, people start asking me questions about why a good-looking man, such as myself, is sitting in the lobby of an obstetrician's office all alone. As if I'm here trolling for pregnant women to date."

I couldn't help it. The laughter bubbled out of me at the ridiculousness of what he was implying. That was up until a woman tapped me on the shoulder from two seats down. I turned to see her smiling at me.

"Are you his sister? Is that why he's here? I don't see any rings, so obviously he's not your husband."

"Maybe, we don't believe in wearing rings as a construct of trust," I explained to her. "Some people might need things like that, and even stupidly believe those symbols will work to keep husband hunters away from their men, but I can assure you, I know women who will go after anyone's man, even if they know there's an attachment." I felt Austin stiffen beside me, clearly thinking that I was talking about Jordan, when in reality, I was warning the weird lady away from my baby's daddy. I would not, at any point in the future, examine why I felt the need to do that.

"I see," the woman stated and leaned back into her own space as her cheeks flamed bright red. Austin finally realized what I'd done and patted my thigh.

"Thanks for being my human shield against unwanted overtures from women in the baby doc's office."

"This isn't the baby doc's office, Austin. That's called a pediatrician. This is a woman's reproductive health doctor."

"Does your doctor delivery babies regularly?"

"Yes."

"So, baby doc."

I rolled my eyes at him. "Whatever you want to call it, Aus."

His grin widened. "I always love when you shorten my name that way." The smile on my face immediately slipped into a frown as I lifted his hand off my thigh, where he'd left it.

"Becs," he pleaded.

"You're here to find out about the baby, not to touch me or get cozy in any way."

"Becs, I'm sorry, please don't shut me out again."

"What would you have said at the movie theater if I'd asked you the same? Oh, right, I don't need to ask because I sent you a text begging you not to do that to me, and you know what your response was?"

"Becs," he moaned.

"No, I didn't even get that much from you. All I got was your silence. Why in the hell should I give you anything more than you ever gave me?" This was the first whisper-level argument I ever had, and somehow it was far more poignant than if we were yelling at one another.

"I'm sorry."

"You know the great thing about apologies?"

"What is that?" He looked worried as he asked, and rightfully so.

"I don't have to accept them to make *you* feel better about what *you* did. And for the record, in case you missed it, I don't accept. You're here for the baby, not me. Let's keep things exactly that simple."

Austin sat quietly until I was called back and then he followed behind me as I was weighed.

"Looks like you've put on twelve pounds since your last visit.

You might want to slow down on the weight gain. The recommended gain for the whole pregnancy is about thirty pounds," the nurse condescendingly informed me.

That was only slightly embarrassing, considering Austin was there to hear it. Then again, it mostly went to my boobs and my butt, so what the hell did I have to be ashamed of? Nothing. That's what. If the nurse had been a little more discreet in weight shaming me, it wouldn't have been a problem.

"Last time I saw Becs, she was underweight. She looks healthy now, what's your problem?" Austin asked the woman, and it seemed like he was determined to take his bad mood out on her.

"I didn't mean any offense; she needs to know…"

"Yes, you did, otherwise you wouldn't have said it like that while staring at me."

"Is there a problem here?" My doctor stopped on her way out of one of the patient rooms to ask.

"Beyond your nursing staff weight shaming your patients, no."

Austin's blunt response caught her attention and Dr. Danvers glanced down at the weight that was written on my chart. "Oh, good. I hoped you put on a little weight before this appointment. This gentleman is right, you were a bit underweight before. That's something we usually discuss in the privacy of the exam room, though." She glared pointedly at the nurse. "I'll see you there in just a few minutes," she directed as she turned her attention back to me.

"I won't turn into an ice cube while we wait this time, will I?" I asked as she got ready to enter another patient's room.

"Oh, I forgot you were here for that last time. No, it will be a normal temperature, and no need to change into the gown this time either."

That was the first bit of good news I'd heard all day. Austin and I entered the examination room and quickly realized there was only one chair. I took the exam table as my seat and he quickly pulled the chair around so that he was sitting beside me.

"So, what are they doing at this visit, if you don't have to take your clothes off?" He finally asked.

"No clue. I was pleasantly surprised by that news."

"Is this one of those times where we'll get to see the baby?"

"No. That's why I was going to invite you to the next visit."

"You're not going to leave me out of that because I made you bring me to this one today, are you?" The panic in his voice was real and honestly, heartbreaking.

"I wouldn't do that," I whispered. "They might be able to tell if it is a girl or a boy next time."

"Really? That soon?"

"Yeah, that soon." I shrugged. "Seems weird to me because last time it just looked like a blob with a beating heart."

"You saw the heart beating last time?" I nodded my head and watched as his shoulders sagged and face fell into a sad little frown that I'd never seen him wear before.

"I missed it," he lamented to the floor. "She fucking lied to me, and I ended up missing out on seeing my real baby's heart beating for the first time."

Aw, man. I would not feel sorry for him. Nope. "She might have lied to you, Austin, but it was your decision to cut me out of your life the way you did that made you miss out. I would have understood if you'd told me why you were doing it. When I found out I was pregnant, I would have included you, if that's what you wanted, even knowing we couldn't be together."

"Then why didn't you anyway?"

"Because I can't trust you to be there for me now. You couldn't communicate with me and left me in the lurch with no explanation, even when I tried to reach out to you. What would you have done if I hadn't run out of your house that night? Would you have left it to Jordan to come kick me out of your bed?"

"No, I wouldn't have done that. I came to tell you that night, but you'd already gone."

"Yeah, I did and once again, you didn't bother to check that I made it home safely, considering you drove me to your house, and it was four in the freaking morning when I left."

He closed his eyes and shook his head. "I hadn't even thought of that. Please, understand, I'd just been told that I was having a baby with the wrong fucking woman, and new that meant I had to let you go. Worse, I thought it meant I had to hurt you in the only way I knew would make an impact, so you'd move on and forget all about me."

"How chivalrous of you," I snapped as I rolled my eyes and looked away from him. The sad part was, I believed what he was telling me. That didn't mean I had to like any of it or forgive him for doing things the way he did. It hurt me, tore us apart, and will have a needlessly huge impact on our child's life as a result. The last part was why I couldn't forgive him.

We both sat quietly after that. Austin smartly realized that there was only so much I was willing to hear about where he'd gone wrong as we sat waiting to get an update on the life growing inside me.

"Ms. Robinson, I'd like to apologize for my nurse's lack of couth earlier."

I waved her off. "It's not that big of a deal, Dr. Danvers."

"Well, rest assured that it won't happen again. Maybe, next time you show up there won't be any catastrophes in the office."

"That would be disappointing. You've built me up with Snowageddon and now Nursegate. I'm just waiting to see how you top those two."

Dr. Danvers laughed and then narrowed her eyes conspiratorially. "Hush your mouth before I end up telling you there are four babies in there," she teased as she pointed to my stomach.

"That is not even funny," I argued.

She continued to chuckle as if she really thought it was. "That shuts the patients up every time when they get sassy with me."

"Touché, madam."

"So, tell me what's been happening in pregnancy land," she insisted. "Morning sickness?"

"Yes, but it's tolerable. If I avoid certain smells, I'm fine and can keep the queasiness at bay. Thankfully, the school took me seriously and assigned a permanent helper for bathroom duty because I can't get near those things. Whatever cleaner they use trips my gag reflex."

"As long as you feel it's under control, we won't worry about it. You did put on a good amount of weight, and I mean that. I am assuming you got your appetite back?"

"Yes, at first I had to force myself to eat so I wouldn't get sick, but after seeing the baby last time, it seemed important to try harder to get food in my system, for them."

"For yourself, too." She reminded me. "Anything else going on that you think I should know about?"

"Not that I can think of right now."

"How are you doing with the prenatal vitamins? They're not causing any upset stomach, are they?"

"No. I usually take them at night before I go to bed. One of the teachers at school told me it was better for her to do it then, since she would fall asleep and wouldn't notice the slightly upset stomach. I drink a glass of milk with them, too."

"Sounds good. I was going to suggest taking them at night if they bothered you at all during the day. Your teacher friend was one step ahead of me."

"I want to address one more thing before we get down to it. You don't have to come up with the answers now, but it's something to think about. You had your friend with you last time, and I see a different friend has joined you this time. It's important to have a support system you can count on during pregnancy, especially the further along you get. If you want to start birthing classes, there are several different types offered through the hospital and a few private places in the area, too. They'll help you discover your birthing plan and teach you and your birthing coach how to handle the important things as they come."

"I'll see what I can work out between mine and Clea's schedule." I heard Austin sigh, but thankfully he didn't say anything in front of the doctor because then, I'd have to point out that she did say I needed people around who I could trust to be there. He did not factor on that list, whether he was the father or not.

"Okay then. Can I get you to unbutton your pants and roll them down to your panty line and lift your shirt up to just where the lower portion of your bra sits on your ribs?"

"Sure," I did as I was told, all the while knowing Austin watched my every move. Dr. Danvers tipped the back the exam table down flat and added a barely-there pillow for my comfort before instructing me to lie down.

She pulled out a measuring tape and started poking around at my lower abdomen, then when she was satisfied with whatever she felt there, one end of the tape was held there while she repeated the process a little higher up. Then she wrote down a measurement and smiled at me.

"You're measuring right on track for the November sixth due date. That's good. Let's take a listen today, too." She popped out a handheld machine that had a tiny little wand thing attached to it and squirted a little gel on my tummy then began rubbing the thing around while pushing rather aggressively.

"It's a good thing I already emptied my bladder, or you might not like me very much, Doc."

She laughed at me as the familiar whooshing sound came out of the machine. I knew my heartbeat when I heard it because it was the slower of the two.

"Is that the baby?" Austin asked.

"No, that sound is unique to Becs." She moved the wand lower and pushed again just before the strong galloping sound of my baby's heartbeat came through the speaker. "That one is the baby's heartbeat."

"It's so fast."

"It's normal at this stage of fetal development," she assured him.

"I saw wands like that at the baby store. Are the at home ones safe to use?"

"There's no reason you can't use a doppler at home, just be sure to pick up the transducer gel, otherwise it won't work for you."

Austin pulled his phone out and typed something in. "Do they sell that gel at the baby store, or is that a special-order thing?"

Dr. Danvers laughed. "I imagine they sell it there, otherwise they'd get far too many returns on those machines." She pulled the doppler machine away from my body and immediately my heart sank as the baby's heartbeat disappeared. It was amazing how calming that little sound could be.

"Everything sounds and looks good. I am pleased with your weight gain, though I don't expect you will continue to pack on quite as much between future visits, even if it starts to look like you put on more than you think you have." Again, she winked as if letting us in on a private joke that I still didn't get. I imagined she was saying when my belly popped, it would feel like I'd gained more than I had. Valid point, I supposed.

"Do you have any questions for me?"

"Yes," Austin stated immediately. "What kind of exercise should Becs be doing? She goes to the gym every morning with her best friend, and I'm worried it'll be too much."

"Becs is her own best advocate. If she feels too tired, or her muscles, especially in the abdominal or groin region, feel too strained, then she should slow down and rest up. If you're feeling fine with what you're doing, everything should be okay. We've had a female body builder in here who continued lifting until her eighth month. I don't recommend heavy lifting, but it's doable. Yoga is great, as long as you are maintaining balance in the poses. That won't be an issue now, but when you're bigger, the center of gravity you're used to is off and you will probably want a spotter just to be safe."

"Spotter, got it." Austin said, since he was apparently transcribing everything the doctor said into his phone. "What about sex?"

"What about it?" Dr. Danvers asked.

"Nothing about it," I interjected, only to be ignored.

"Is it safe for her to have intercourse throughout the pregnancy?"

"Of course. Unless there's bleeding, heavy spotting, or cramping she can continue regular sexual intercourse right up until it's time to deliver. Some women swear by sex that ends in an orgasm to trigger labor when they're close enough to their due date. As with the workouts and yoga, you will have to experiment with what feels comfortable for you." Dr. Danvers said to me, instead of Austin.

"Will massage help with the rapid growth?"

My doctor chuckled at his latest question. "Rapid growth?" She asked but didn't wait for him to elaborate. "Prenatal massage has been known to lower stress and help with the ligaments that pull tight in the groin area and lower back as the body prepares for childbirth."

"When do you think she'll need to start wearing maternity clothes?"

Dr. Danvers made eye contact with me that time and grinned widely. "That is a good question and one that Becs will answer for you as soon as her clothes stop fitting her. It is different for every woman and depends on how many pregnancies they've been through too. For most first timers, they start growing out of their clothing around the fourth or fifth month. Sometimes, that can happen sooner. It really just depends."

"Okay, I had more questions, but I can't remember them all right now."

"You can always write them down for next time."

"And you'll be doing another ultrasound next time?" He asked.

"Yes, we'll do another ultrasound next time where I can get measurements again, and with any luck, we'll be able to tell the baby's gender if you want to know. I will warn you though, my office does not play the gender reveal game. Those parties have become dangerous. It was one thing when people just wanted to color the cake and cut into it to find out if it was blue or pink, but with all the outlandish smoke poppers and fireworks people are using these days, we don't allow that information out to anyone beyond the patient and whoever she has in the room with her that day."

"I understand and would never do anything that could harm either of them."

Dr. Danvers had clearly put two-and-two together. "Shall we go ahead and fill in the blanks on the father's side of the family while we're here?"

I nodded my head, letting her know that he was indeed the father-to-be. Then she turned the tables and started grilling Austin about his medical history and that of his closest relatives to make a full profile for our little one.

I wondered if Austin had been to the baby store with Jordan, looking at things for their fake baby, and that's how he knew what they had on their shelves. I hadn't even taken a trip to the baby store yet. It made me feel like shit that she had that one up on me still, even if she couldn't carry a child. That probably made me an asshole, but all my residual anger was stuck focused on what she'd taken from me, and it didn't leave a whole lot of room for me to be nice about anything that happened to her to make her unable to carry a child.

Once Dr. Danvers got all the information she needed from Austin about his side of the family and their medical history, she headed out with a reminder to stop and schedule my next appointment. The minute we agreed on a date and time, Austin typed it into his phone, and then grinned the whole way to the door.

"Do you want to grab lunch?" He asked as we walked out.

"I don't think that's a good idea."

"Look, Becs, I know you're still angry with me and I understand that, but we have to learn to talk to one another again."

"And we did. We managed to get through an entire checkup together. I think that's a good enough start."

"I don't think it was. You plan on using Clea as your birthing coach," he reminded me.

"Yes, because I know that I can count on her to show up."

The hopeful demeanor he possessed, since I informed the doctor that he was the father, slipped away completely. "I'll be there," he promised quietly.

"I don't trust you." I turned to walk back to where my car had been parked and didn't stop moving. I couldn't feel sorry for him. He had burned me twice now, three times if you counted the first few dates we ever went on and the way everything came out about Jordan outside that movie theater. The thought of movie theaters made me physically ill these days. Considering Austin and Jordan factored twice in breaking my heart at one, it was safe to say I had no plans to go back to one – ever.

When I got to my car, there was no choice but to face the direction of the doctor's office, where I'd left Austin. He still stood there, watching me as I got into my car and took off. One day, maybe things wouldn't hurt so much. That day hadn't come yet, and I imagined it was a long way off since I'd have to deal with Austin for the next nineteen years and then special occasions afterward, too. There would be our child's college graduation, marriage, grandchildren being born. It seemed so daunting when I thought of that length of time, especially if I allowed myself to throw in that Austin would eventually fall in love with someone else or forgive a certain evil witch and end up playing happy couples with her throughout my child's life.

THREE DAYS AFTER MY APPOINTMENT, there was a quick knock on my door and by the time I got up to see who it was, no one was there. A rather large box had been left behind though. I struggled to push the damn thing into my apartment, after I checked to make sure it was addressed to me, since I hadn't ordered anything.

When I opened it up, there was a card on top.

BECS,
I KNOW YOU DON'T BELIEVE ME YET, BUT HOPEFULLY I'LL CONVINCE YOU ONE DAY SOON. I'M NOT GOING ANYWHERE EVER AGAIN.
LOVE ALWAYS,
AUSTIN

My hands shook as I dropped the card and started pulling smaller boxes out of the larger one.

The first box had several onesies in it for a baby in neutral colors. The one on top had, *My Mom and Dad do great things together!* written on it. I wanted to cry because obviously the great thing we had done together was make our baby. I didn't have the heart to read the rest of them, so I tucked them aside and pulled out the next box.

It had an assortment of burp cloths, baby bath towels, and an assortment of baby shampoos, soaps, lotions, and powders.

"What have you done, Austin?" I asked, even though he wasn't there to answer.

The next box had an assortment of bottles, pacifiers, and two different breast pumps. The box beneath that, the largest one, was full of clothing. Maternity clothes, to be exact. There were two pairs of jeans with that stretchy material top to fit a growing belly, a couple pair of leggings, and some flowy maternity tops. Buried at the bottom of the box was a top that had been made using the print from Van Gough's famous Sunflowers.

I couldn't hold back the tears at how thoughtful the whole box had been. I also didn't think Austin realized how painful it would be either. His heart was in the right place, but I couldn't look at Van Gough's painting without thinking of how the best night of my life turned into the worst morning I'd ever experienced, and I was still dealing with the ramifications. That shirt would never be worn and went right back into the box.

> Becs: You should take all the baby stuff to your house since you'll need it there. I'll get my own. Please, take the clothes back, too.

> Dickhead Baby Daddy: I wanted you to have everything in that box. It's all yours.

> Becs: So, you purposely meant to remind me of the worst night of my life?

> Dickhead Baby Daddy: What? No! You said that our Van Gough date was the best night of your life.

> Becs: Obviously, you forgot how that one ended.

He didn't send a text back right away, so he must have realized what I was talking about. Eventually, as I worked to pack the boxes back up, my phone dinged.

> Dickhead Baby Daddy: I'm sorry. I wasn't thinking. I don't think of those two events as happening on the same day. The nightmare happened when someone woke us up, not during the best date night ever. Please, don't let what happened steal that memory from you.

Becs: Too late. That happened the moment she showed up and once again, you didn't tell her to leave right away. You invited her inside for a chat, that ended with me being discarded and forgotten again.

Dickhead Baby Daddy: You'll never know how many regrets I have.

CHAPTER SEVENTEEN

"Hey, you never said if you got either of those summer camp art director jobs," Clea mentioned as she sipped on her coffee. I stared longingly at her cup, wishing I could trade mine for hers. Caffeine was no good for growing fetuses, which sucked. It would be cool, if I could drink all the coffee I wanted, and the side effect was a kid who came out with superpowers.

"Maggy Grayson got the short one and I don't know who got the summer-long program, but I did hear through the grapevine that they didn't want an unwed pregnant woman running the show."

"What is this the 1950s?"

"I know, right? That's what I said. It's not like they could come out and say that to me, but still. The rumor is out there, so it must be true."

"At least you got the job teaching at both schools next year, that still enables you to be a twelve-month employee, right?"

"Yeah, I get to keep my full-time status, benefits, and the thrill of being paid less all year so that I have bills covered in the summertime. What I don't get is tenure at either school because technically, I'm only part time at each."

"No!" Clea grumbled. "That's not fair. At least you're staying in my house now, so you have plenty of room for the new baby without having to upgrade to a two-bedroom."

I could honestly kiss my best friend for her generosity. A week ago, she offered her house up to me, for the same amount of rent I was paying on my crappy one-bedroom apartment, and she'd included my utilities with that, which actually lowered my monthly expenses.

Clea had inherited the house free and clear from some crazy aunt when she passed and now, I was going to benefit because she and Houston decided to move in together. I didn't even have to worry about moving all my stuff. She left most of her furniture behind, since Houston's house was already furnished, and he didn't want anything she's shared with Jeff to accidentally come to his place. It left me with far better furniture and her boyfriend found people to move the rest of my shit for me, too. The transition had been easy as could be.

I shrugged thinking about just how easy the move to my new house had been in comparison with my job situation. "That's the life of an art or music teacher," I explained to my best friend. "We are always at the mercy of people who think culture and creativity doesn't matter as much as sports. Do you know the elementary school got all brand-new gym equipment this year and the other stuff was only a couple years old?"

"That's not okay," Clea murmured.

"No, it's not. I had to buy the clay the kids used for their pots this year out of my own pocket, but there was no way I could skip that lesson. What if one of them ends up being a famous sculptor one day? What if they didn't because there wasn't enough money in the damn budget for some stinking clay?"

"Aw, I love how you love them so much."

"I just wish the schools loved them enough to give them the arts full time," I griped before taking a sip of decaf latte that tasted just like caramel milk with a splash of defective coffee in it.

I scrunched my nose up at the offensive drink. "The things I do for the little people," I added as I pushed the cup further away from me.

Clea glanced around nervously, then settled her eyes back on mine. "So, have you heard from Austin lately?"

"I hear from him every day."

"Seriously? Why haven't you told me?"

"It's not important. He sends at least one text a day."

"Do you respond to them?"

"Only the ones that directly relate to the baby."

"Are there ones that don't?" She asked curiously, while eyeing something in the café behind me. I turned to look and Clea shouted, "Damn!"

I turned back around immediately, to see my best friend picking up her purse that had been hanging off the side of her chair. Her cheeks were suspiciously red, though.

"I guess someone bumped it," she stated without looking up at me. Something was going on with my best friend. She was acting weird. "So, you were talking about Austin," she encouraged.

"No, I wasn't. You were asking about him, and I was trying to give you short answers that hinted at how much I didn't enjoy the subject."

Clea giggled. "At some point, you're going to have to get used to it, since you know," she pointed at my belly as if it was too taboo to say out loud that I was pregnant with his baby.

"Fine, he's been sending gifts."

"What kind of gifts?"

"The kind that are meant to help care for a baby when it gets here." I rolled my eyes and poked a finger at the stupid drink that taunted me. It was so not what I wanted, but at the same time I was hungry. "I think another muffin sounds good," I mumbled.

"Way to lose your train of thought," Clea teased. "This pregnancy thing is really doing your brain in, isn't it?"

"Well, there are all these stupid emotions, then there are the things I can't enjoy anymore." I stared longingly at the coffee she sipped before slowly putting it down, like it might bite her for the simple fact that I wasn't able to enjoy it. "Then there are all the irrational fears and the real worries."

"What worries?" Clea asked, suddenly more serious than she'd been all morning.

"What if something goes wrong? What if no one is around to help me? What if I need to be on bedrest and can't go to work, so then I can't pay my bills and my insurance gets canceled before I have the baby? What if the hospital then tells me my baby is dead, but really they're selling it to the highest bidder on e-Bay by disguising the sale as some ancient diaper pack that no longer exists, but everyone knows that's code for a baby girl or a baby boy?"

"Wow, that escalated so quickly into a whole black market, underground baby-selling conspiracy. Are you okay?"

I groaned and leaned forward to bang my head on the table. "No. No, I'm not okay. See, I just went from rational to completely irrational in two point five seconds flat. That's my brain these days."

"At least you still know the difference."

"Well, there's that," I agreed before my friend started laughing at me. Then, the strangest thing happened. A blueberry muffin appeared on our table like magic. Well, not quite like magic, since I'd seen the café employee deliver it and walk away.

"Um, I think she got the wrong table," I suggested to Clea, who smiled warmly at me.

"I don't think so," she argued.

"But I didn't order this, so clearly she got the wrong table."

"Didn't you just say you were thinking about getting another muffin?"

"Yes, but this isn't a fantasy novel where food appears when you ask for it," I explained to my ridiculous bestie. "On second thought, lets test the theory." I closed my eyes and when they popped open again, I voiced my demand to the universe. "I'm thinking of getting a million dollars today."

"What the hell, Becs?"

"What? It worked with the muffin. Tell me you weren't thinking the same thing!"

"I can't say that I was," she mentioned before laughing at me once again. "You're ridiculous."

"A muffin appeared at our table, not five minutes after I voiced wanting another." I eyed my friend suspiciously because she was wearing her guilty face, complete with red-tinged cheeks. "I know you didn't order it because I've been sitting here with you the whole time." I turned to look back in the direction that kept grabbing my friend's attention. When I did, it was to see a familiar back walking out of the café.

"Was that?" I asked before turning back around to see Clea busily staring off in the opposite direction, like that wasn't suspect. "Did Austin just buy me this muffin?"

"Maybe?" Clea answered, though it sounded more like a question.

"A part of me wants to throw it away now," I huffed.

"But you're going to eat it anyway?"

"Yeah, because I'm starving and honestly, it's his fault that I'm starving. You know?" Clea grinned as I took a dainty nibble of the crumbly goodness on top of the muffin.

"I think your boyfriend's brother might be stalking me," I whispered across the table after swallowing another bite.

"Maybe, he's just trying to show you that he's there without being too pushy and making you angry again."

"Why aren't you still angry with him?" I asked her, sort of hurt that she seemed to be taking up for the asshole.

Clea sighed. "It's not that I don't want to kick him in the balls for what he's put you through, because I do. It's just that, you're having his baby and I'm marrying his brother, and that's going to make us all family in a strange way. I want to be able to support my future brother-in-law when he has my future niece or nephew with him without you getting angry with me. If you two work your shit out, I won't have to feel like I'm walking on eggshells around you."

"I would never begrudge you being there for my child, no matter which parent had custody at the moment." My explanation was weak, but it was dawning on me that my best friend would be stuck between a rock and a hard place eventually if this rift remained between Austin and myself.

"While I don't agree, at all, with how he handled things, you have to admit he was put in an impossible situation when Jordan lied to him."

"I'd still like to punch that whore to the moon," I threatened.

"I know. I would, too. Houston said he thinks she's planning on leaving town. Maybe it's for good this time."

"I very seriously doubt that. The bitch is evil, and she didn't get what she wanted. I'd bet money she'll come back and try again."

"You really think so?"

"I would put down good money, that I don't even have, that if I were to start up a relationship with Austin again, his evil big sister would run off and tell Jordan, who would come charging back with some comically unbelievable, yet somehow gullible people believe it anyway, reason why they need to be together. Then the bastard would have no choice but to drop me again, immediately." I laughed after stringing together that blubbering ball of ridiculousness, no matter how accurate it might be. Then, I forgot all about it and took another bite of my muffin before tacking just a little bit more.

"It wouldn't surprise me if she tried to convince Austin that I wasn't actually carrying his baby."

Clea winced and perked a brow up.

"I may have already overheard Victoria asking her family just that. It was in the middle of her taking up for Jordan, too. That was weeks ago when they first found out you were pregnant."

"Don't worry, I'm not surprised. I ran into Mrs. Mercer and her eldest wildebeest while grocery shopping one day and Momma Texas had to apologize for her daughter's behavior. Apparently, Victoria is still team 'Jordan loves Austin' all the way."

"I still don't understand why she's so invested in them ending up together. All their other siblings, including Dallas, can see right through Jordan's shit and don't want her anywhere near Austin. And for the record, Austin cut her out of his life, and I don't think she'll ever be welcomed back again."

"That's all a little too late, isn't it?"

"It doesn't have to be, Becs."

I finished my muffin in silence while my best friend sat and watched. I knew she felt like she went a step too far by telling me that, but I couldn't assure her that she hadn't. Clea meant well and she still believed in happily ever after.

"He came here specifically to buy you a muffin this morning, since he was too late to pay for your latte."

"And how did he know to come here?" I asked, mad at her for giving him that information.

She held her hand up. "That part wasn't on me, but Houston knew where I was going, and he feels the same about at least making sure you guys are friends again before the baby comes. We're not saying you ever have to date him or anything."

"I know," I groaned. "You want everyone to get along so it's not weird around my baby."

"Exactly. Babies can pick up on stress and people's discomfort." She was stretching her argument to appeal to the irrational fear side of my brain, and I knew it. Still, my best friend had a point that I couldn't avoid much longer. The baby would be here before the year was out and I didn't want to always have awkward handoffs and resentment bringing everyone down. It sucked that I was the one who had to be the bigger person, though.

CHAPTER EIGHTEEN

LATER THAT DAY, I RECEIVED A TEXT FROM AUSTIN.

Dickhead Baby Daddy: How was your breakfast?

Becs: Surprisingly, fifty percent off since I didn't have to pay for my second muffin.

Dickhead Baby Daddy: That must have been a nice surprise.

Becs: Something like that.

When he didn't send anything else back, I bit the bullet and decided this would be the moment where I started trying to be the better person, for my baby.

Becs: Thank you.

Dickhead Baby Daddy: Any time, Becs.

That was the beginning of me no longer ignoring the majority of Austin's texts. It was also the beginning of reestablishing a friendly relationship with him. We didn't see one another in person until the end of April, when my next doctor's appointment was. While that had been a little disappointing, it also made perfect sense. Our friendliness was strictly texting business.

> Baby Daddy: Can I pick you up to take you to your appointment today?

I chewed on my lip as I thought about that. While our relationship had been repaired on one level with the friendlier texts, it was still fractured. I didn't think that was something that could be fixed. Just seeing the man could send me into a tailspin of mixed emotions. I never stopped loving him because my heart seemed incapable. Then again, I also didn't trust him at all anymore.

Waiting for the other shoe to drop seemed inevitable. Honestly, my irrational fears had me searching for Jordan to pop up at a moment's notice. In my crazy pregnant mind, she knew we had been texting one another and would eventually show up to put a stop to it. The bad thing was, I didn't trust Austin – even in a made-up scenario – to do the right thing.

Still, we had to move past texting eventually. It wasn't like I'd be able to hand him a baby emoji a few months down the road and call that our 'baby swap'. I'd have to see and interact in person with him eventually, too.

> Becs: Sure. Can you be here about thirty minutes earlier than the appointment, just in case the stupid parking lot gets blocked off again?

> Baby Daddy: Anything you need.

If only. What I needed was never anyone else's priority. I'd learned that the hard way, repeatedly. I groaned at my own negative, though true, thought.

A few minutes later, forty-five minutes earlier than necessary, there was a knock on my door. I opened it to let Austin in.

"Sorry, I wasn't quite ready." I tore through my house with one shoe in hand, searching frantically for the other one. Dammit, the thing had pulled a runner on me. I wasn't even sure how one shoe ended up next to the door while the other was missing. A mystery for the ages.

"Can I help?"

"Not unless you can magically produce my other shoe," I explained. Austin immediately moved into my living room and lifted the chair, then the front side of the couch, where my other shoe magically appeared. "How in the hell did you know?"

"Where do you take your shoes off?"

"Usually by the door, but sometimes…" It dawned on me as I attempted to explain, that he'd seen me sit on my couch before in my old apartment, take my shoes off, and throw them toward the door. I only did that when I was wearing tennis shoes though. No way would I harm any of my beautiful pumps that I barely ever got to wear thanks to my dirty job.

"I guess you were too tired to toss this one," he said as he offered the shoe up to me.

"Thanks." I took the shoe and then sat to put both on my feet. My belly had popped into a slightly rounded, tight ball at my waistline, so I had on a pair of the leggings Austin had purchased for me the month before. Judging by the smile he wore; the man knew exactly which pants I was wearing.

"Do you think we'll really get to see if it's a boy or a girl today?"

I glanced up at him. "I don't know. It's supposedly within the window for when we can find out since I'm thirteen weeks along now. Do you want to know, or did you want to wait to find out in the delivery room?"

He sucked in a sharp breath and stared at me as if I'd just turned to gold. "You're going to let me in the delivery room?"

It was only then that it dawned on me what I'd just accidentally offered him. That was my damn dreamy mouth running away with me. In all my good dreams, he was there when our baby was born, and we were a family. A happy family. My nightmares were closer to reality.

"It's your baby, too. I think maybe you should be there to see them come into the world, if you want to."

"I want that more than almost anything else," he declared. I wondered what the 'almost anything else' was, but I'd never ask that question.

"Okay, well the same question stands then. Do you want to know the gender now?"

"Do you?" I nodded my head and his smile widened.

"Yeah, me too. I'm too excited to find out. Waiting sucks."

"Try growing a human inside your body and knowing you have to wait nine months to meet it," I suggested.

He came closer and sat down beside me on the couch, so our thighs were touching. "I know you have the difficult job here, but it eats me alive every day knowing you're growing our baby and I can't do anything to help you along the way."

Oh damn. I forgot how potent up-close-and-personal Austin could be. Text-level Austin was easier to be friendly with. He pinched a bit of the material on my thigh.

"Glad to see these fit you."

"Thanks. My stomach popped out a little bit and made some of my jeans a bit too snug to wear."

"Can I…" He hesitated as his eyes trailed down my body to my middle. The sweater I wore was too bulky for him to tell anything had changed in my body, except maybe my boobs. They had grown quite a bit and I'd been forced to buy new bras to accommodate them.

"There's really not much there to see," I explained, picking up on what he wanted.

"I'd still like to see, if you don't mind."

I stood and moved so that I was in front of him and then slowly lifted my sweater out of the way. The way his eyes immediately misted up sent flutters straight to my growing belly. He reached out and ran a hand over the slight mound that was now present.

"Becs," his reverent tone captivated me as he spoke. "This is amazing. Can you feel the baby move yet?"

"I felt something last night when I tried to go to sleep."

"What was it like?" As he asked that question, he moved his hands to my hips and pushed and pulled at each side to get me to turn so that he could see the baby bump in profile.

"It was just the tiniest little flutter, like butterfly wings on your skin, only from the inside out." I laughed then as I remembered what I thought it had been at first.

"What?" He asked as his eyes met mine and twinkled with shared amusement.

"Honestly?" He nodded. "I thought I had gas at first. It almost felt like the beginning of having bubble guts when you eat something that doesn't agree with you."

He chuckled at my assessment. "I read that it's often mistaken for that in the beginning."

"You did?"

"Yeah. Well, for a while there, you wouldn't really tell me anything, so I went online and started reading through a pregnancy forum on Reddit. The descriptions of what women go through ranged from subtle things to so descriptive it was a bit disturbing."

"Hmm," I hummed out because he may have inadvertently read a few of my posts about my crazy pregnancy brain. People were not always kind on that forum and some of them told me to go get counseling. If they'd been through what I had, they'd prob-ably be a little paranoid about everything, too. Stupid judgey internet judgers.

An alarm on his phone started going off, and Austin easily slid me back a step as he stood from the couch. I wanted so badly to take that step forward and hold onto the man I'd once dreamed of starting a family with. My body ached with the need to feel his arms wrap around me and hold me close. That was too much though. It would break something inside me. Maybe it was just the wall I put up between us, maybe it would be whatever was left of my heart. I didn't know and wasn't willing to take the chance that it would do permanent damage to get close to the man again.

I took a step back, and then another, until we were standing a few paces apart and no longer in touching distance. "That was the alarm to leave, since you said you wanted to be there a little early."

I nodded and turned to go grab my purse.

"Thank you, for letting me have that," he muttered as he moved to the door and held it open for me. There weren't words for what I wanted to say to him, and 'You're welcome,' seemed a stupid thing to say, so I just nodded instead and walked out to where he'd parked his truck.

"ARE you ready to see your baby?" Dr. Danvers asked us. We both nodded our heads so aggressively that the woman laughed at us. "We seem rather eager today. I supposed you want to learn the sex of the baby?"

"Yes, please," I requested.

"Let's see if the little one will cooperate." She squeezed the gel on my already exposed belly and then pulled a different wand out than she'd used last time, thankfully. It went on top of my belly, like the doppler heartbeat thing, rather than the original ultrasound that went inside me.

"Holy shit!" Austin's exclamation puffed out as he sat closer, almost leaning across my body to see the image on the screen. "I can see a hand and fingers," he said. "Wait, is the baby waving at us?"

I concentrated on what he was seeing and damn if that didn't look like what was happening.

"Sure is," Dr. Danvers confirmed. "Your little one is just learning how to open and close that fist."

"Oh my God! That's so adorable. I didn't realize they could do that."

"Sure can." She clicked and measured and moved the wand around my belly and clicked some more. "Give me one more moment to get these measurements in, and we'll get down to the good stuff. Do either of you have a preference?"

"Healthy," Austin stated without a moment's hesitation.

"That's what I like to hear!" Dr. Danvers nearly shouted with her enthusiasm. "What about you?" She asked, addressing me since I hadn't answered.

"Well, I'll feel like a copycat if I say healthy, too. Honestly, I can picture either a boy or a girl. It doesn't matter because they'll be loved no matter what."

"You two are perfect. I wish all my parents-to-be were like you." She moved the wand around one more time and grinned. "All right, your little one is not shy. Last chance to place your bets," she teased. Austin and I were waiting, though I thought I saw the tell-tale sign of... "That's your son's penis," she pointed out.

"We're having a boy?" I asked at the same time Austin said, "That's our son!"

"Technically, it's his penis and we should be ashamed of ogling it to appease our curiosity," I teased to break the tension in the room. The awe in his voice as he'd seen his son for the first time made me want to kiss him in celebration and I couldn't do that. Dr. Danvers laughed at the joke I'd made to cover for what I really wanted to do.

"I don't think he'll mind this time," she winked as Austin grabbed hold of my hand and squeezed it tight.

When I glanced up, it was to see the man had tears flowing freely down his face and he didn't seem to care one bit that the doctor or I might catch him in his moment of elation. His tears spurred on my own. We were having a little boy who would one day look just like his father. I had very little doubt of that, considering all the Texas-themed Mercer brothers favored one another, even if Dallas did have a paler complexion than the other two with his blond hair and light eyes that he got from his mother's side.

"I'll have a little video you can take with you on a flash drive as well as the usual ultrasound pictures when we're done here," Dr. Danvers assured us.

I think the rest of the visit was a wash because I don't remember a thing after finding out we were having a boy. Once we got to Austin's car, he handed me my latest appointment card, and I realized I'd zoned out through the whole process of making a new appointment.

"Thank you," I offered as I took the card.

"I hope the time works for you. I made it late in the day because I wasn't sure if you were still in school then or not. She made it for May 29th."

"That's perfect. We're still in school until the first week of June."

Austin nodded then reached over and grabbed hold of my hand. "Thank you for letting me be here for this. I can't imagine not being able to see that in person. It was amazing. He was moving around inside you and waving his hand at us, Becs. Our boy is already doing things on his own and we can only guess what he's normally doing outside of that small little glimpse we got."

His amazement leaked over into my own excitement. "I know. I wish it was safe to be hooked up to something like that for the whole pregnancy, or at least to be able to check in once or twice a day and see what's going on."

"That would be cool, but then you'd have to put up with me living on your couch because no way would I want to miss those check-ins."

"Austin," I whispered his voice. "How are we going to do this with the baby when he's here?" He'd just brought up a good point. Neither of us was going to want to miss out on the milestones when the other had the baby.

"We'll work it all out, Becs." He patted my hand, and I missed the warmth of his touch when he let go. "Will you do me the honor of having lunch with me this time?"

"Can we go to that one place?"

He grinned, so I felt like he already knew what I was talking about, but he asked anyway. "Which place is that?"

"The one with the animal themed foods?"

"You're dying for their potato soup again, huh?"

"How did you know?"

He grinned but didn't answer as he put his truck in gear and backed out of the parking spot. "Seems like the perfect place to celebrate finding out we're having a boy!"

"It really does," I admitted. "I can't wait to tell everyone."

"About that," Austin started to say, and then he looked at me before taking off in the direction of the highway. "Do you think we could hold off until the weekend and maybe go to my family's Sunday dinner, so we can tell everyone at once?"

"Um, I haven't exactly met all of your family."

"No, but it would be a good time to do it, so that there aren't any strangers to you in our son's life when he gets here. No matter what, I want you comfortable with everything that happens, including who he's around." I nodded because that had been a legitimate worry of mine.

"Okay, we can do that. Clea's going to kill me, since she knows my appointment was today."

"I'll handle her."

I laughed at that. "Okay, buddy. I'll be sure to tell her you thought you could handle her."

"Well, I'll handle her adjacent. I happen to know her boyfriend and I think he can keep her off your back and busy on hers instead for a few days."

"Oh my God! You did not just say it like that."

"Oh, come on, everyone knows all they do is eat, sleep, work, and fuck."

"That's actually pretty accurate."

Our lighthearted banter kept up all the way to the restaurant and until we were seated at a table. Once we ordered, Austin took my hand across the table. Flashbacks of our first date there hit me like a freight train and I immediately pulled back from him.

"Sorry," he mumbled.

I shook my head. "No, it's fine. I just…"

"Remembered last time we were here?"

"Yeah."

"Was it so bad to remember that?" He asked and it was evident he wanted a sincere answer.

"Austin, nothing was ever bad when we were dating, it was the fact that it ended so abruptly, without any discussion, that makes it hard to remember the good times. It's like they didn't matter or count for anything."

"They mattered, Becs. Every damn minute I got to spend with you mattered."

"Just not enough."

"You once asked me to put myself in your shoes with that whole Clarence nonsense." I nodded in agreement. "Well, I'm asking the same of you now." He explained how his conversation with Jordan that night had gone down.

"She never helped with my house, not when it was being built, not after." He sighed. "I don't know why she lied about that, since I could call her out on it. Jordan never helped pick out anything for my house, never spent a single night there, and not once was she ever allowed inside my bedroom."

"Why are you telling me that?"

"Because it's true, but also because she knew exactly why she hadn't been allowed to do those things. I told her, back when I was building the house, that it was for my future family and the only woman who would ever sleep over, besides my mom or sisters, was going to be the woman who would one day be my wife."

"You think that's why she showed up that night? She knew you brought me home somehow?"

He shrugged. "I don't want to speculate on what was going through her mind. I want you to understand what was going through mine." He took a sip of his drink before continuing.

"Jordan told me I couldn't tell you about the baby. She also said that if you were involved with me in any way, she would run."

"That's a horribly manipulative thing for her to have done, so why in the hell did I see you kissing her only days later, like she hadn't done anything wrong?"

He shook his head. "I was trying to force it. I chose the baby, not her. You need to understand that. I chose my child not another woman. The kissing, that was me trying to forget you. Trying to force something with Jordan, that was never there before, for the sake of my kid. I knew she would be difficult if I didn't at least try, and I couldn't..." He shook his head as if talking about all of this was too hard.

"If it had been her, I wouldn't have been as happy to go to doctor visits, but it still would have been amazing to see my child grow and move and find out the sex. Please, understand, I didn't want to miss out on that because I pissed Jordan off."

"What kills me is that you knew on some level that she was

that manipulative, that you would have to placate her through childbirth, but you still kept going there with her over the years. What would you have done if she had really been pregnant and I was, too, Austin? Would you have continued to placate her and ignored me and our child for hers?"

"No. You already know the answer to that because you found out you were pregnant before the truth came out about her. I asked you to marry me right away, without even thinking about it, because that was the natural response for me. I never did that with her. If I had to give anyone up at that point, Becs, it would never have been you and our baby."

"It's hard to believe that all things considered."

"I know it is. That's on me, and the only way to change your mind about it is to keep proving to you that I'll be right here by your side for everything."

"We'll see," I conceded.

By the time we finished our meals and got back to my place, it was almost dinner time. Austin walked me up to the front door, and I kept it open for him once I walked through. "Why don't you come in for a minute, and I'll download the flash drive onto my laptop, then you can take the copy Dr. Danvers gave me?"

"Thank you, I'd like that."

We sat there in semi-awkward silence as the video of our ultrasound downloaded and about the time it finished, Austin finally spoke up again.

"Can we watch it together one more time before I go?"

"Yeah, we can do that," I responded softly as I pulled the video up and pushed play. We watched together as Dr. Danvers's cursor moved all over the screen taking her measurements. Austin reached up to trace our son's fingers that stuck straight up in front of his face before closing into a fist again.

"I can't wait to hold him," he admitted.

"I know. Every time I think of his tiny little fingers, I can't wait to feel them wrap around my finger and hold on while I feed him."

Austin smiled down at me. "Do you plan to breastfeed, or did you want to just use formula and a bottle?"

"Do you have a preference?"

"It's not my body, sweetheart. Whatever you decide, we'll work it out. It'll be difficult on you if we're splitting custody to pump breastmilk when you don't have him here. Maybe we should just think about you keeping him here all the time, and me coming here to visit until he's old enough to be weaned off, if that's what you want."

"You would do that?" I asked, awed by the sacrifice he was willing to make.

"I'd be an asshole if I wouldn't consider it. You would have to agree to me being in your space more often though, so it's not just me who would have to be accommodating."

"Yeah, I get that." My heart thudded away in my chest at the prospect of having both my baby and Austin here, almost like we were a family. The dream I'd once had of just that came to mind and wrapped me up in its warm embrace. No, wait. That was a real body wrapping around me.

"What are you doing?"

"You looked like you could use a hug," he told me.

"Dammit," I muttered against his chest because my willpower to push him away waned as his scent filled my nostrils. The heat of his body warmed me in a way I didn't want to lose either.

"I missed this," he whispered into my hair.

"Me too," I admitted because there was no point in being stubborn. It was obvious, by the way I clung to his waist, and nuzzled my face into his chest to inhale his intoxicating aroma. "You always smelled so good. It's addicting."

"Good to know," he teased. "And right back at you, Trouble."

I chuckled. "Jesus, that was the dumbest costume to ever wear to a college party and Clea never did show up because her Game of Life spinner wheel kept falling off her costume."

"I wouldn't say it was the dumbest costume. It caught my attention from across the room, remember?"

"Yeah, I guess it did."

We stood there clinging to one another for what seemed like hours but was probably only a few drawn-out moments. Then, reluctantly, I pulled away before I lost my heart to the infuriating man again.

"So, I guess the next thing we need to decide on is a name for our son."

"I imagine that's going to be one of the first questions my family ask after they find out that he's a boy on Sunday."

"Ugh, don't remind me. The thought of going there to your family's house for their Sunday dinner makes me want to hurl."

"Tell me how you really feel," he said, though I could hear the hurt in his tone at the callous way I'd just implied his family made me sick.

"I didn't mean it like that. I meant my nerves are going to get the best of me, especially having to wait four days."

"You've met my mom and my brothers. That's half the family already."

"Yeah, I also met your older sister, and she wasn't exactly pleasant."

"When did that happen?"

"I ran into her and your mom at the grocery store a month or so ago."

"Fuck. If that ever happens again, I want to know about it right away. Victoria is in the middle of her own shit, and she won't talk to anyone about it, but it's clouded her judgment on a few things."

"Like Jordan," I insisted.

"Among other things." He huffed. "I'm sorry she was a brat, but I promise she won't be this weekend. Everyone already ripped into her the last time she tried to defend Jordan and insinuated you might be faking your pregnancy as well."

"So, I heard."

He smiled then. "Clea told you?"

"Yes, but not until recently. I don't think she wanted to hurt my feelings by letting me know that someone in your family was less than thrilled about my situation, but it slipped out, and I made her fill me in. I promise, she's not spying for me."

"Oh, I know. She has a pact with Houston. Neither one of them will get too involved in our shit, beyond being supportive. Houston put his foot down about meddlesome involvement."

That made me laugh. "I wondered why she hadn't been pushier about things." I held my hand out to Austin and he placed his in mine without question. "Come on, let's go get settled in and see if we can't decide on what we're going to call our boy, so he doesn't get tormented throughout school."

"I'm guessing, we shouldn't name him Christopher Robinson then?" He teased.

"Ew, I would poke your eyes out with Eeyore's missing tail, thumbtack and all, if you tried to Winnie the Poo our son."

Austin laughed. "Noted. Besides, I kind of hoped he could have my last name," he admitted.

"I figured as much, and you won't get an argument from me on that point because my family isn't that great. Yours apparently is, and I'd rather him feel those ties."

"My mom and dad would love the shit out of you for that answer."

"Good, you can let them know I said that, and butter them up before I have to meet your dad on Sunday."

"Becs, I don't think you have to worry about impressing my dad."

"Why is that?"

"He threatened to kick my ass across town and back if I didn't put things right with you."

"Aw, that's sweet. I love him already."

Austin's eyes went so soft, it looked like he would melt right there in front of me. It was a look I couldn't resist even in my angriest moments. I was damned with the emotionally beautiful day we shared. That was why, when he leaned in to kiss me, I never stopped him.

CHAPTER NINETEEN

AUSTIN'S LIPS SINGED MY OWN WITH THEIR HEAT, FORCING ME TO immediately open to him so he could cool that fire with a deeper kiss.

It didn't work. The fire only grew between us until there was a raging damn inferno on my couch. I didn't even realize when he picked me up and shifted us, so that my body rested fully on the couch, while Austin's form hovered over mine. His kisses were frantic as my fingers clawed at his shirt to get it untucked from the pants that he'd worn that day. Why in sexy man heaven had he worn pants? Or a shirt for that matter?

Eventually, I had the man stripped down to his boxer briefs as he worshipped the mounds of cleavage that spilled out of the top of my bra. I hadn't even realized my shirt had come off along with his. That was the drugging magic of his kisses. They were meant to be bottled and sold to induce euphoria among the masses, but I was a greedy thing and refused to share. Everyone else would have to live with the misery of never knowing how it felt to be worshipped by Austin.

I knew there was a certain level of crazy talk going on in my mind again, but I couldn't fathom being wrong about this. About him. Not again. I just knew that my body needed what his could give and I'd deal with the consequences later.

"Becs, I need you," he whispered. I fully agreed until I felt his underwear sliding down between our legs and then a tiny bit of clarity bounced back into my brain.

"I don't have condoms."

His hand landed on my belly to caress the skin there with the barest tickle from his fingertips. "I think the damage is already done."

"I'm not worried about pregnancy," I argued.

He swallowed and looked me straight in the eye. I had a checkup when we were apart and I'm clean, but Becs, I haven't been with anyone else since you."

"That's a lie, or did you forget that Clea and I saw you and Jordan together?"

"You saw us kiss, and that is the only time that happened, since you and I reunited in February. I explained before that I tried to appease her, but when I saw you…"

"I watched you go in for a kiss specifically that day," I reminded him.

"It was because she tried to feed me the popcorn with Reese's Pieces in it," he admitted sullenly. "I was trying to stop her from doing it."

"You had to remind me about that," I muttered and pushed on his chest to move him off me.

"That's not something I ever shared with her. I used to do it when I went to the movies with Houston and Dallas, and they talked about it in front of her at some point, I guess. I don't think Jordan ever realized that was something I started because of you, considering I never did it when I was with her. She ordered everything, to try to cheer me up, when she dragged me to the movies that night, thinking that it was something special I usually did with my brothers."

He must have seen the indecision on my face because he

leaned in and placed a gentle kiss on my lips. "I swear to you that I'm telling the truth about all of it. I haven't slept with her since last year, a couple months before you and I got back together. You can ask Houston about the candy in the popcorn if you need to, he'll tell you."

"I believe you," I muttered.

"Still, killed the mood, huh?"

"Little bit," I answered as we both took in the fact that he was still sitting there with his boxer briefs tangled around his ankle and I was stripped down to my bra and panties. "Well, this was one way to come up with names for our kid, I guess," I joked.

"Did you want to name him Randy?" Austin teased.

"Oh, no! That would be awful, especially if he ends up anything like your younger brother. Did Clea tell you about the chocolate sauce and the blow job queen in the back room of the club on Valentine's Day?"

Austin laughed. "No, but I'm not surprised. Dallas marches to the beat of his own throbbing dick."

"Well, that was obvious, what with his penchant for diaper wearing."

Austin kicked his underwear off his foot and turned to me. "Do you think we could discuss baby names from the comfort of your bed?"

"While naked?" I asked.

He grinned. "We should be comfortable while trying to decide our son's future name, don't you think?"

I smirked at him and stood up, reached behind me to snap my bra clasps open, and let it drop as I walked back to my bedroom. Austin followed immediately. By the time we crawled in the bed, my panties had been tossed to the side of the room somewhere as the mood was most certainly found again. Thank you, pregnancy hormones.

"Is it just me or have your breasts grown along with your baby bump?" Austin asked as he spread his hands out and palmed the underside of my breasts. What used to be a handful for him now overflowed.

"They've definitely gotten bigger and more sensitive," I admitted.

"Oh yeah? How sensitive?" He leaned in and kissed the tips of each nipple before licking first one, then the other, with his tongue. When I moaned, he sucked one tight peak into his mouth while his nimble fingers pinched and teased the other.

"Oh shit," I hissed when I realized that my climax was imminent. I had never, in my whole life, had an orgasm from someone playing with my breasts.

He switched nipples and treated them to the opposite interactions. "Austin!" I panted his name out on a shaky breath.

"Are you going to come for me?" His eyes met mine and the lazy, half-lidded expression he wore undid me as he slipped my nipple back in his mouth and gave an almighty suck that made my nerve endings tingle all the way down to my toes. There was no need to answer him as my belly tightened with the contractions the orgasm brought on. Quickly, I placed his hand on my belly.

"Do you feel that?"

"Wow that got really hard. I can feel you coming."

"Yeah, that was wild."

"Nah, that was just the beginning, Trouble. We're going to explore just how pregnancy affects other areas of your body, too. It sounds like more fun than playing board games." He chuckled as he nipped and kissed his way down my abdomen.

"I see what you did there," I laughed until there was nothing funny about what the man was doing with his mouth. "Oh God, please don't stop."

"Didn't plan on it," he mumbled against my sex before going back to licking and teasingly scraping across my clit with his teeth. "Everything is so swollen down here," he commented, "and darker than before."

"Really?"

"Yeah, it's sexy, so stop worrying about it." He smacked my pussy lightly as if to drive his point home when I bit into my teeth and watched him like he might bolt at any moment. My body was going through so many changes, I hadn't yet catalogued them all. Not that I could, if I wanted to, considering how often everything changed.

Austin worked hard to take my mind off all of it though, as his tongue slid back up my center and then he suckled at my clit in a way that had me pulsing and ready to come again far too soon. Pregnancy was like being a part of an instant orgasm factory.

"Wow," Austin whispered against my skin as he made his way back up my body, so that he was face-to-face with me. "You fucking gushed all over me. I don't think I've ever seen anything sexier, Trouble."

"Why are you calling me that again, all of a sudden?"

"What?"

"Trouble."

He slicked the hair back from my face and placed a sweet, too-brief kiss on my lips. "I've had a lot of time to think about us lately, and in my reflection, I went back to the very beginning."

"The Halloween party," I remembered.

"Your first birthday that we spent together, even though I didn't realize it at the time."

"It was my only birthday we ever spent together," I added.

"I know, and that was part of why that memory stuck with me so hard. The only birthday I've ever been able to spend with you, in going on seven years, was one I didn't even know to appreciate. I still knew that there was something about you, even then." His fingertips slid over my eyebrow and then down my nose. "It might have been the way you stared at me like I was the only person in that party. Then again, it could have been because you were the only woman who dared to show up in a creative costume instead of..."

"The usual slutbag attire that has become popular for Halloween?"

"Yeah, that." He leaned in and kissed my lips again. "I keep going back to that night and how I should have gone straight home the next day and made sure that nothing could come between us."

We both knew he was talking about the way he hadn't let Jordan know that they were 'off again' with their fuck buddy situation.

"I can't change the past, as much as I want to," Austin finally told me. "I can only make sure that your future is secure."

I got ready to protest, but he kissed my words away. "Not tonight," he muttered against my mouth a moment later. "I promise, we'll talk through everything and more than that, I'll prove it with my actions, but can we just be together for tonight?"

I nodded my head at the same moment Austin slipped inside me. It felt like I'd finally come home and that made a tear slip free from my eyes. He kissed it away and slowly withdrew and thrust back into me in a languid push and pull that built in that delicious slow burn way that you could luxuriate in for hours.

"Missed you so much," he whispered in my ear. I felt the same but couldn't bring myself to say it back. "I love you, Becs. Never stopped. Never will."

Ah shit, he was really trying to rip me wide open on an emotional level while he decimated me in the best way on a physical one. I didn't know how I was supposed to resist falling for him again. Not that I'd ever gotten over him the first or second time.

CHAPTER TWENTY

THAT WAS NOT THE LAST TIME AUSTIN AND I ENDED UP TANGLED in my sheets together. It happened every night leading up to the family dinner we were supposed to attend together.

"Are you ready for this?" He asked as I hopped into his truck.

"No," I replied honestly.

"Why did Houston tell me that Clea doesn't know you're coming to dinner tonight?"

"Because I didn't tell her."

"Yeah, I gathered that. Why didn't you tell her?"

"I didn't want her to…" How the hell could I tell him that I didn't want my best friend to get her hopes up that there was more between Austin and me than there was? I still didn't trust him, and I had a boatload of issues to work through before we could ever be anything more than friends, who fucked nightly. I wanted to smack myself for being so stupid as to fall back in bed with him, but it always felt so right in the moment.

"Didn't want her to…?" He prompted me.

"I don't know. I'm nervous enough," I changed tack, not wanting to explain my feelings because I didn't even understand the damn things myself.

"You know you have nothing to be nervous about, right?"

"Says you," I argued.

He chuckled. "Yeah, says me. I promise, everything will be fine." His hand rested on my thigh for the entirety of the drive and if I was being honest with myself, it helped. His warmth felt like a security blanket, even if it was just wrapped around a small portion of my leg.

When we finally got to his house, I noticed someone peeking out the window of whatever room was nearest the front door. Austin got out and came around to my side before I could even think of moving to get myself out of the car. There was no reason for me to be so nervous. Austin was right. I'd already met over half his family. The only people left who I hadn't been introduced to, were his younger sister, Katy, and his father.

Austin held his hand out for me, and I immediately placed mine in it and allowed him to gently pull me out of his truck. He kept pulling, until I stood there in his embrace as he wrapped his arms around me and leaned down to whisper in my ear.

"Everything is going to be okay, promise."

"I'm going to hold you to that," I mumbled against his chest.

"Wouldn't have it any other way, Becs. Let's go introduce you to my dad since he's standing on the porch watching us now."

"Oh man!" I whined much to Austin's amusement. He turned us around, and it was only then that I realized his dad was not the only one standing on the porch waiting. Clea's jaw was damn near to the deck while Houston seemed amused by her reaction. Dallas rolled his eyes and went back inside, probably to steal all the food while no one was watching over it. There was a younger version of Victoria standing on the porch next to her mother and then Austin's Dad stood on her other side. All of them, minus my flustered best friend, had giant smiles on their faces.

I noticed the lack of Victoria but didn't say anything about it. I figured it was better she didn't show up, than be there and cause a scene that everyone ended up blaming me for.

"I'm so glad you finally agreed to come to a family dinner," Mrs. Mercer gushed as she moved forward to give me a hug. I met Clea's questioning glance over Austin's mom's shoulder and mouthed, 'Later' to her.

She nodded and took Houston's hand and led him back inside. "Come on, before Dallas eats everything," she commanded her fiancé.

"Shit, I didn't even realize he slipped away," Houston complained.

"Watch your mouth, Houston!" His mother called after him before she handed me off to her husband. "This is my husband and Austin's father, Jacob." I held my hand out, but the man ignored it and pulled me into a hug, too.

"Glad to see you show up with my boy, even if he is a pinhead," he teased.

I laughed. "Thank you."

Once he let me go, Austin's sister pounced and hugged me. "I'm Katy, the only normal one," she announced.

"Normal? You?" Austin teased her.

"Well, yeah. She already knows the rest of you, so that's not a big stretch."

I laughed at her. "You're probably right, so long as you can beat out Houston in that department."

"My biggest brother wears ginormous shoes, so they're hard to fill," she mumbled as her cheeks turned pink.

"I'm sure you do just fine."

"Can we keep you?" She asked.

I patted my belly. "I guess one way or another, there's really no choice in that anymore."

She reached out as if to touch my belly and then stopped at the last minute. "Is it okay?"

I shrugged. "There's not much to feel. It's more like I have a giant food baby than a real one. I've felt the little one move around a bit, but no one else can feel it yet."

"That's so cool," Katy gushed.

"Not too cool though," her father reminded her.

"Don't worry, I just started college. I have no plans of going out and getting myself pregnant."

"I didn't either," I whispered conspiratorially.

"Shirley, this one's trouble," Mr. Mercer announced to his wife who playfully swatted him.

"That's what I've been telling Becs since the moment we met," Austin announced proudly.

"Come on, let's get everyone inside before Dallas and Houston eat us out of house and home."

"Might want to keep an eye on Clea, too," I informed her. "That girl can out eat most grown men on a good night."

Everyone laughed, but Katy was the only one who bothered to agree. "We noticed, but mom loves it. You'll probably have to keep up with your friend, especially with a baby on the way or Mom will keep loading up your plate anyway and force you to take whatever you don't eat back home with you."

"I'm sure that won't be a hardship, since I love a good home cooked meal."

Austin's hand never left my lower back as he guided me into the dining room. Then, the man surprised everyone by pulling my chair out for me. I'd never had anyone, including him, do that before. Things got a little awkward when he tried to slide me back in toward the table and nearly overdid it, then slid me back, and caused Dallas to burst out laughing.

"Damn, Bro, chill out before you give your baby momma motion sickness."

Everyone laughed as my face flamed, but a quick glance at Austin as he tucked himself into the seat beside me showed that his ears were on fire, too. I thought it was adorable that he was trying to take care of me, even if he bumbled it a little bit.

"So, Clea was telling us that you had a doctor's visit a few days ago. How is everything progressing?" Mrs. Mercer smiled as she waited for me to answer. I turned to Austin to give him the go-ahead to tell everyone what we were having.

"Are you sure?" He asked. I nodded and kept my eyes on him as he announced our news. "We found out it's going to be a boy!" He damn near yelled it, as if it had been painful to hold onto that information for four whole days. Oddly enough, Houston didn't seem the least bit surprised. Clea did, though."

"You knew all this time and didn't tell me?"

"We wanted to tell everyone at once," I explained as my eyes shifted to Houston and narrowed on him. He shrugged his shoulders and smiled at me. Yeah, Austin had blabbed, but obviously his brother was capable of keeping a secret.

"You knew?" Clea hissed at him in an accusing tone.

"I think that's lovely news," Mrs. Mercer interjected in an attempt to keep everyone positive. Then she looked at her husband. "Our oldest grandchild is going to be a boy who can look after any who come after him," she announced proudly.

"Like a girl being the oldest would have been a bad thing?" A woman asked from somewhere behind me. I turned to see Victoria standing there with someone else, half-assed hiding behind her. Oh no she didn't.

I had just been about to feel bad for her, since she was the oldest child and a girl, and her mother's announcement must have sounded like only a boy could be the protector of the others – even though I don't think she meant it that way. There was no way I was going to feel bad for her after she showed up with Jordan though. The whole family knew I was coming tonight, minus Clea. I'd asked Austin to spread the word to keep it a secret, to surprise her.

"Victoria Marie, what have you done?" Mrs. Mercer asked as she stood and turned to face her eldest daughter.

"What?" Victoria snapped haughtily at her mom.

"Vic, you should have told me," Jordan stated calmly, though she didn't bother moving from where she was mostly hidden behind the elder Mercer sibling.

"Why?" Vic asked as she turned to look at Jordan, which opened up the view for the rest of us to get a good look at her. "You've always been welcome to family dinners. I don't see any need to change that now." The eldest Mercer child turned her glare my way. "Not for anyone."

Wow. What had I ever done to piss her off?

"Vic, I don't know what's going on with you, but this is just making things worse. Why would you put me in this position?" Jordan cried. Then she glanced over and the pitiful look on her face, as she noticed Austin's arm wrapped around me, damn near made me feel sorry for her. Damn near, but I wasn't stupid and certainly hadn't forgotten what she'd put me and Austin through over the years.

"I'm sorry. You'll never know how sorry I am that I interfered with things between you." She was speaking directly to me. I nodded because it felt like everyone expected me to acknowledge her. I wouldn't go so far as to invite her to sit at the same table with me, but that seemed to be enough.

"Would you like to take a seat?" Mrs. Mercer asked her.

"No," Jordan shook her head as she backed up. "I didn't realize Austin or…" she trailed off, unable to say my name. "I didn't realize they'd be here, or I wouldn't have come. There's been enough trouble from me."

If that wasn't the truth, I didn't know what was. We all watched her leave before Victoria turned back to face her family.

"What?" She asked, as if she didn't already know the answer to that question. Her brother stood up from the table and I felt the lack of his warmth as his hand trailed away from my back.

"You knew that Becs would be here tonight."

"So?"

"So?" Austin mocked. "So, you decided to be a complete bitch and invite Jordan without telling her we'd be here? You didn't bother to warn me so that my pregnant girlfriend wouldn't be upset?"

"I didn't know you had a girlfriend anymore, pregnant or otherwise," she replied snidely.

"You know what I mean," he demanded. "Why would you hurt everyone this way, including Jordan?"

"It's not like you care about Jordan anymore," she spat at him.

"I will always care about Jordan. She's been in my life since we were babies. I might not like her very much right now, and she won't ever be close to me again the way we once were, and that's partly my fault for getting too involved when I shouldn't have, but that doesn't mean I want to see her purposely hurt by this family."

I couldn't fault him for anything he had to say.

"The worst part of what you did, is that you know Becs is pregnant with my baby and stress isn't good for pregnancy. You decided to put her in undo stress anyway all because you're miserable with whatever is going on in your own life and you decided to take it out on everyone else. You might be the oldest, Vic, but you need to grow the fuck up!"

Austin held his hand out to me. "I promised you nothing like this would happen if I brought you to meet the rest of my family. I've let you down and I'm so fucking sorry. Come on, we'll go somewhere else for dinner."

"It's not your fault," I tried to calm Austin, because it wasn't. I didn't blame him for this latest bit of drama, and for once, I couldn't blame Jordan for showing up either. This all fell on Victoria, who hated me for some reason.

"Why are you placating the bitch who helped you cheat on your lifelong girlfriend?" Victoria screamed at her brother.

"Jordan has never been my girlfriend and I have never cheated on anyone. Jordan had expectations that didn't align with mine, and if anything, she was the one who constantly tried to sabotage my relationships with Becs. All three times I tried to date Becs before, Jordan did everything in her power to drive her away. The crazy thing is that Jordan didn't try to do it this time. My own fucking sister did instead."

"She said…" Vic hesitantly tried to explain but was cut off by a voice from behind her.

"Sorry, I just realized I couldn't leave because Vic brought me here. Victoria, the first time they dated, I was angry because he hadn't said anything to me about our arrangement being over. It felt like he cheated on me, but that wasn't really true, since we were never together that way. The other times, we weren't together either. I just wanted us to be."

"But you said…" Victoria tried to argue with her.

"No. I'm sorry. I shouldn't have misled you, I just needed someone to hear how I felt, not what was true."

"Are you kidding me?" Victoria lashed out at her friend. "All this time, I thought my brother was doing you wrong and that woman was the one trying to ruin your relationship. Now, you're telling me it was the other way around? I should have known, I guess, since you faked a Goddamn pregnancy to try to trick my brother."

"Victoria," Mr. Mercer warned his daughter. "I think we've all had about enough drama. You brought Jordan here on a night when you knew she wasn't invited, you need to take her home. When you get back, you can apologize for ruining dinner and your brother's announcement."

"Oh God!" She cried before she turned and ran from the room with Jordan hot on her heels.

I felt sick to my stomach knowing that I was at the center of this family's pain. "I'm so sorry." The apology came out as a whimper.

"Stop," Austin ordered. "You don't have a damn thing to apologize for."

"I do, though. All of this is because of me," I argued.

"Becs?" Mr. Mercer called out to me. Hesitantly, I shifted my focus to the family's patriarch. "Seems to me you're the innocent party who got dragged in the middle of the mess my son made. Do not take that blame on yourself, none of us are putting it there, because it doesn't belong. I apologize that your first visit to our home was uncomfortable for you, and hopefully that won't ever be the case again. We welcome you back any time. We're a family with flaws like any other, so unlike my son, I'm not going to promise that everything will always run smoothly when you're here, but we will try to make sure everyone is respectful."

Mr. Mercer turned to Austin then. "Son, you make a promise to your woman, it better be one you can keep. Otherwise, you make the next best promise you know is in your power to honor. Don't make a fool out of yourself, and worse out of the woman you love."

"Understood," Austin answered back.

"I don't blame you for what happened here tonight," I told him. "Obviously, this was beyond your control."

"Well, tonight only happened because I didn't get my life under control years ago, when I should have," he admitted before he turned to look at everyone who was still gathered around the table. "I'm sorry for all the damn drama that everyone got dragged into because of me."

"S'ok," Dallas said with a mouthful of food. "Takes the heat off the rest of us for the stupid shit we do."

"Dallas!" His name was a warning from Mrs. Mercer. "Why don't we all take our seats and eat before everything gets cold?"

"No point wasting good food," Mr. Mercer added as he went back to loading his plate up.

"Are you okay? We can leave if you want?" Austin asked me. I shook my head and sat back down. Eventually, these people would be my son's family, and I needed to be able to work through the bumps in the road with them before he got here.

"Do you have a name picked out?" Katy asked excitedly.

I glanced at Austin and be both started to laugh. "We've ruled out a few, but haven't come to any decisions yet," he told his sister.

I wasn't about to tell his family that we ruled out Randy, and why that one had come up. Though, thinking about it did make me giggle.

"Oh, there must have been some doozies in the discard pile," Katy surmised.

"You could say that," I agreed and decided to give them a little something to laugh about. "My last name is Robinson." I hitched a thumb at Austin who grinned, knowing what I was about to divulge. "He threw out the suggestion of Christopher Robinson," I told them much to Dallas and Houston's amusement while Katy threw him a horrified look.

"You didn't, Aus. That's awful. Do you want your son to be bullied?"

"Did you not plan on using Mercer, then?" Mr. Mercer asked.

"It was my first joke of a suggestion," Austin explained. "Becs agreed that our son should have the Mercer surname, since she said our family is more of a family than hers and she wants him to feel that connection."

"Oh, honey!" Mrs. Mercer cried out before getting up from her seat and coming around to hug me yet again. The Mercer clan were a family of huggers that was for sure.

Clea made the 'I love you sign' to me from down at the other end of the table. I smiled back at her as Mrs. Mercer let go and allowed me to breathe again.

After the ice was officially broken on something other than mine and Austin's relationship drama, dinner ran smoothly. Victoria never did come back from taking Jordan home. I assumed her embarrassment kept her away, not that I could blame her. She had been fed the wrong information, just as Austin had many times over the years.

I didn't think Jordan would be randomly showing up, or invited, to family dinner anymore after this latest round of truth telling. Everyone seemed more than a little fed up with the way she had started to tear their family apart at the seams.

When we finally said our goodbyes, Austin yawned as he started the truck and pointed it in the opposite direction of my apartment.

"You're tired. You should just take me home."

"I am," he insisted.

"Um, no." I pointed in the opposite direction. "My place is that way, in case you forgot."

"Yeah, but my place is this way and it's closer. Besides, I wanted to show you something."

"No. Please, take me home – to my home." I reiterated in a frantic tone.

"What?" He slowed the truck, realizing that I was dead serious, and it wasn't up for negotiation. "Why?"

"You really need to ask me that?"

"Becs, I don't understand. I really wanted to show you something at the house. That can't happen unless you go there."

"If you think, for even a minute, that I will step foot inside that house ever again without there being a life-or-death emergency involving my son, you are sadly mistaken."

"You're serious?"

"As a heart attack."

Austin sighed, then checked his mirrors and blind spot before pulling a U-turn and heading back toward my house. "I explained that Jordan had no part in helping with that house, it was another one of her lies."

"It was also where we fell apart. It's the reason I have to plan on being a single parent. It's the reason I couldn't even function for weeks until I realized someone else was counting on me to pull my shit together," I yelled at him as I clutch my belly to indicate who that 'someone' was I had to get my stuff together for.

"Becs, Jesus. What the hell am I supposed to do to fix that? I own my home."

"Good for you, I guess."

"I planned on one day being able to bring my son and you home there," he tried to explain.

"Not happening."

It may have seemed stubborn, but that place had too many crappy memories attached to it. I didn't think I could even stomach looking at it from the street, let alone being forced to go inside.

"I don't get it, Becs. We've been getting along so well."

"How can you not get it? The last time I was there, you chose her. Our future together, the happy one I'd been dreaming about where I'd one day be your wife before we ever started a family, ended that last day I was at your house. I don't ever want to go there again."

"You know why. I thought she was pregnant and that I had to cut ties with you for my baby – not her! It was never about choosing her over you. I've told you that before."

"I was owed a damn conversation, Austin. I don't care why you did it. You just left me alone with my imagination and the last place I had to imagine you in was that house. The one I left you alone in with her. The one that was the last memory I had of you until I saw the two of you looking so much like a couple at the movie theater, then my imagination of what went on in that house grew by leaps and bounds. It doesn't matter what you say to me now. It doesn't matter that I know the truth is different. I had too much time to picture what was happening between the two of you, and that house was the backdrop for every single one of my nightmares."

"Fuck!" He yelled. Not at me, at himself, I think.

We both remained silent for the rest of the ride to my house. When he walked me to the door, I expected him to turn around and leave, but he shocked me by walking right inside behind me.

"I'm not going anywhere. Our problem is that one of us always runs from the nightmares instead of fighting them. I'm staying. We're not even going to talk about it. It's been a long night, we're both beat, and we need some sleep. I want to do that while holding you. We'll figure everything else out in the light of a new day, okay?"

"Okay," I agreed quietly. He was right. One of us was always taken the silent road. The first time he ghosted me, I'd ghosted him, too. It was just easier to forget my part in our lack of communication. That needed to change.

CHAPTER TWENTY-ONE

OVER THE NEXT FEW WEEKS, AUSTIN AND I TALKED ABOUT WHAT we wanted for the future. He was very adamant that he still wanted to be a family unit. I was still on the fence. While that had been the dream, our past left me worried about how long it would last before something spooked him or held more importance for whatever reason.

My hormones weren't helping with the decision-making process either, as I pointed out to him every time I shared one of my irrational fear flights of fancy.

"What nightmare scenario did you dream up today?" He asked when he came to pick me up for my appointment.

"I have to take a gestational diabetes test today," I admitted.

"Okay and what's that exactly?"

"They give you this sugary drink, make you chug the whole thing, and then test to see how long it takes you to process the sugar. I think." I shrugged because I wasn't a fucking doctor and didn't really know the mechanics behind the test. "I will have to wait an hour between drinking the crap and being tested. Are you sure you want to hang around that long?"

"I think I better because you haven't gotten to the weird part yet." He grinned at me as I gave him the stink eye.

"Well," I hedged, because of course I had a weird fear of the stupid test that every pregnant woman had to take. "What if the test is what gives me the diabetes?"

The jackass laughed at me.

"Why are you laughing? I'm serious."

"That's not how it works, Becs."

"That's how all the books claim it works. Haven't you seen all those jokes about the people who eat the sugary crap and end up with diabetes?"

"Yeah, I have and it's a bunch of shit. One of the guys from my fraternity was Type One. He had to be genetically predisposed to get it and he said his doctor told him it didn't matter what he ate, that his diet didn't cause it. The guy grew up with vegetarian parents who never allowed him to have soda or many sweets. I promise that drink is just a test and won't cause you to have it. If you do end up with it, we'll adjust to make sure you and our son stay healthy."

"Fine," I mumbled, though inside I was hopping around like a giddy schoolgirl. He wanted to help me adjust to stay healthy, if necessary. He meant business, too. Austin had rarely left my side unless one of us was working. Dallas stepped up and took over running the club at night, especially on the weekends, so that Austin could be with me. Houston had his other business to run. Austin went in during my work hours to get all the ordering, payroll, and business side of things taken care of.

They were eventually going to hire a management team to run the place when it was open so that Dallas could go back to whatever it was Dallas did and Austin could continue to work whatever hours he needed to between me and the baby, so that hopefully we wouldn't have to put our son in daycare when my maternity leave was up.

I still hadn't confided in Clea what was going on with Austin and me, though I had a feeling she already knew there was more to us than I ever let on.

I couldn't tell her now for the same reasons I never confided in her to begin with. I was worried that it wouldn't last, and she'd think I was an idiot for putting myself out there with him again. Okay, that wasn't it either, because as much as I valued her opinion, it wouldn't really matter in the end. My decision boiled down to what I felt in my heart. The problem was, I was afraid to admit it to myself, and if I told her everything, then that would be admitting to myself that I'd already given Austin the power to hurt me irrevocably.

As it turned out, I did not have gestational diabetes and the drink they made me chug, which was a gross orange concoction, did not make my pancreas stop producing the insulin the baby and I needed.

"You want to head back home, or do you need to go back to work?"

"Home. I took the day off just in case," I admitted.

Austin laughed at me again. "Just in case your drink gave you the sugars?"

"Hush!" He continued laughing at me as he drove. "You're a jerk."

"You still love me," he teased, though there was an edge to it when he ended and cringed over how I might react to that phrase.

"I do, you know. Despite everything that's happened between us, I've never fallen out of love with you. I've been angry, confused, and disappointed but underneath it all was still the love I've always felt for you."

"That's something I can work with," he said before pretending that driving took far more concentration than it did. Considering I saw a bit of moisture collecting in his eyes to go along with the relief he must have felt, he might have needed to concentrate a bit harder.

CHAPTER TWENTY-TWO

CLEA AND HOUSTON'S WEDDING WAS TWO DAYS BEFORE MY NEXT baby doc check-up, as Austin called them. I was in my third trimester with six weeks to go until delivery day. Hopefully. Dr. Danvers kept warning me that most women went over their due date. I refused to believe that bit of nonsense. I was not most women.

"Are you sure you want me wearing this?" I asked Clea for the third time.

"Yes, it looks gorgeous on you."

"But it's white," I argued.

"So, what. It's my wedding and you can wear white because I said so."

I chuckled at my best friend's testiness. She was the opposite of a bridezilla. Except where her shoes were concerned. "I'm really not too sure about this dress with these heels." She was like a broken record with that crap all morning.

"Oh hush, you'll be fine."

"Says my knocked-up bestie who gets to wear flats."

I laughed at her view of how unfair things were. "Well, you're the one who wouldn't wait until I got my figure back to march down the aisle toward your lover man."

"I still don't know why you aren't the one marching down the aisle, considering." She had the audacity to point at my burgeoning belly. I wanted to laugh about it, but I couldn't, so I offered a weak smile instead.

"It wasn't an option," I reminded her.

"I know he-"

I cut her off mid-sentence. "He asked, but you and I both know that it was done reluctantly." It had been a hair-trigger reaction to finding out I was pregnant. "Let's face it, we dated years ago for a short time." I pointed to my belly, still ready to perpetrate the lie I'd stuck with to convince myself, through my bestie, that my heart wasn't already down river with Austin's somewhere. "This happened as a result of a one-night stand years after he ghosted me for something that wasn't even my fault and didn't directly concern us. I couldn't agree to marry him." The truth was, he had never asked again, so I assumed it wasn't what he really wanted, despite all the time we'd spent together in recent months.

"He asked you to marry him," she spit out fully, as if I hadn't just contradicted his proposal.

"I know. I was there."

"Right, but I'm saying that he never asked Jordan to marry him when he thought she was pregnant with his kid. Even when he thought that's what was going on, the minute he found out that *you* were pregnant, he asked *you* to marry him."

"Probably because it was already a given that they were supposed to marry," I supplied, since she seemed to have forgotten about their stupid marriage pact.

"So, what? He was going to have two wives?"

"Those people in Utah do it, why not?"

Clea laughed at me. "Those people in Utah? Really Becs?"

"Yeah, I'm not trying to be some sister-wife and making

charts for who gets the asshole on which night. Plus, she would have seniority and I'm not playing second fiddle next to crazy-town who tried to fake a pregnancy when she doesn't even have a uterus."

Clea's eyes grew saucer-wide at my callous description. I pretended not to notice while adding on to one of my nightmare scenarios.

"Can you imagine? What if no one knew about her medical shit and she tried to cut me open and steal my baby like in those Lifetime movies or something?"

"I would never allow that to happen," Clea promised.

"Agh! Shit!" I yelped as I noticed Austin standing there in the mirror's reflection. He glared at me, as if I had grown two heads and both of them were hideous.

"You think I'd ever let anything happen to harm you or our baby?"

I was in a mood because I had to attend my best friend's wedding while forever-months pregnant with a full bladder, because it was perpetually full these days. And I was going to be a single mom in a matter of weeks. It was depressing and I was taking it out on Austin and anyone else who would accept my stupid, hormonal abuse.

"You harmed me, and you did it for her, so yeah."

"Son of a bitch!" He groaned before giving his attention to Clea instead of me. "This is for you. A gift from your groom. Your something blue," he told her before stomping out of the room in a tizzy.

"You could have said something," I fussed at my best friend. She had been facing the door and knew he was there.

"I gave you the eyes!" She insisted.

"What? No, you didn't. Your eyes always look wild." She had given me the eyes, but I thought she was scandalized over some-thing I said. "What am I supposed to do with that?" I doubled down as if I wasn't wrong.

I tried to distract her by pointing in the mirror. She looked amazing. We were wearing almost the same dress. Well, it was exactly the same style, but hers was made for skinny people and mine was made in whale size, or pregnant belly size, as Clea told me I needed to refer to it. The only difference, other than mine having way more belly room, was that hers was more of an ivory while mine was pure white, which I thought was kind of backward, but whatever. It was her wedding.

"Here, let me put this on you," I offered as I held up the gorgeous necklace her groom had just made his brother drop off for her. It was a platinum chain with a sapphire stone that was surrounded by a bunch of diamonds in the shape of a heart. Too cute.

"There's something here for you as well," Clea informed me as she opened a box up. "This is also your something blue," she told me. What the hell I needed something blue for was beyond me. She put the necklace around my neck, and I looked into the mirror to see what it was. The pendant that dangled off the chain was an angel with her hands spread out around a blue stone. I imagined that represented me and my baby boy.

"Thank you, this is beautiful. You didn't have to," I cried and swiped at the stupid tear that threatened to ruin my makeup.

"I didn't do it," Clea informed me.

"Then who?" I tried to take it off because I didn't like accepting gifts from unknown people. When I thought it was a thank you gift for participating in my bestie's wedding, I'd been willing to take it. Not that she needed to get me anything to be in her wedding, but you know. Who was I to break traditions?

"Leave it!" She ordered. "He's trying to make amends. Let him. For your peace of mind and the baby's."

Oh! It had come from Austin then. God, I was stupidly in love with that man, but my worries about him never went away. I wish I could chalk them up to my weird irrational fears, but with everything we'd been through, I was afraid it just boiled down to not wanting to repeat history.

"Yeah?" I finally managed to get out. "What if he flakes on us after the baby comes?"

"Then we bury him where no one will ever find his corpse."

"I have a shovel," a gravelly voice called out from the door. Oops, someone else we failed, or at least I failed, to notice.

"Hi Daddy!" Clea shuffled to the man, in the heels that I was surprised she still managed to keep on her feet. Then she threw her arms around him and hugged him tightly. I wished I had that. He hadn't been there much while Clea was growing up because he was off doing the military thing and earning money. Still, he was there for her on her important day.

I'd supported my parents for a little over a year after my father lost his job. I even worked a second job to do it, and when I called to tell them I was pregnant, they were too put out about being grandparents to even ask if I was doing okay.

"You ladies ready?" Clea's dad asked.

"Yep," she grinned at the man as she spoke.

"Let's go," I offered as I lifted my dress up in my hands and headed for the doors that would open so my best friend could walk down the aisle to her own Mr. Texas and their future together.

When I got closer, I realized the doors were already open and saw that Austin was making a fool of himself at Clea's wedding. Damn him.

"Um," I hesitated to tell her.

"Something wrong?" She asked as they moved closer. Clea looked guilty as she asked though, almost like she already knew what I'd seen.

"Either you made my baby daddy your Maid of Honor or he's standing in the wrong place," I explained.

That was when Mr. Mercer popped out of the shadows and

yanked me into a hug. "Take a leap of faith and let me walk you down the aisle to a better future with my boy."

"But he…"

"Is your one, just like you're his," Mr. Mercer explained in no uncertain terms. "He messed up big time, and if he does it again, I'll bring my own damn shovel along to help with that body." He pulled back and winked at me. I couldn't help but smile at the man as his eyes twinkled with humor and something else that I'd been missing all my life. The love of a father.

Dammit. My makeup probably wouldn't survive the next five minutes, never mind the rest of the day. I honestly couldn't tell you where Clea was or why I was the one being walked arm-in-arm by my very soon-to-be father-in-law first. All I could see was a blurry version of Austin waiting for me at the end of the flower-strewn aisle.

"You take care of her and love her until your dying breath," Mr. Mercer told his son before he placed my hand in Austin's.

"That's a promise I intend to keep," he told his dad. The conversation they had at the first family dinner I ever attended came back to me then. His father had warned him to never promise me anything he didn't know for sure he could deliver.

Austin reached up and swiped away the tears that started to fall as Clea made her way to his other side, where her father gave her away to Houston. Something red grazed mine and Austin's arms just before another hit Clea in the butt. I turned to see Dallas standing there looking like a complete idiot in a diaper with a bow and arrow dangling from his hand.

"I think I got it right this time," he shouted, winked at Clea, and then took off running. Austin tipped a finger under my chin to drag my attention back to him before I could see where Dallas ended up. His momma was probably going to tan his hide later, whether he was an adult or not.

Houston and Clea mumbled something to one another, but I didn't hear what it was as I got lost in those deep, soulful eyes of my husband-to-be. I was trying to figure out how in the hell I managed to be a surprise guest at my own wedding?

I hate to say that I barely recall the actual ceremony. I was in a state of shock as I repeated vows when the minister asked me to. Austin tried to slip a ring on my finger, but my knuckles were too swollen, so he left it in his pocket and teased that he'd attach it to my necklace later. I didn't have a ring for him, considering I didn't even know I was getting married, so our vows took a little less time than Clea and Houston's who shook as they each placed a ring on the other's finger.

"Austin and Rebecca," the minister addressed us before turning to the other couple. "Houston and Clea," I now pronounce you all husband and wife, you may each kiss your own brides, but not each other's," he teased in the end much to everyone's amusement.

I chuckled through the kiss Austin smooshed onto my open mouth. "I'll do better later," he promised.

"I'll hold you to that." It was the first coherent thing I think I said throughout the ceremony.

"Are you okay with this?" He asked worriedly.

"Yeah. Kinda wish I knew it was coming, but it was the best sort of surprise."

"Good. Now, let's go get the party started before you fall asleep on me."

We turned and started down the aisle in the opposite direction, smiling at the well-wishers who stood on either side. We were about halfway down the aisle when I was tugged back a bit because Austin was stopped by someone holding him back. The first thing I noticed was the woman's hand, then my eyes traveled up to find Jordan there pleading with her eyes and Austin smiling down at her.

You had to be kidding me.

On. My. Wedding. Day.

I glanced around, looking for Mr. Mercer, so he could fulfill his promise and bring his shovel, but I didn't see him, so instead, I dislodged Austin's arm from mine and took off at a fast-paced waddle. Luckily for me, the leach – I mean Jordan – didn't seem inclined to let him go so he could follow me. That gave me a head start as he attempted to peel her hand off his arm without hurting her.

Someone had to invite the bitch to the wedding. If it had been Austin, I was going to file for an annulment immediately. Actually, I hadn't signed any paperwork, so I didn't think an annulment would even be necessary.

"Becs!" Austin called after me as I made it through the door of the little chapel where we'd just gotten married. His family, along with Clea – who I guess was his family now, too – were all hot on my heels as well.

"Becs, wait!" Clea called out. For her, I stopped and turned and let everyone get a load of the hurt, anger, and betrayal I felt.

"Why would you invite her to a wedding I didn't even know about?" I screamed at Austin.

"I didn't invite her. I haven't even seen her since the last time Vic tried to bring her to family dinner."

I glanced around at everyone else who gathered near us. Someone had shut the doors once the family was through, so that none of the guests would witness the drama.

"I invited her," Mrs. Mercer spoke up, shocking just about everyone present. She used to be one of my favorite people.

"Why in the hell would you invite the woman who tried to ruin my relationship with Becs, three times over, to our wedding?" Austin fumed at his mother. His palpable fury was the only thing stopping me from thinking about that unnecessary annulment.

His mother looked at me when she answered. "She needed to see that Austin was serious about you. She needed to see him marry someone else, so she could move on. It was the least I could do for my friend Lydia, since she can't be here to help her daughter."

Nope. That was not going to fly with me, and I didn't care who didn't like what I was about to say.

"So, to hell with the fact that what *I needed* on my surprise wedding day, was to **NOT** see the woman who attempted to destroy my relationship on more than one occasion?" A sinister chuckle left my mouth before I could speak again.

"What am I saying? She didn't just attempt it. She did destroy it. Three times. And you invited her to what was supposed to be my special day. Austin and I have been working hard on rebuilding a relationship that is still not on completely solid ground. I just went through with a wedding after your husband asked me to take a leap of faith, only to find out that another Mercer family member, my supposed mother-in-law now, betrayed me by putting that woman above my needs yet again!" I growled what must have sounded like an absolutely insane noise of frustration.

"You ruined my wedding day so that Jordan could get closure?" Austin asked his mother.

"I'm so sorry. I didn't think of it like that at all. I thought you would support anything that meant she would never be an issue for you again." Her apology was directed at me, once again, and not her son.

"You made her an issue for me again. That vile woman touched him. She reached out and held onto him, not five minutes after we said our vows, and Austin stopped escorting me down the aisle to allow it and rewarded her with a smile. What exactly did she learn? Beside the fact that she was once again prioritized over me ON MY OWN WEDDING DAY."

"I was smiling because you just married me," Austin corrected. "I only stopped because someone grabbed hold of my arm and I didn't want to accidentally trip you up. My reaction had zero to do with Jordan and everything to do with you on all counts."

"Do you think Jordan will see it that way?" I asked him.

"Fuck!" He hissed through his teeth and then turned an icy cool glare on his mother. "I wish you would have informed me that you invited her. I would have told you what a horrible idea that was."

"I'm sorry. I thought I was helping everyone move on."

"Let's get this clear right now. The only helpful thing to do where Jordan is concerned, is to not have her in the picture at all. If she's going to be at your house visiting you, then make it very clear to us, so that we aren't there."

"She's been your best friend your entire life. I realize things are messy and that she screwed it all up, but she doesn't have anyone else. Her mother was my best friend and I promised to look after her."

I understood where Mrs. Mercer was coming from. I truly did. Some people were beyond helping though. If Jordan had learned her lesson, she would have turned down the invitation, knowing that her presence would cause problems. Not only did she not turn it down, but she had to insert herself, too. Looking back, I was surprised she hadn't objected at some point. Then again, I didn't recall the minister asking if there were any objections. Someone must have instructed him not to.

"Mom, Jordan threw our friendship away when she lied and attempted to destroy every single chance I took at dating someone else. But she burned that bridge completely when she faked a pregnancy, that she wasn't even capable of, to ruin things for Becs and me again. If you want to honor your relationship with her because her mom was your best friend before she died – then you can do that. If there are any further surprises of Jordan being invited into our lives," he insisted as he waved his hand back and forth between us, "then you will be severing ties with my new family for Jordan's sake."

Holy crap. He really just threatened to cut his family out for me. To keep us away from Jordan.

"Whoa!" Austin's father called out as he came inside, with Jordan in tow. "What the hell, Austin?"

"Get her out of here, now!" Austin yelled at his father.

"I was just escorting her out, as I didn't think she should be here today, all things considered."

"Austin," Jordan pleaded.

"Never mind. Enjoy the party without us. We're leaving," Austin said to his parents while ignoring Jordan who started crying. My new husband took my hand in his and began to lead me out of the chapel.

"Austin!" His father called. We both stopped so he could look back. "I'm taking care of this. Why don't you and Becs go get changed and by the time you're comfortable, there won't be any reason left here that you can't enjoy the party, too."

I supposed that was his nice way of saying that Jordan wouldn't be there any longer. Truthfully, I was tired and just wanted to go take a long nap, after crying, maybe with a gallon of ice cream in my lap for comfort.

Austin's mom had good intentions. I knew that. She didn't do what she'd done to hurt anyone. That didn't mean that her actions hadn't felt like another blow to my self-esteem. Jordan's issues always came before my comfort. Except tonight, my husband had put me first, above her, above his family. He had placed me at the top of his priorities to keep safe. His promise remained intact, and I felt a bit more trust fall into place between us as a result.

CHAPTER TWENTY-THREE

ALL OF US SAT DOWN TO DINNER AT THE MERCER'S FAMILY HOUSE two weeks later. It was the first time I'd been in the same space as Shirley since the wedding, though Jacob had come to see us the following day. He apologized for his wife's misguided efforts to make Jordan see that Austin was not meant for her.

Once everyone was settled around the table, Shirley stood. "I owe everyone here an apology," she stated succinctly. "I took a special day for all of you," she looked at Clea and Houston, then Austin and myself, "and I ruined it by trying to force Jordan to see that Austin was never meant for her. I felt responsible because I'm the one that put the idea in Lydia's head, and she pushed it on Jordan in an unhealthy way for years. I felt completely responsible for everything that girl has done to try to get my son's attention, including destroying your relationship by lying to him," she added while looking right at me. "I thought I was fixing things not making them worse, and I apologize because I didn't see the bigger picture or how precarious things still were for you and Austin.

"I'm happy to see that the two of you are still together and working through everything. That's all, I just… I don't expect any of you to forgive me. I just wanted to explain and apologize."

"I understand, Mrs. Mercer," I started to say.

"Oh, sweetheart, stop that and either call me Shirley as I deserve right now, or Mom when you can stand to look at me again. There are three Mrs. Mercers sitting at this table right now, it'll be pretty darn confusing if you keep that up."

I laughed at her unintentional humor because she was right. Clea and I had both legally taken the Mercer name as our own. "Okay, I just wanted to say that I understand and while you don't need it, you have my forgiveness. Jordan grew up like another daughter to you. When we weren't in the thick of things, I remembered that."

Shirley swiped at the tears that started to fall as I spoke. "You are too good for all of us," she commented before taking her seat again. Mr. Mercer, Jacob, rubbed his wife's back before leaning in and placing a sweet kiss on her cheek.

"Proud of you," I heard him mumble to her.

"Why is my mother crying?" Victoria asked as she blew into the house. She had been the only Mercer not present for her brothers' joint wedding. There was very little surprise there.

"It's of no matter to you," Shirley explained to her daughter.

"Okay, whatever." Victoria moved around the table to the chair she was supposed to sit in, that usually remained empty. Then she looked at me. "I hope you're happy with yourself."

"Fuck, Vic!" Austin groaned. "What now?"

"Jordan is moving away, as in out of town. It isn't fair that I couldn't even invite her over for one last family dinner, so she could say goodbye before she leaves tomorrow, all because *she's* here."

The woman just couldn't let things go, and I didn't understand why, especially now that she'd heard the truth about what had really gone down between Austin, Jordan, and me.

"All you had to do was text your brother that she was coming to dinner tonight, and we wouldn't have shown up," I explained.

"So, you're just going to hold my brother hostage and not allow him to say goodbye to his life-long friend?"

I shook my head and looked at Austin. He could handle his cranky, belligerent sister. I was done with her bullshit and the attitude she threw my way.

"As I told everyone at my wedding, you know the one you failed to even show up to?" He questioned her. "I already said my goodbyes to Jordan. She burned all her bridges with me."

"Because of her," Vic pointed at me as she lobbed her accusation my way.

"No," Houston stood and approached his sister. "Austin let Jordan go because she could never be honest, and she was always sabotaging his life. Shit, Vic, she tried to bring down our fucking bar, too."

"No, she didn't."

"Yeah, she did. Ask her about the sexual harassment claim she lobbed against your brother. It wasn't just the drama with the fake baby, or any of the other lies to get Becs away from him over the years. She lied to the authorities about him sexually harassing her and threatening to fire her if she didn't 'perform' for him."

"What?" I asked as I turned to Austin to see his reaction. It was the first I was hearing about this.

"It happened during the time when we weren't really speaking, but after I learned she faked her pregnancy. We let her go from her job and she tried to make a claim for unemployment, despite getting a severance package. She tried to claim that was hush money."

"Oh, dear Lord," Shirley called out from her end of the table. "Why didn't you boys tell us? That makes what I did even worse."

"No, it doesn't," I assured her and reached over and patted her hand. Mr. Mercer beamed at me. Victoria threw me a hateful look, but it was mellowed a bit compared to the norm.

"Why would she do that?" Vic asked.

"Why did she do any of the bullshit she did?" Austin asked. "The girl was fucking disturbed, and it took unraveling her lies to finally see it because none of us wanted to notice before."

"Hopefully, she gets some fucking therapy wherever she ends up," Dallas chimed in as he continued to take advantage of everyone else being caught up in the drama, so that he could fill his plate.

"Vic, I know you want to believe the best in her because you took her under your wing after her mom died, but it's no one's fault she's leaving town. She made that choice on her own, just like she chose to start all the drama she did." Houston sat back down and tucked his wife up in his arm. Her eyes were on me though.

"Sorry," she mouthed to me.

I shrugged my shoulders back. What could we do? I'd entered into this family with a bunch of drama, and it didn't seem to be going anywhere anytime soon. Truthfully, I'd take the drama over the whole lot of nothing I experience with my own family.

"You all act like Austin's girlfriend-"

"Wife," Austin corrected quickly.

"Whatever, you act like she's not the real reason."

"That's because she's not, Vic," Houston cut in again. "I don't know why you felt compelled to come throw this fit tonight, but it's not cool. Get your facts and priorities straight before running your damn mouth. One day, you're going to realize life isn't as simple as you try to make it out to be," her younger brother lectured.

"Oh, she knows, since she's dating a married man," Katy tattled on her big sister.

"What the fuck?" Dallas snarled as he turned toward her. "Tell me you're not!"

Every bit of color that had been there before, drained from Victoria's face, before she turned and fled. Dallas charged off out of the house after his sister while the rest of us sat there in stunned silence for a full minute before Jacob growled at Katy.

"Explain!"

"Vic's been seeing Devin behind Dallas's back for years, even before he married his long-time girlfriend. Honestly, I think he only kept the girlfriend around to keep Dallas off their backs because he caught them once and forbid them from being together again because his friend was such a player. He only forbade them to protect Vic. The thing is, Dallas wasn't wrong to do it, because Devin wasn't exactly using Justice as a typical beard, since they were having sex, too."

Katy took a quick breath and then jumped back into her synopsis of what had been going on with her big sister.

"Justice ended up pregnant, so Devin married her, but I don't think he ever stopped seeing Vic. His wife lost the baby a few days after the wedding. So, Victoria thought she still had a chance to be with Devin, who she's been in love with for years, only I think Devin actually fell in love with his wife after everything they just went through together."

"Where in the hell did we go wrong with these kids?" Mr. Mercer asked his wife.

"Maybe family dinner isn't such a good idea this week," Shirley mumbled. "I'll pack food up for all of you to take home."

She left to go to the kitchen and Houston and Austin got up, as if to go ahead and leave. That was when angry Jacob came out. "Don't piss me off by making your mother more upset than she already is," he warned his boys. "You will stay long enough to accept the food she packs for you. Then, you can go and talk about the latest Mercer family drama in private. Until then, keep quiet." He got up and headed for the kitchen to go help his wife, all the while he muttered to himself something about how he should have raised dogs instead of kids because they were easier.

CHAPTER TWENTY-FOUR

THREE WEEKS LATER

"I STILL THINK YOU LOOK LIKE THE BEST KIND OF TROUBLE," AUSTIN whispered in my ear as he came up behind me at the party. He reached around my shoulder and held his palm upright with a beautifully wrapped gift box sitting in it.

I glanced back over my shoulder and smiled at him as I took the gift and began unwrapping it while it rested on my ginormous belly. When I got it opened, there was a charm bracelet inside.

"It tells our story," Austin explained. He pointed to the charm on the far left near the catch. It was a tiny little die in a bubble. "This is because you were trouble from the start."

I giggled. "Where on Earth did you find that?"

"Special request from a jeweler," he admitted. "This one, was for the second chance that I blew." It was a miniature replica of a popcorn container. "The bow and arrow is actually two-fold. It represents the end of my second chance and the beginning of the third."

That was a no-brainer, since both happened on Valentine's Day. The next charm nearly made me cry because it was a sunflower, and I knew exactly what day that represented.

"The best date ever," he said. Then he pointed to the next charm. It was a ghost. "My worst mistake came next." He skimmed past that one and tapped the next. It was a baby bottle. "Happiest day of my life, knowing that I'd have a chance to have a family with you, even if it wasn't how I always pictured it." Yup, the tears that threatened a moment ago started making wet tracks down my face. He pointed to the last charm on the bracelet. The one that wasn't a charm at all. It was my wedding ring.

"I think you know what this one was. One day, we'll move it to your finger." He lifted the charm bracelet and moved around in front of me to hold my wrist up between us. Austin worked the clasp so that it locked around my wrist and dangled there with the weight of our relationship between us.

"I don't want to forget a thing because I never want us to become lax and forget that we're always worth fighting for."

"Why are you trying to turn me into a blubbering sap at a Halloween party, Austin?"

He leaned in and kissed my nose while sneakily wiping away my tears. "I'm not. I just wanted you to know how much I love you on your birthday."

Dammit. My husband was too sweet for his own good these days. "I love you, too. Thank you." I traced the black letters on his white t-shirt that said, "This is my costume." He kept it simple yet again. That's okay because I did too. I wore a simple white dress and pinned a nametag on my chest that said: Virgin Bride. I thought it went well with my huge, pregnant belly.

The same belly that hardened and scrunched painfully for a minute before the feeling went away. "Are you okay? You went quiet and pale for a minute there."

"I think my birthday and another Halloween party in combination might be a bit too much…" I was about to say excitement, I swear, but then my stomach did that crunch thing again and I lost my breath.

"Holy shit, Becs! Are you going into labor?" Austin asked.

"What?" I huffed the word out because it was hard to catch my breath. "No. I still have…" Fuck me! The tightening of my belly happened again before I could remind him that I still had a week until my due date and Dr. Danvers kept telling us at each visit that first time moms almost always go into labor late.

"I'm calling Doc." He pulled his phone out and while he dialed, he yelled across the noisy bar. "Houston!"

I swear to God, everyone in the room quieted and even the music turned down a notch or seven.

"What?" Houston yelled back as he dragged my best friend along with him to come see what his brother bellowed for.

"Becs is in labor," Austin announced just as a gush of warm liquid trickled down my thighs and onto the floor below me.

"Please, tell me that didn't just happen," I begged. When I glanced back up, everyone's eyes were trained on the floor and my wet feet.

Houston caught one of the servers, who was passing by, and directed her to put the wet floor cones up and get one of the dishwashers to come out and clean up the 'spill'. Then he moved ahead of us to clear a path to the back door, so we could get to the employee parking lot.

"I'll run to the house and grab your bag and meet you guys at the hospital," Clea offered helpfully.

"Hurry," I told her as Austin guided me to his car. We were still living in Clea's place while Austin waited to see if not-so-hormonal-me wanted to keep his house and redecorate or sell the damn thing and buy a new one. My vote was still to buy something new. It might have been his dream home, but I couldn't shake the negative feelings associated with it.

Luckily, he understood.

~*~

Five hours later

"We never did come up with a name for him," Austin reminded me as he held our son for the first time.

"I did."

"Were you going to share with the class or keep it secret until you had to fill out his school paperwork?" I laughed along with Dr. Danvers as she took care of the afterbirth situation that I had going on.

"Jacob Austin Mercer," I blurted out my idea for our son's name. My poor, beautiful, emotional husband cried big fat tears all over our newborn son.

"It's perfect."

"I know."

BONUS CHAPTER 5

AUSTIN'S POV

"Stop blaming yourself," Houston growled, again. As if that would happen just because he insisted. We'd both watched as Becs' friend, Houston's blind date for the night, fell all over herself to get to another man.

"I never would have set you up with the chick if Becs hadn't talked up how virtuous she was so often. It was like a broken fucking record hearing how perfect her best friend was and how choosy with men. I'm really sorry, man."

Houston offered little more than a nod of his chin. "We all know shit happens. Never met the woman before, not like she cheated on me and got knocked up with someone else's kid after dating me for years."

"Fuck man! That's exactly why I thought she would be a good trial date to get back out there. After what Samantha did to you, a good girl was exactly what you needed. Unfortunately, my girlfriend lied to me about everything."

"Stop, Aus. She didn't lie. Shit happens. Another man got to her first. It's my loss because I was supposed to wait by the front door so we wouldn't miss one another, and then fucking Dallas had to go around nailing everyone with his arrows."

Our younger brother showed up to the party dressed as Cupid. The idiot shot several people in the ass and other questionable places, forcing Houston and me to clean up his messes while he ran off, presumably to duck out of the party before he got his ass beat by someone.

His antics made it impossible to track down Becs and Clea until it was too late, and we watched the latter leave the party hand-in-hand with another man. Houston might act like he wasn't affected, but to a man who had his ego crushed by his ex-girlfriend, or fiancé, I wasn't quite sure of their status before it was all called off. Either, way, he already suffered a major blow when he learned she'd not only been cheating but was pregnant by someone else.

So, to have another woman agree to go on a date with him and then end up in the arms, or hands, of another man couldn't have done anything good for my brother. The setup had been about getting him dating again, not delaying the process.

Still, I took a deep breath and tried to think through my anger logically. Becs couldn't help the things her friend did. She would probably come here later, apologize, and tell me exactly that. There had to be a good damn explanation for what happened to set my brother back again.

"I'm headed upstairs to study. I'll have my headphones on, so no worries about bothering me when Becs gets here."

"Night," I called out as he headed up the stairs toward his bedroom. It was weird that Houston really didn't seem bothered. It was almost like he just didn't care and maybe that was worse. He was still too numb from the whole Samantha thing.

I managed to grab a beer from the fridge and sit in my comfy chair in the corner of the room to take a load off, when I heard the key turning in the door. That was weird, considering Houston was upstairs and the only other people who had a key had been Samantha, before she became Houston's ex, and Jordan, who was only supposed to hold my extra key for emergency situations. It couldn't be her anyway since she was supposed to be out of town.

When I glanced up, the beer nearly slipped from my fingers at the sight that greeted me. Jordan stood there in nothing more than an open coat and some very tiny, baby blue lingerie.

"What in the hell are you doing here, and dressed like that," I asked her.

Jordan grinned at me. "What are you doing sitting all alone in the corner of your living room on Valentine's Day?"

"Honestly, Jordan?" She nodded her head quickly, apparently waiting to hear that my night went to shit, and I no longer had a girlfriend.

"My girlfriend is dealing with a mess her best friend made tonight, and when she's done, she's supposed to head over. So, what I'm doing is sitting here waiting for her. What you're doing right now is trying to ruin everything."

She rolled her eyes as if I was being ridiculous. "Did it ever occur to you that your supposed girlfriend and friend messed things up tonight on purpose?"

"What the hell do you even know about tonight?"

"I know what your sister told me. That bitch's bestie was supposed to be Houston's blind date. I went to that party to see you, to apologize for how I reacted before."

"Why the fuck would you go there to do that on Valentine's Day when you knew I had a date?"

"Just shut up and listen, I'm getting to that."

"Fine, but hurry up, because Jordan, if Becs shows up and you're still here, especially looking like that," I pointed at the almost non-existent clothing she wore, "things will not go well. If you ruin this thing I have with her, we won't go back to being fuck buddies because we will no longer be friends."

"Nice to see who your priority is," she sniffed. "Anyway, your girlfriend and her buddy set you up."

"What the fuck did you just say?" My calm tone belied the war raging in my mind. I sat my beer down on the table beside the chair and kicked back, legs spread, in what I'm sure looked like a relaxed position, but was more about keeping my ass in the chair instead of strangling the woman I once called my best friend.

"You humiliated her when I was there after your movie date that night. Truthfully, you humiliated me too, but that's something I can get over. Apparently, she couldn't. She told you about her saintly friend, but have you ever even met the woman?"

Shit. Jordan unknowingly hit a nerve. I wondered why Becs spoke so highly of Clea, who happened to be her roommate and best friend, yet she seemed to go out of her way to keep us from interacting. I'd been wondering why lately, but when she suggested setting Clea and Houston up because they sounded perfect for one another, I thought maybe it was just me over-thinking things.

"You never met her because you weren't supposed to. They've been plotting a way to get back at you. A woman like Becs doesn't give men second chances. She has a reputation on campus of going through men like water. Usually, she's the one to do the dumping and humiliating."

That last part didn't sound right at all, but I wasn't about to stop whatever tear Jordan found herself on.

"They planned it out," she insisted when I said nothing.

"What do you think Becs will say about that accusation when she gets here? That is, if she'll even entertain hearing me out considering you're standing in front of me wearing only a couple scraps of lace."

"She won't show up. That's why I'm here, wearing this." Jordan waved her hands in front of herself, indicating the ensemble she chose to wear that night. "I didn't want your Valentine's Day to be completely ruined by that hateful woman who only pretended to be understanding about our relationship."

"You have that much wrong. She never pretended to be okay with you, or your place in my life."

Jordan huffed. "That's exactly why she's playing this game, Aus. She realized that you would never let me go. I'm too important to you. I am more important than she'll ever be. She can't compete with our history or the link we have with our families, and how they've wanted to see us together from the very beginning."

It was disconcerting to hear Jordan's twist on the same worries that Becs had thrown in my face about my best friend and what my family thought of her. My girlfriend had been right about the problems she would face in a relationship with me if Jordan remained a part of the equation. Jordan had just proved that point herself.

"When was your ex-girlfriend supposed to show up?"

I glanced at the clock on the wall, above where Jordan stood, and ignored the way she added 'ex' before girlfriend when she asked. It had been an hour and a half since I left the party. That meant Becs was thirty minutes late already. A quick peek at my cell phone showed no missed calls or messages. There was no way Jordan was right about all this. There had to be a plausible explanation. I continued to think that as Jordan finally took a seat on the couch. My best friend stared at me, as if waiting for me to come to the realization she'd presented for me.

Three hours later, my phone was still dark, Jordan had fallen asleep on the couch, and Becs never showed up. An ache developed in my chest the likes of which I thought would send me to the hospital. Was it possible for someone in their early twenties to have a heart attack? It sure the fuck felt like it. I rubbed the spot over my chest as my brother came strolling through.

"Sorry, thought you went to bed already," Houston whispered before he glanced down and noticed Jordan sleeping on the couch. It was the first time I'd given anything more than a modicum of attention to her. Her legs were splayed, the coat she'd been wearing earlier was discarded on the back of the couch, and every asset she had to work with was available for anyone to see.

"You're a fucking idiot," Houston grumbled as his eyes returned to meet mine.

"Why is that exactly?"

"Becs is a good person. Are you really going to throw her away for a cheap roll in the hay with that?" He asked while pointing at Jordan. I could have sworn I saw the woman flinch, and maybe Houston did, too.

"She may be your friend, but she's been obsessed with you since childhood, and hasn't really given a fair shake to anyone else who has come into your life, thanks to her parents pressuring her all those years. She isn't the woman for you, Aus. All three of us know that. Jordan doesn't want to lose you and she's desperate. That, I get. What's your excuse?"

"Excuse for what, Houston?"

"What's your excuse for sitting here in the dark with your naked best friend within reach, not to mention within view of the windows, while your girlfriend is out there probably thinking your angry with her for a choice her friend made?"

"She said she would meet me here before she took off to go check on Clea."

"Yeah? How receptive to knocking on the door do you think she was when she noticed Jordan's car outside?"

"How the hell would she know what Jordan's car looked like?"

"You really are an idiot. Aus, Jordan was there, standing by her car that she conveniently parked behind yours, at the movie theater that night you almost lost your girl. If you don't think Becs noticed exactly what she was driving, you are even more of a dumbass than I ever thought you were."

"Fuck, do you think that's why she never showed or called?"

"You told her that Jordan was out of town for a while, and at the first sign of trouble, there she is naked on our couch. Not that Becs would know that. It does bring something else to question, though. Why the hell didn't you kick Jordan out the minute she showed up at the door?"

"She let herself in with the key," I informed him.

"You should have taken her key back when you had your talk months ago."

"I didn't even remember she had a key until she used it tonight. I only gave her a copy in case I lost or forgot mine and couldn't get a hold of you."

"Do me a favor and get it back. The last thing I need, is to start dating someone and have them get the wrong idea about the woman who showed up to the house in a barely-there panty and bra set. What would you have done if Becs did come last night and saw Jordan here dressed that way?" Again, he pointed to Jordan as if I didn't know what he was talking about.

"I honestly don't know. It's not like I had any control over the situation."

"That's just it, Aus. You had plenty of control, you just didn't use it. The minute you heard that key in the door, you should have been on your feet, going to see who it was. The second you realized it was Jordan, you should have sent her packing, but especially if you realized that was all she was wearing. If I were Becs, even if I'd shown up and nothing was going on, I would have dumped your ass for not turning her away immediately."

"She's my best friend," I tried to explain. "I couldn't just turn her away like she didn't matter."

"And isn't that why Becs had a hard time trusting you with a second chance?"

"What?"

"Man, you can't have a female best friend hanging around, who you've been fucking for years, while you try to establish a relationship with another woman. The 'she's my best friend' excuse stopped being plausible the minute you stuck your dick in Jordan. As far as any woman is concerned from here on out, she's an ex who is competition that won't go away, and if you tell them that you allowed her to stay in your house wearing only her underwear because she matters, you're basically saying she matters more than they do."

"That's bullshit."

"No, it's not, man. No woman would be okay if she showed up to your house and saw that. I can see her pussy from here," my brother pointed out, which of course made me look. I winced to see he was right. Jordan hadn't even bothered to class things up. She went straight for cheap and visible with her look.

"Aus, if you allow Jordan to get away with this level of bad behavior, only minutes after getting mad at your girlfriend for the first time, then I'd say Becs' point was proven. Jordan will always be a problem for you. You keep putting her first, and Becs won't be the only woman you lose because of her, and we already know there have been others, but this one meant something to you too. Are you really willing to lose her for that?" Again, he pointed at my best friend while using a tone that felt more like he was calling her trash.

My brother shook his head as he glanced between Jordan and me one more time before nailing me with a heated stare. "You may have already lost Becs, tonight."

"You're right about that."

"Why do you say it like that?"

"Houston, Jordan pointed something out to me last night," I started to say only to have my brother lose all decorum and laugh so loudly there was no way Jordan could have slept through it.

"Seriously? Your crazy best friend showed up at our place, let herself in with a key she shouldn't still have, wearing only lingerie, and she doesn't have an agenda she's speaking from? Aus, you can't be that fucking stupid."

"If she was wrong, then where is Becs?"

"I don't care what story she whipped up to get you to turn on your girlfriend that quickly, but I will remind you that your girl gave you the benefit of the doubt and took you back when Jordan got in between you two before. Funny, that you're not willing to give the same benefit of the doubt to Becs, and instead you're taking whatever bullshit Jordan slung your way as the truth when she clearly meant to fuck things up for you by coming here like that tonight."

Houston made a good point. Plus, he was right earlier, if Becs had noticed Jordan's car outside, it would explain why she wouldn't even bother to come up to the door and knock. She would also be angry enough to refuse to call. Why in the hell was I still sitting in my living room, with Jordan lying in her lingerie only a few feet away, when I needed to make things right with my girl? I blew out a frustrated breath because I felt like I was being ripped apart by my girlfriend and best friend. Neither of them wanted me to have the other in my life, and it fucking sucked.

"I'll fix everything in the morning," I promised my brother, and myself.

"You're still an idiot. Good luck fixing things after Becs thinks you spent the night with her," once more he pointed at Jordan before turning his back on us and the room. "There won't be any way for you to get around telling her that either, because I have a feeling your supposedly innocent little bestie will make sure she knows if she doesn't already. Get that key back, I mean it!"

"Will do," I called out to his retreating form.

Thirty minutes later, Jordan stretched, and the movement caused her breasts to thrust upward, almost unnaturally, in the air. There was no physical reaction on my part, which is what I wished I could make Becs understand. My cock didn't even stir at the sight. I didn't think of her that way anymore, and only barely had before Becs came along. My eyes drifted to her face in time to see the woman yawn before she fluttered her eyes open to meet mine.

"Hey," she called out to me in a sweet, sleepy tone.

"You need to leave your key on the table and then get your car out of here."

"So, basically, you're kicking me out?"

"You weren't invited to begin with," I reminded her.

"Since when do we need invites into one another's lives, Aus?"

"You know why, now it's time you leave. I have to go straighten things out with Becs and I can't do that while you're sitting on my couch damn near naked."

"If you like what you see, there's no need for you to go anywhere," she caressed a finger down her breast as she spoke.

"I don't like what I see. The wrong woman is sitting in front of me in her bra and panties. It shouldn't be you. Now, you need to get your ass into that car of yours and get yourself back home because I have places to be."

"I thought you believed me last night," Jordan pouted as she sat up and worked her fingers through the long strands of her sleep-mussed hair.

"Well, Houston made a good point while you slept. Becs would have turned away immediately if she saw your car parked here that late, on a night when things didn't go well for us."

Jordan laughed.

"What's so damn funny about that?"

"Vic dropped me off here."

"Vic?"

"Victoria," she rolled her eyes as she delivered the name.

"As in, my sister?"

"The very one."

"Why did my sister drop you off at my apartment?"

"I told you, we both figured out what was going on, and she left it to me to break the news to you." She trailed a hand down her body to indicate the way she'd dressed. "That's why I showed up like this, to make sure your night didn't completely suck."

If that was true, there was never a car outside my place to scare Becs away. That meant she'd never shown up and didn't have a reason to worry about what I was up to with Jordan. I grabbed my phone and looked again to see if maybe I'd nodded off and missed an incoming text notification or something. There was still nothing to see. She hadn't reached out to me at all.

The only reasonable explanation for her silence, was the one Jordan had given me. It was all some elaborate plan to hurt and humiliate me. Well, she'd done damage to my brother too and made him a pawn in her game. Even if everything else had been forgivable, that wasn't.

"Come on," I told Jordan as I stood and grabbed my keys off the table.

"Where are we going?"

"I'm taking you home."

"But I thought…"

"Nothing has changed between us, Jordan. I meant what I said before about not doing the friends with benefits thing. It won't work for us, especially since you never date anyone else. We do still need time apart for you to go date and try to find someone who makes you happy."

"*You* are the person who makes me happy, Austin!"

"No, I don't. You can't be happy with the fact that things are basically over with my girlfriend and you being here in front of me, wearing almost nothing, has had no effect on me. You can't be happy with someone who doesn't have anything more than friendly feelings for you."

"You only think that because you're still rebelling against what our parents want."

"Jordan, stop. I'm taking you home and that's the end of it. We are just friends. Nothing more. That isn't going to change."

Not even after Becs stomped on my heart and hurt me in a way I'd never been hurt before. I didn't tell my best friend that part, because it wasn't something I was willing to admit out loud just yet.

*LINK BACK to Chapter 6

BONUS CHAPTER 12

AUSTIN'S POV

BECS WAS IN MY BED, IN THE HOUSE I'D BUILT FOR MY FUTURE family, after admitting that our date tonight had been the best night of her life. She drifted off to sleep more than an hour ago in my arms, but I wasn't able to follow her, despite how exhausted I felt. Having her here, for the first time, felt too precious somehow and I didn't want to miss a second of her warm body lying next to mine, in the bed that would one day be ours.

The Van Gough exhibit wasn't something that normally would have ranked as one of the best moments of my life but watching the excitement in her eyes and feeling like we were being immersed in her world, made all the difference.

I'd do it again in a heartbeat to keep my woman satisfied. The night had gone off without a hitch, the same as the past two weeks. If it hadn't been for my sister jumping my ass the day before about Jordan, I'd say the past two weeks had been perfection.

My best friend was still a touchy issue that I didn't know how to work around. Jordan wasn't happy with me basically disappearing from her life again as I tried to work on my relationship with Becs. It couldn't be helped though, after everything that went on in our pasts, I was lucky my girlfriend even allowed this opportunity for a second, or was it third, chance.

Still, it didn't feel fair to Jordan because, as my sister pointed out, she didn't do anything wrong to get the shaft from me. I wondered if I'd be able to reintroduce Jordan to our lives over the next couple weeks, in the hopes of settling everyone in with the reality that I was dating Becs and Jordan was still my close friend.

I'd asked Jordan about the things Becs accused her of, like meeting her on campus two weeks after we broke up to rub it in her face that Jordan and I were fucking again. She claimed it never happened. I had a hard time figuring out who was lying and who was telling the truth because I didn't think Jordan would do anything to impede my happiness, even if she did think she had a crush on me.

Then again, how else could Becs have known some of the things Jordan supposedly told her? I didn't think Becs would purposely try to remove Jordan from my life, but there was a tiny bit of doubt that went both ways. Both women thought the other was trying to keep me from them. It meant they each had their own motivation.

I tried to ask my dad, the week before, what he thought I should do about everything. His advice had been vague.

"Son, you have to figure out what, or who in this case, is the most important to you and focus on that part of your life. It's going to require sacrifice on your part. If you're lucky, you get to keep them both. If you're not, you have to choose who you want around more."

"That's not fair," I'd told him because there wasn't a world where I could imagine not having either of them. I'd already lived in a world where Becs was no longer part of my life and it had sucked. Aside from a couple weeks, where we'd been apart when I first started seriously dating Becs years ago, and the past two weeks where I'd barely seen my best friend, Jordan had always been in my life. How could I even wrap my head around her not being there in the future?

"This is one of those times when you have to realize life is rarely fair, it's just a series of choices we have to make on the path to contentment."

"Contentment?" I scoffed.

"Contentment," he agreed with a huff of his own. "You can't feel happiness, or even elation, without experiencing the opposite emotion. Just like you can't know love without hate. It's how the universe balances itself. Contentment is the middle of the road, that place between the extremes where we reside more of the time than not."

"Then what's the opposite of contentment?"

"From the way you talk, it's been the past six years that you lived without your woman by your side. It's the moderate level of misery you carry with you when you know you somehow ended up traveling down the wrong path. Contentment is the place in your life where you know you found your path and you can breathe easily again."

In a weird way, my father's explanation made a lot of sense. I couldn't lose Becs again, because he was right, there was a sense of wrongness that followed me around for years, like I was forgetting something important when I knew everything was in order. Everything except the fact that she had been missing from my life.

"Won't I just be trading one misery for another if I have to choose between them?"

"How should I know?" My father asked. "I'm a simple man, Austin. I believe that if your heart needs something, you must act. Need and want are two different things. You need one of those women in your life. I have a feeling you just want the other one there because it's a comfortable choice to make, not necessarily because she does anything to better your life."

"Which one are you talking about?"

My father smiled at me and then winked like a fucking lunatic. "That's what you need to figure out."

While his answers had been insightful, his lack of clarity just made more of a headache for me. If the last two weeks were anything to go by, Becs was the woman I needed. Not that I didn't already know that, but it had taken a while for me to understand. Even though Jordan had been my friend since we were kids, I didn't need her. In a lot of ways, she held me back from experiencing true happiness. I was always more worried about how she would react or feel than doing what I truly wanted. Then there was the worry that the next decision I made might unravel the shitty framework that was our friendship.

The woman whose warmth seeped into my side, who I'd just made love to, and spent one of the collective best nights of our lives together, was something I couldn't give up. I knew that even as I tried to come to grips about what that might mean for me and Jordan. I wasn't an idiot, like my brother kept trying to tell me. There wasn't a way to keep them both. Having Becs in my life meant the dynamic between Jordan and me had to change.

I turned and snuggled further into Becs, aligning our bodies so that I was wrapped around her like the big spoon. Having her in my arms, after our perfect night together, there was no choice to be made. I'd already made it. For better or worse, Becs was my future. Where that left Jordan, I couldn't be certain. It all hinged on how well she took the news that my girlfriend was my priority and would eventually become my wife.

I finally drifted off to sleep, knowing in my heart that I'd made the right decision this time. Becs didn't want to possess me the way my best friend did, she simply wanted to be loved and love back. I could have kicked myself for ever doubting her, or our relationship, before.

~*~

I woke to the sound of someone beating down my front door. That was unlikely since it was a solid oak door sitting in a steel frame, but whoever was at my house was giving it their best try. I slid away from Becs and rolled out of the bed as she groaned her disappointment.

"It's probably Dallas being an ass as usual. You would think he didn't have his own place to go at night," I quickly placated her as

I pulled on a pair of sweatpants that had been sitting on top of my dresser. Becs didn't say anything, and I hoped she would roll back over and slip back into a peaceful slumber, but for that to happen, I needed to go take care of whoever was banging my door down.

I slid out of the room and down the stairs to the door before disarming the alarm and opening up to find a harassed looking Jordan standing there.

"What in the hell is going on?" I asked her.

She pushed past me into the house, which wasn't going to fly if Becs woke up and came downstairs to find her there. At least my friend wasn't wearing lingerie this go round, as she had been in the past.

"We need to talk, Austin."

"It's the middle of the fucking night, Jordan." She laughed at me, but it sounded more unhinged than humorous.

"It's morning, you giant dick! Ask me how I know exactly what time it is. Go on! Ask me!"

"I don't have time to play stupid games with you, Jordan. You need to come back at another time and call first while you're at it. This shit," I pointed to my door that had actual fucking scuff marks along the bottom from where she must have been kicking it to make the ungodly noise she'd been making, "is not okay."

"Do you really think it's okay to have me work your shifts, so you can go galivanting off with the whore who keeps causing trouble in our friendship? She doesn't want me around you, so you drop me, and worse, think it's okay to make me work your shift while I have to imagine all night what you're getting up to with her?"

I was stunned stupid for a minute. What in the absolute fuck was she babbling about? If I didn't know any better, she sounded more like a jealous wife, who was being cheated on, than a platonic friend who had to work at the bar because she was scheduled to.

"It's not like that, and you know it, Jordan."

"Oh, no I don't. I'm sick of her ass coming into your life and pushing me out. The last time you two got together, I had to leave town for you, so that she wouldn't see me. Now, I'm working *your* shifts for the same damn reason."

My brother, Dallas, had been the one working my shifts for me, so that I could come in and get the business end of things taken care of while Becs worked at the school. Jordan didn't know that though because we hadn't spoken much over the past couple weeks, and it wasn't her fucking business to know what Dallas, Houston, or I arranged for the schedule, since we were her bosses in that respect.

"I was right to ask you to leave back then. You proved that by the stunt you pulled showing up to my place in your underwear on Valentine's Day. My girlfriend saw you that night and never bothered to come to the door again. You can't tell me you didn't arrange that on purpose."

The smirk, and smug set of her jaw behind it, made me take a step back in complete shock. I didn't know the woman who stood in front of me. Becs had been right. Jordan orchestrated that whole thing and probably stood in that window, for as long as she had, to make sure she'd was seen that night. When Jordan started to chuckle lightly, my temper flared.

"I don't think it's amusing," I bellowed at her, wanting to thrash her with my words, since I couldn't do it with my fists. If my best friend had been a man who tried to sabotage my relationship with Becs, I'd have thrown punches already.

"Well, too fucking bad, Austin! I've been in love with you my whole life. Do you think I find it amusing that I'm working extra shifts so that you can go play with some whore you have a temporary infatuation with?"

"Keep your voice down!" I knew she was being loud on purpose, and I glanced up to see if her antics had managed to rouse Becs from our bed yet. Jordan didn't miss the look I sent toward the stairs.

"What. The. Fuck. Austin?" My former best friend screamed at me. "Did you bring your whore to this house? You promised you wouldn't do that. This is *our* space."

Jordan had well and truly fallen off the deep end. This house had never been a shared space. She had only been to the house a few times, and that was when Victoria brought her, because I didn't want her to start feeling too comfortable here.

"Jordan, this is my house, and I can-" She cut me off before I could tell her that I could bring whoever the hell I wanted home with me, and she needed to get over the fact that it had never been a choice to bring my her there. The space had always been meant for Becs – the love of my fucking life.

"We picked everything for this house together, including the bed you probably have that bitch tucked up in."

The outright lie sent my anger into the stratosphere as I took a few deliberate steps further back from Jordan. "I don't know what fucking game you think you're playing here, Jordan, but you just crossed a line that can't be uncrossed. You're going to scream lies and bullshit in my house to drive Becs away? Really? I'm standing right here and know that shit isn't true. You never even liked this house, let alone picked shit out for it. You've certainly never even seen my bed here, let alone been in it."

Her eyes tracked something upstairs while I'd been talking and then the look of triumph that crossed her face, told me Becs must have overheard at least part of our conversation. I'd go reassure her in just a minute and then we wouldn't have to worry about Jordan ever interfering again because she'd just burned our friendship to the fucking ground.

"We're fucking done here. You need to get out and don't even think about coming back." Jordan's eyes widened in surprise before they dropped to her feet. Her shoulders slumped in defeat before she raised her eyes to meet my furious ones again.

"I'm pregnant," Jordan whispered, though she might as well have shouted those words for the impact they made.

It felt like my heart took a nose-dive right out of my chest and hit the fucking floor only to bounce away and shatter somewhere just out of reach. Those two words shouldn't have packed that much punch, but I knew in an instant that they did.

It was over.

Becs might have eventually come around and accepted Jordan in my life as a friend, though that train of thought had been a moot point after the display Jordan just put on for her. There was no way in hell that Becs would stick around while I had to coparent with Jordan, especially after the lies she'd spewed tonight.

I knew just as surely that Jordan wouldn't tolerate Becs being around to play mommy to a kid we had together. She was already beyond territorial over me and even my fucking house apparently. I knew Jordan had been loud on purpose earlier. She was trying to prove a point to Becs, just in case she was listening and God, I really hoped like hell that I'd been wrong about Jordan seeing Becs on the landing, standing there to witness her lies.

Jordan hated my house. She hated the wood and stone construction and preferred the clean lines and smooth features of modern architecture instead. The closest she had come to helping pick anything out for my house was when I invited my sisters and mom to help me go get curtains and blinds for the windows because I didn't know jack shit about shopping for things like that. Victoria had dragged Jordan along too, but my friend refused to help unless I bought a different house – one that she helped me choose instead. We all thought she had been joking that day. Suddenly, I didn't think that was the case.

The way Jordan twisted the truth to make it sound like we'd planned the house together, cast doubt on everything that happened in our past too. I knew who had been telling the truth about what happened before. Becs had been right all along, about my friend manipulating all the relationships I tried to have, to ensure their failure. Unfortunately, it didn't fucking matter anymore. Jordan just said the two fucking words that would change everything. Now, I had to figure out how to tell Becs that we were over.

"How exactly are you pregnant? I thought you said you had birth control covered?"

Stupidly, there had been a time or two, a couple months before Becs came back into my life, where Jordan and I hadn't been as careful as we should have. Both times, Jordan had hopped on my dick too quickly for me to stop her long enough to put on a condom.

She'd giggled and said, *"I have birth control covered, but the damage is already done. You can pull out if that will make you feel better."*

Stupid me, thinking with my stupid dick, and wanting to know what sex felt like without a condom for once in my twenty-eight years, had reluctantly agreed to continue with the condomless sex. I'd also pulled out before climaxing, but apparently that hadn't worked out so well.

Jordan shrugged. "Nothing is totally effective. I guess we got our miracle shot, and I'm taking it, no matter what you say, Austin. I'm having this baby and I won't allow my baby to be around your fucking whore."

And there it was, the ultimatum I knew would come. I could have my kid with Jordan, or I could have Becs, but not both. I would choose Becs over any other human in the world, with one exception, and this was it.

This was my kid, and I would never do that to a child of mine. They were supposed to come first. That was something both of my parents had drilled into our heads, right along with being responsible about sex. Becs would never let me choose her over my child anyway. Then there was the part where she wouldn't be able to be in my life and watch as I had a baby with Jordan. I think it would kill her. It was fucking making me sicker than hell as I tried to comprehend everything.

That was when I knew what I had to do. I would have to make Becs hate me. It was the only way to give her the clean break she would need to move on from the fucking misery I always brought into her life.

"Austin?" Someone questioned from above me, which was how I realized I'd fallen to the floor at some point. My ass was on the hardwood and my face was buried in my knees. How had I fucked my life up this bad? Becs words came back to haunt me. She'd warned me that I'd fall right back in with Jordan when she was gone, the last time we were together. She told me something about not learning an important lesson since I didn't understand the lengths Jordan would go to keep me.

I glared up at the woman who I thought had been my best friend all these years. She had done this on purpose. Her eyes were wide, shocked by my reaction to her news, obviously. I don't know what the fuck she expected.

"Austin, are you okay? I know it's a shock, but we'll work through it. We were destined to be together anyway, so this just speeds up the inevitable."

There it was.

Becs had been right all along. Jordan was obsessed with the thought that we were meant to marry one day because her mother had drilled the idea into her head when we were kids. I couldn't even fault her for it. That was an expectation that should have never been placed on her shoulders. Did my mother hope for a union between me and her best friend's daughter? Yes. Did she ever force the idea down my throat? No. She told me her greatest happiness would be to see me find a life partner like she found in my father, no matter who it turned out to be.

I found that connection with Becs. Now, I was stuck with Jordan because I couldn't keep both the woman I loved and the baby that was on the way. My baby with the wrong woman.

"I need you to leave," I told Jordan who immediately puffed up, ready for a fight. "I need you to leave so I can break the news to Becs."

"I don't want her to know about the baby yet. She'll make our child into some awful monster who is coming between you two, and I won't allow our baby to be a pawn for her to use against you."

That wasn't true. If I knew Becs at all, she would sacrifice our relationship immediately for the sake of my child. That was the kind of woman she was. That's why I had always pictured her as the mother of my children. I'd never even imagined having a kid with Jordan, and it made me sick all over again to think that it was about to become my reality.

"I'm not going to tell her about the fucking baby, but I do need to let her go, and you will not be here for that."

"Fine." Jordan glanced down at the phone she pulled from her pocket. "It's quarter after four now. I'll be back by eight, so we can have breakfast and talk over where we go from here. Maybe it's time to sell your monstrosity of a house and think about getting something we both like," she demanded.

"Funny, I thought you helped me pick everything about this house out. Isn't that what you yelled, so that my girlfriend would think I built this house for our life together?" Her cheeks turned bright red with embarrassment at being called out for the games she tried to play.

"Sorry," she whispered. "Honestly, Aus, the hormones are doing my head in. I can't think straight," she whined and even that felt fake, but what the fuck did I know about pregnant women and hormones? Jordan's sweet, apologetic tone disappeared almost immediately as she started speaking again, and I swear it was like witnessing her turn into someone else before my very eyes.

"Make sure you do it right this time, because I meant what I said, that woman will not be involved with my baby. If she stays around, I'll run, and you'll never get to see your child, and neither will your family."

Jordan really went there while I was still stuck on whether it was truly pregnancy hormones making her crazy or if I'd missed that she had been all along. All I knew was that she was about to cost me my happiness and hurt the one woman I loved more than anyone on the fucking planet.

Funny that this was the moment that forced me to admit that feeling to myself. I was so fucking lost in love with Becs. I always had been, from the very beginning, but more so now that we'd spent time really getting to know one another. Knowing that I had to go upstairs and end it all, for the sake of my child, felt like I was living through her death. At the very least, I was living through the death of our relationship.

After the front door closed, I picked myself up off the floor and trudged up the stairs with the weight of the fucking universe on my shoulders. I didn't even know what to say, considering I'd just told Jordan I would respect her decision not to mention the baby just yet.

I hesitated outside the bedroom door for a minute. It was still cracked open, so unless Becs immediately fell back to sleep, she had at least heard the worst parts of that conversation. Jordan manufactured that argument to get loud during those moments on purpose, after all. She'd just admitted as much.

When I opened the door, the emptiness of the room hit me immediately. The complete and utter quiet, and the lack of clothing spelled one thing. She obviously hadn't passed us on the steps to get to the front door. That left one option. I ran across the expanse of the open loft area to the back staircase I'd told her was there in case of emergency. It led straight down to the back door. The proof was there. The door had been left unlocked when she fled into the darkness of the far-too-early morning.

I wasn't sure which part she overheard that sent her running, but it couldn't have been the pregnancy announcement, since

Jordan had whispered that much. Becs thought I'd built the house with Jordan, and maybe that was the thought I should leave her with, since I couldn't tell her about the pregnancy. My life was not my own anymore and it felt absolutely fucking miserable to know the last thing the love of my life would remember about me was that I was the bastard who brought her to the home I'd supposedly built with another woman in mind.

I screamed, at the top of my fucking lungs. The noise was so loud my neighbors ended up calling the cops, who I had to deal with about twenty minutes later, while looking completely ravaged when they showed up to my door. When they asked what was wrong with me, I told them I'd just been given the news that the love of my life was gone. They thought I meant she'd died, and truthfully that was what it felt like. Only, it felt like I was the one who died and had found my new home in hell.

*Link Back to Chapter 13

WHAT'S NEXT?

Resolving Rumors
Loved for the Holidays #3
Anne Storm

.●

Chapter One
Victoria

"Why?"

That one stupid word was all I could manage, and even as it left my lips, I knew I wasn't ready to hear the answer just yet. Instead of listening to him, I turned around and left.

"Victoria, wait! Aren't you even going to hear me out?"

"Why should I, Devin?" It hurt too much to turn back around and look at him. All I could see was the scene I'd just walked in on. The one that let me know that my boyfriend's public girl-friend – his beard to keep people from looking too closely at our relationship – wasn't as fake as he'd always led me to believe. His dark hair was mussed like someone had been running their fingers through it, and I couldn't be too sure at that point if it had been him or her.

"Come on, Vic." He sighed. "That's not fair and you know it. It was once and you were out on a date with someone else."

"You've been out on a date with someone else how many times? The difference is that mine was a set up by my mother and I didn't even remotely enjoy it. Yours has been with the fake girl-friend that you swore you weren't sleeping with, but suddenly I walk in on her talking to you about the baby you two are respon-sible for?" A dark chuckle escaped me. "Tell me which scenario seems fair. I never slept with anyone else and you were appar-ently fucking your fake girlfriend the whole time."

"It's not like that. If you'd just let me…"

"No. As far as I'm concerned, you made your choice when you stuck your dick in Justice – apparently raw – and got her preg-nant. That went a little beyond the whole, 'fake relationship' terms that were set up in the beginning. I'm assuming you two have had your own rules all this time that I knew nothing about."

"You're the one who insisted on the secrecy and you're dead wrong. It was one time, Vic. Once."

"Well, Devin, that's one time too many, especially since you managed to knock your girlfriend up in the process."

"Wife," he huffed the word out reluctantly.

"Excuse me?" The question exploded from me as if painful shards of glass had just ripped me apart from the inside. I didn't want to, but I had to turn back around to see his face as he tried to explain to me how he could have possibly married someone else. Someone who wasn't me.

"When she told me, we ran off and got married because…" I couldn't bear to see him look so wrecked by his admission, as if it pained HIM. The love of my life married another woman. A woman he apparently knocked up at some point while we were dating. If it was possible to die of a broken heart, I might just crumple to the ground on the spot.

"Stop!" My shout bordered on the hysterical. "That's enough."

I was not proud of my actions, but I turned and ran from the only man I'd ever loved. I couldn't do it any longer. I couldn't stand there and face him as the woman he got pregnant, and married behind my back, stood in the background smirking at me.

I'd always thought our situation was ideal because she was involved in a taboo romance with her father's best friend – who happened to be a married man. It meant that she and Devin formed the perfect beard relationship. He helped to conceal her activities, and she kept my little brother, Dallas, off our backs.

I should have known if she didn't have any issues carrying on a clandestine relationship with a married man, especially one so close to her own family, that she would have zero qualms about sleeping with her fake boyfriend – my man. The thing that made it easy to overlook that possibility had been that I had absolute faith in Devin.

I really should have known better. She was age appropriate for him, and didn't come with the baggage that was my brother and the rest of our family. She was also a petite blonde with unnaturally large tits. They were natural, but didn't look as though they fit her otherwise tiny frame. Then there was her faux innocent denim blue eyes that everyone always raved about – including my boyfriend when he played the doting partner at her side.

They were married now and expecting a baby together. They were both 22. I was closing in quickly on 29 and 30 loomed in the not-too-far distance. I'd spent the past three years in a relationship with the man. Well, we spent two years in a secret relationship after a year where Devin chased me until he finally wore me down.

My eyes blurred with unshed tears as I made it to my car, got inside, and flipped the locks before Devin could come after me and grab it open. I had the car turned on before I glanced up and realized he never even bothered to follow me. Instead, he made his way back toward the bitch, who conveniently had her arms wide open for him to step into.

I guess that picture was worth a thousand words and all of them pointed to the fact that I'd been the toy. All along, I'd been the other woman in my own relationship and hadn't realized it. How fucking stupid was I?

Chapter 2
Devin

"I'm so sorry, D."

I stepped into Justice's waiting arms and allowed her to hold me for a minute because I felt like my whole body might fly apart at seeing the damage I'd done to the only woman I ever wanted to marry. Newsflash – it wasn't the wife who was there to hold me when everything fell apart. No, the woman I wanted to build a life with had been too busy keeping me hidden in the shadows. One night of resentment on my part meant everything was over.

"Wow, she just gave me a hateful look," Justice sniped. I glared up at her and took a step back before I glanced back over my shoulder to see Victoria swipe angrily at the tears on her face just before she flew out of the driveway.

"What do you expect?" I growled angrily. "We both made promises to her. Promises that we broke and then compounded by the decisions we made on top of that."

"Well, my promise didn't mean shit, since she doesn't factor into my life."

"She factored into mine. Did that not mean anything? Do I not mean anything to you?"

Justice grinned at me. "Of course you do, husband."

"Don't call me that!" I snapped.

The marriage had been another in a series of complete panic-induced fuckups on my part. We didn't even know if the baby Justice carried was mine or Brody Hinton's. Brody being her 43-year-old married boyfriend. I shook my head free of that mind fuck. Justice had been panicked, too. She begged me to make it look legitimate or else her parents might find out, disown her, and she wouldn't be able to take care of a baby on her own.

How I convinced myself that it was my problem was beyond me. It really wasn't my problem. The chances that I'd impregnated Justice were slim-to-none.

We slept together once, and I didn't even remember the part where I was supposedly inside her – though she swears it happened. I believed her, considering she told me as she apologized for allowing things to go that far while we were both drunk off our asses.

"We are married now," Justice insisted.

It took me a minute to sort my thoughts before I was able to respond. "We need to go back inside and sit down for this conversation."

"Fine." Justice turned on her heel immediately and walked into the house while I meandered in slowly, wondering if the one thing I always dreamed of was now lost to me forever. I'd been in love with Victoria Mercer since the day I met her when I was 12-years-old. My chest cracked wide open thinking that today would be the last time I saw her. That wasn't even the worst case scenario. She was my best friend's big sister, that meant we'd probably see one another again. The problem was, who would she be with when I saw her next? Judging by how everything worked out today it wouldn't be me.

When I finally made my way back into the house, I sat next to Justice and turned so that we were sort of facing one another while still sitting side-by-side. I pulled her hand into mine – the one that now had a ring adorning it that tied her to me. I felt sick to my stomach at the sight and let her hand go to run my fingers through the short hair on my head in frustration. As luck would have it, the ring she placed on my finger snagged on my hair as a reminder of just how fucking off the original plan we had gone.

"You know that I'm in love with Victoria."

Justice shrugged her shoulders and pouted her lips as if it was news to her and it made her unhappy. "It doesn't really matter, considering she wouldn't hear you out!"

I stared at Justice, as if seeing her for the first time. "Are you kidding right now? How would you react if you just found out your boyfriend of two years might have gotten another woman pregnant and married her too?"

"She's the one that agreed to this whole situation to begin with. She had to know it was possible that we would end up hooking up."

"She literally put down rules that we both agreed to, that stated otherwise. Not to mention she thought you were in love with Brody. I imagine that's the only reason she did agree, was that you already had a man you loved."

"Still, you would have to be stupid to throw a younger, better looking woman at your secret boyfriend and not expect things to happen between them." She giggled. "I mean," she tossed her hand back-and-forth between our two bodies, "look at us. We're both gorgeous people. Of course, we were going to fuck at some point. I'm honestly surprised it took you as long as it did."

"I don't even remember ever being naked with you, let alone fucking!" I reminded her. "You are not the woman I want."

Her brow arched higher as I stated that. "Well, I'm the one you knocked up and married."

"Stop. We both know the chances that kid is mine are almost nil."

"We don't know anything yet," She insisted.

"I may have acted out of a knee-jerk reflex when I married you, but only a DNA test will convince me that the baby you're carrying is mine." Her lips puckered like she tasted something sour.

"That doesn't change the fact that we're still married and everyone will know that soon enough."

"An annulment is easy enough to obtain, since we never consummated our vows."

"Or we could consummate our vows and give this a shot," she insisted as her hand trailed up my chest and she attempted to wrap her fingers around my neck.

"Stop!" I shook her off and stood to move across the room. "We're not doing that. What about Brody?"

"He has a wife of his own, in case you've forgotten. I don't know what you want from me. You promised you would be there to help protect me from my situation. Just because your situation blew up in your face doesn't mean you aren't obligated to keep helping me. We are married. I am pregnant. My family still can't know that this baby might not be yours."

"If we tell everyone that it is mine, then it means that I can never fix things with Victoria."

Justice pulled her hair around as if to shield herself behind it and then she shook her head like the thought was easy enough to shake off. "And what will you do if the baby is yours? You'll lose her anyway. No matter what happens between us, there is no way that Victoria will help you raise a baby we made together. Our child will always be a reminder of how she didn't mean that much to you."

"What the fuck is that supposed to mean? She means every-thing to me!" I argued.

Justice made a noise of disapproval. "Really? Then why in the hell did we get drunk together and end up having sex?"

"I wish I knew."

My unwanted wife rolled her eyes at me. "Oh, you knew exactly what you were doing that night. You might have been thinking about your precious little Victoria, but those thoughts revolved around fucking me to forget she was out with another man that night. It's really convenient how she forgot she was on a date with another man."

"Did you set this up on purpose so that Vic would be here to hear us discussing the baby and marriage?" There was a little niggle at the back of my mind that told me something wasn't right. Justice pushed too hard to get me to accept the end of my relationship with Victoria. I had to change the subject though because just thinking about how Vic went out on a date with some other man still made me feel downright homicidal. I hoped like hell no one ever told me who she was out with.

I was so lost in thought I almost missed the sarcastic sounding giggle that came from Justice. "How was I supposed to know she would show up here today? Besides, maybe you should have been honest with her since the first day we woke up together. At the very least, you should have clued her in the minute I told you I was pregnant, or any time before you married me. Don't try to put this on my shoulders, D. I didn't do anything that you're trying to make me guilty of. You need to accept responsibility just like Victoria does."

"She didn't do anything wrong."

"She has kept you locked in a hidden relationship for two years because she's embarrassed to tell her family that you're together. What part of that isn't wrong? At least in my case, I'm not ashamed of you or anything else. I'm protecting my lover from the fallout of us having a relationship at the wrong time. She's just protecting herself."

Justice wasn't wrong about any of that. I had gone about everything all wrong, starting with Vic's demands to keep our relationship secret. I should have forced the issue long ago. It had been two years since we officially started dating. The minute she said yes to that first date, I should have told her brother. The only reason I hadn't was because she knew it would cause a strain between her and the rest of her family. I had to respect that, but I think we took it all too far and made everything worse. My fake relationship to throw everyone off our trail, and to help Justice out with her situation, made it impossible for her family to take me seriously as her boyfriend if and when we did finally come clean.

Now, with a pregnancy and a marriage in the mix, everything was infinitely messier. Hindsight was a bitch because we should have seen this coming. We should have already factored in how Vic's family would perceive things after we fooled them for so long with my fake relationship to Justice. Our story was never going to have the happy ending I always envisioned, and that was on me for not standing up for our relationship from the very beginning.

ALSO BY ANNE STORM

Loved for the Holidays Series

Cupid Broke my Heart

Ghosted by Texas

Resolving Rumors

Cheating Hearts Series

The Homewrecker's Fate

The Regrettable Mistake

Savage Vipers MC Series

Wait for Me

Devastate Me

Surprise Me

Baby Me

ALSO BY CHRISTINE MICHELLE

Standalone Romances

Bad at Love

His Bittersweet Regret

Letters to Lily

The Groupie Journal

Winter Wolves (PNR)

The Fortunate Ones

Robeson Family Novels Series

The Forgotten Wife

When the Last Petal Falls

Aces High MC - Charleston Series

The Other Princess

A Love so Hard

The Princess and the Prospect

The Killing Ride

A Twist of Fate

Everlasting

A Year and a Day

The Broken Beginning - Part One

The Broken Beginning - Part Two

Aces High MC - Dakotas Series

Dancing with Danger

Whiskey Tango Foxtrot

The Restart and the Remedy

Aces High MC - Tallahassee Series

Crushed

Aces High MC - Cedar Falls Series

Redemption Weather

Smoke and the Flame

Proven

Aces High MC - Sierra High Series

Walker

Trouble

S.H.E. MC Series

Angel Girl

JoJo

Keys

Dark Leopards MC Series (PNR)

Ridden by Darkness

The B Team

T.I.E. (The Infinite Everything) Series

The Infinite Something

The Infinite Beat

Valhalla Rising Series

Revived

Mirage island Mates (PNR)

Into the Grasslands

Beyond the Grasslands

The Ancients Series (PNR)

Shadows of the Ancients

Falling into the White

Branches of the Willow

Bound by the Moon

Vukodlak Brew Series (PNR)

Entwined

Enraged

The Awakening Trilogy

Birthrights

Revelations

Incarnations

Death Viewers Series (Paranormal Suspense)
Breathless

Other Works (YA/NA Paranormal and Dystopian):
The Voodoo Follies
Catch a Falling Star

ABOUT THE AUTHOR

Anne Storm is a pen name for Christine Michelle.
Anne Storm's books:
Dark romance/subjects with major triggers
Christine Michelle's books:
(mild) MC Romance, Rock Star Romance, and other
Contemporary Romance
Paranormal Fantasy & Romance

If you want to learn more about Christine, her books, or her crazy adventures into the wilderness, you can find out more through the following links:
Website & Newsletter sign up:
www.moonlitdreams.org
Signing up for the newsletter also gets you first option at future Beta reading and ARC (advanced reader copy) giveaway opportunities!
**Universal links to everything
(social media, book links, and more)**
https://linktr.ee/christinemichelle

facebook.com/M00nlitDreams
instagram.com/christinemichelle_annestorm
tiktok.com/@christine.michelle.books

www.ingramcontent.com/pod-product-compliance
Lightning Source LLC
Chambersburg PA
CBHW020941260626
47169CB00006B/1766